To Donna,
Enjoy this story of
the "wild" west!
Cheryl

Saving Legacy Springs

CHERYL KOSHUTA

abbott press®
A DIVISION OF WRITER'S DIGEST

Abbott Press books may be ordered through booksellers or by contacting:

Abbott Press
1663 Liberty Drive
Bloomington, IN 47403
www.abbottpress.com
Phone: 1-866-697-5310

Because of the dynamic nature of the Internet, any web addresses or
links contained in this book may have changed since publication and
may no longer be valid. The views expressed in this work are solely those
of the author and do not necessarily reflect the views of the publisher,
and the publisher hereby disclaims any responsibility for them.

Any people depicted in stock imagery provided by Thinkstock are models,
and such images are being used for illustrative purposes only.

Certain stock imagery © Thinkstock.

ISBN: 978-1-4582-1000-5 (sc)
ISBN: 978-1-4582-0999-3 (hc)
ISBN: 978-1-4582-0998-6 (e)

Library of Congress Control Number: 2013910588

Printed in the United States of America.

Abbott Press rev. date: 06/21/2013

To Michelle, Kathleen, and Stephanie

Who wants to understand the poem,
Must go to the land of poetry.
Who wants to understand the poet,
Must go to the poet's land.

—Johann Wolfgang von Goethe, *West-Eastern Divan.*

ACKNOWLEDGMENTS

This book would not have happened but for a serendipitous conversation on October 30, 2004. I was having a late Friday afternoon coffee with Michelle Gaines when I asked her what she was going to do for the weekend. Her response was, "Write a novel." November is National Novel Writing Month, and, on a whim, I decided to accept her offer to join her and our colleague, Kathleen Paul, on the venture to write fifty thousand words in one month. And so began my writing career.

Back in 2004, to keep each other motivated, Michelle, Kathleen and I formed a writer's group. Stephanie Hallock Cummins joined us a few years later, and we have been going strong ever since. Their advice and encouragement—about writing and life—has been priceless. They had incredible stamina for endless reviews, and there is no doubt that this book would not exist without them. They challenged me, critiqued me, complimented me, and made everything about this novel better. They are all better writers than I am, and I hope their books are published soon. I can't thank them enough.

Many thanks go to three other women who were instrumental in helping get this book to publication. My best friend, Lani-Kai

Swanhart, not only helped conceive the original trajectory of this story, but she always believes I can do whatever crazy thing I set out to do and then gives me unwavering support. Gayle Marie gave me advice on both my writing and the specifics of the equine scenes in this book. Last, but not least, my mother, Ann Weth, has given me the unique combination of a solid foundation to stand on and wings to fly.

This book is about strong women and I've drawn my inspiration from the scores of women I've worked with, played with, and met in passing. It is impossible to thank each of you individually, but read this and know that you were a part of it.

CHAPTER 1

The plane climbed steeply out of Ronald Reagan National Airport in Washington, DC. From her window seat in first class, Leslie Montgomery looked down on the familiar landmarks. *Twenty-nine years*, she thought. *I can't believe he called it quits after twenty-nine years.* Leslie felt tears stinging and willed them away, pretending everything was fine when the flight attendant asked if she wanted a drink. She wasn't going to let Hugh's decision ruin her plans—her dream. She had found what she hoped would be the perfect place, the perfect town in Montana, to eventually retire in, and this was the trip when her dream would start to become real. Even without Hugh.

Maybe I should have worked harder to fix the marriage after Kelly left for college, she thought. *But he didn't either. In any case, it wasn't so bad that he had to end it. Especially without any warning. We had a comfortable life, even if it wasn't exciting. Twenty-nine years invested in a relationship, a family, a career, a town . . . all turned on its head because he wants a divorce.*

Leslie took a deep breath and a sip of her drink. She made herself smile at the businessman beside her and made small talk. She could do this. By herself. Four days in Legacy Springs should be enough to check out the town and find a place to buy. And if not, she could go back again next month. She was so busy at work that she shouldn't be gone at all, but she had to get away. Had to do something to feel like she was in control of her life after Hugh's announcement. She opened the work file on her lap and tried to concentrate.

The landscape below became more rural as the plane flew west, the myriad greens of spring spreading across Ohio and Indiana. She wondered when she had fallen out of love with Hugh. Or when he had fallen out of love with her. He said he was in love with someone else. When did that happen? Was she just too busy to notice or too lazy to care?

The what-ifs ran through her mind for the hundredth time, but she knew it didn't matter. She had banked on the future instead of paying attention to the present. She had always pictured them growing old together in a small town in Montana with wide-open spaces and views of mountains all around. Now she would grow old alone, but by god, she would do it in Montana.

Leslie gave up trying to work and pulled her tote bag from under the seat in front of her. She slipped the file inside and took out a small book called *Venus is Singing* by her favorite poet, Maggie Madison. She loved the way the cadences captured the essence of the West and the words always seemed to be perfect for whatever she was feeling.

She took a deep breath and tried to forget about Hugh. She opened the book to one of her favorite passages.

> The gift the mountains give
> Tranquility and peace,

A place the mind can hold,
Throughout the storms of life.

She closed her eyes and repeated the words to herself. She'd had her share of storms, but nothing like this. Nothing that she felt so powerless to change or that was so contrary to her plan for her life.

Eventually, she dozed a bit, waking when the plane's rhythm changed as they started the descent. Looking out the window, she hoped they might be flying over Legacy Springs, but there was a heavy cloud layer and she couldn't see anything until they were almost on the ground. She'd picked Legacy Springs because it was a real town, not a tourist destination like the other places she had considered. Close enough to an airport and some amenities but far enough away to have open space and cattle ranches. And mountains. Everything she wanted. She couldn't wait to see it in person.

Leslie felt a tingle of excitement as she got off the plane and walked down a concourse lined with Western art. The airport felt friendlier than in DC, and she realized it was because of the natural wood and stone throughout. She found her rental car company, where even the counter was made of wood instead of plastic.

"We've got you a nice little SUV," the agent said. "The cars are outside in the lot next to the terminal building."

"Thanks. How long do you think it will take me to drive to Legacy Springs? I've got an appointment at four and I was hoping to get there early enough to check into my hotel and freshen up a bit."

"Shouldn't take you much more than an hour unless the pass is bad. You should have plenty of time."

"What do you mean 'unless the pass is bad'? Is there construction?"

"No, but there might be snow. Just doesn't seem to want to quit this year. Don't worry. You've got all-wheel drive. You're comfortable driving in the snow, aren't you?"

"Sure," Leslie said, although it had been a while. When she had learned to drive growing up in Vermont, the roads were often snowy or icy, but she didn't get much practice in DC. She signed the form he had put in front of her and dated it. *April 18, 2008. I will remember this date as the beginning of my new life. Or, at least what I hope will be my new life.*

She left the warmth of the terminal building and felt the cold stinging her face and hands. Luckily, the SUV wasn't far down the row. She quickly threw her bag in the back and got in, pushing the heat to maximum. The car thermometer read thirty-four degrees, and the steering wheel was icy cold. Thank god, she'd thrown in a pair of gloves at the last minute, even though it had been almost seventy degrees in DC the past few days. The sky was dark and heavy, and there was still snow on the ground anywhere that hadn't been plowed or shoveled.

"Welcome to Montana, Leslie," she said out loud once the mirrors were adjusted and she'd found her way out of the rental car lot. She was finally here.

From the highway, the landscape was beautiful. She concentrated on the cloud-shrouded mountains she could barely see in the distance and the fat snowflakes that had started accumulating on the windshield. There were only a few other cars on the road, and she shivered slightly. She couldn't remember the last time she had traveled somewhere by herself. It felt odd not to have someone with her. Not to have Hugh attached, sitting in the other seat.

Well, she thought, *now I really am alone.*

She could feel the tears start up again, and her chest tightened. She didn't want to feel that way; she wasn't going to feel that way. She wanted to be happy. With a practiced effort, she straightened her shoulders and pushed the feelings aside. She forced herself to smile and looked ahead, seeing the road again, seeing what was in front of her. *Who would have thought it would still be snowing in April?*

"Stop leaning on me, you old bugger, or I'll punch you in the stomach and make you sorry." Peg Hamilton leaned her shoulder against the thick, brown hindquarters of the horse, lifting the left hind leg and bracing the hoof onto her knee so she could clean it. She had broken this horse as a colt, and they knew each other well. Which was why she wasn't surprised when he tried his favorite trick of leaning his twelve hundred pounds into her as she pried mud away from his shoe.

Peg finished the cleaning and then patted the nose of the old horse before feeding him a carrot. Heading back to the house, she stopped by the breaking corral, where Manny Watkins, her oldest hand, was working with a young mustang that had been rounded up during the annual federal effort to cull wild horses from the open range. Breaking them took an extra effort, but if you managed to win them over, they were the best working horses. And their stamina was unmatched.

The sides of the small breaking corral were high, wooden slats, and she squinted through the cracks to see Manny holding the horse tightly, forcing him into obedience, and battling him step-by-step. The horse's head reared continuously up and down, up and down, like an oil well pumping; the snorts from his nostrils punctuated the motion. Manny believed in the old ways. For years, Peg had tried to convince him that talking softly to a horse would get better results, but even though Manny respected Peg's way with the horses, he continued to literally swear by his own methods.

Peg looked at her watch. If she was going to get into town this afternoon to run those errands, she had better leave soon. She shoved her hands into her pockets to keep them warm. It looked like it might start snowing again too.

Inside, she grabbed a pair of gloves and her purse before heading back out to Lee's pickup that was parked in front of the garage doors. She didn't want to take time to move the truck to get her smaller sedan out of the garage, so she slid in and adjusted the seat.

The snow was coming down hard by the time she got to town half an hour later. She parked in the grocery store lot but decided to go down the block to the fabric store first. She bent forward into the wind, the tips of her ears freezing where they poked above the scarf wrapped around her neck. Crystalline snowflakes landed lightly on the long braid streaked with gray that hung down her back.

She stepped into the store, stamping snow off her boots.

"Hi, Peg," the woman behind the counter said. "How are you today?"

"I'm fine, Elaine." Peg loosened her scarf. "I'm making outfits for the grandkids, and I need black thread and about a yard of accent fabric."

"Sure." Elaine grabbed a handful of the spools and placed them on the counter. "What kind of fabric?"

"That green plaid up there would be perfect." Peg pointed at a bolt on the top shelf.

"I'll get the ladder."

"No need. I can reach it." Peg went behind the counter and pulled the bolt from the shelf.

"Need anything else?" Elaine rolled the cloth out to measure it.

"Just a shoulder to cry on. I listed forty acres of the ranch with Judy Baker last week, and it makes me sick that I had to do it. I only hope she can't sell it."

"Oh, don't be silly. Of course, it'll sell. And you'll be happy when you get the money. What do you need with all that property anyway? Someone might as well get some use out of it."

"Unfortunately, I do need the money. That latest scare about mad cow disease has the beef market way down again."

"Did you hear that Angus Foley signed one of those contracts to let them drill on his property? He's supposed to keep it quiet, but you know how news travels here." The shears slid through the fabric with a zipping sound.

"No, I hadn't heard that. That's not good news. I'm surprised at Angus. He's usually got a good head on his shoulders."

"Money talks. Have they been round to see you?"

"No, and they'd better not set foot on my property. I have no use for speculators." Peg paid for her purchases and pulled the scarf tightly around her neck. "Say hi to the family for me. Thanks."

She did her grocery shopping, gassed up, and was almost halfway home when she realized she had forgotten to stop at the hardware store. The snow was falling even harder now, and the wind had picked up considerably. *Better to go back now than have to drive all the way in again tomorrow,* she thought, pulling over to the side of the road to let cars pass before making a U-turn. A few shafts of shimmering light illuminated the horizon ahead where the Hamilton ranch nestled, the mountains on either side of the open valley now obscured by the storm. Although Peg had spent most of her life here, she never tired of the landscape, the ever-changing weather, or the magical light. *Thank you,* she said in a silent prayer. *Thank you for reminding me that the beauty of this land does not belong to any of us to buy or sell. It will always be here, no matter what.*

She turned the truck around and headed back into town.

Senator Sam Curtis walked through his rambling ranch house to a large room at the back that served as his office. It was a cold and snowy afternoon, so he made a fire in the old stone fireplace. He sat behind the huge mahogany desk that had belonged to his father, opened the bottom drawer, and pulled out a thick file marked "Subsurface Mining Rights." He hadn't looked at it for months and needed to refresh his memory on the issue before tonight's meeting. He wanted to be fully prepared.

He leaned back in the worn leather chair and looked out the window at the horses huddled together in a corner of the pasture, snow accumulating on their manes. Being home in Montana energized him and made him happy to be a US senator. *If only we could run Congress from our home states instead of sitting in DC,* he thought, *the nation would be better off. Lobbyists wouldn't have the same influence. The good of the country might take precedence over party politics. And I sure wouldn't miss all that travel time.* Flying back to Montana at least every other weekend and sometimes more often was a grind. Of course, even when he was home, he spent a lot of time flying or driving to events around the state, making sure he was in touch with the people who had elected him. But that was his job, and he loved it.

Sam opened the file and began to read. First, the newspaper clippings, then the letters from constituents asking for help, and finally, the collection of court cases. He'd had a thriving law practice when he ran for the Senate and took pride in his ability to quickly grasp the legal underpinnings of any issue he was dealing with.

After about an hour, he glanced at his watch. He would need to leave soon for the dinner meeting in town with Macfarlane and Harbinger. Sam shrugged his shoulders from front to back, trying to relieve the tension in his neck. *I have to be careful with this one,* he thought. *They wouldn't have invited me to dinner if they didn't want something.*

Sam barely knew Andrew Macfarlane, president of Xandex Exploration, but ran into him periodically at business functions and fundraisers since Xandex and Macfarlane were definitely players in Montana. Sam was pretty sure that Macfarlane's campaign contributions were insurance in case he wanted something someday, not actual support. But despite that, Macfarlane was always professional and pleasant when they met. On the other hand, Cortez Harbinger, the Xandex lobbyist, was somebody who made his jaw tighten up. Harbinger had been around for a long time and Sam had never heard anything good about him either in Montana or DC. Luckily, he'd managed to keep Harbinger at arm's length, and he didn't intend for that to change now.

Sam finished reading and put the file back into the bottom drawer. He looked at the photo on his desk of himself and his wife, Karen. Palm trees framed the two of them holding hands across a table on a Costa Rican beach, a spectacular sunset behind them.

I miss you so much, he silently said to the photo. The picture had been taken a year after the breast cancer diagnosis, at the beginning of the long, but eventually losing, battle. Karen had died almost three years ago. He thought about how she would have counseled him before a dinner like tonight's—about corporate greed and the need to protect the environment. She had always stood on the side of the environment, bucking conservative Montana politics, and he had often heeded her advice: "Do right, Sam."

He leaned back in his chair and put his feet up on his desk. *Do right, Sam,* he thought. *Sometimes easier said than done.*

CHAPTER 2

Leslie drove toward Legacy Springs, excited to see if the town looked like what she had imagined or if the Internet photos had, as so often was the case, captured the one good thing about a place while ignoring the rest. So far, so good, she thought as she drove over a small pass and down into the far end of a wide valley. The rental car agent had gotten her worried about the drive, but it was fine. Snow covered the road, but the visibility was good. She could see mountains on both sides of the valley, but she couldn't tell how big they were since the tops were shrouded in gray clouds.

She drove a long straightaway from the pass into town, her excitement growing. One minute, she was driving past open pastures with horses looking at her across wooden fences, and the next, she was in a scene that could have been a movie set. She immediately loved the feel of the place, the tired storefronts looking very homey in the snow. Just like in the pictures. Except that it was snowing and freezing cold in April while cherry blossoms were blooming in DC. She wondered if she was being dumb about the weather—she'd only been to Montana for skiing in the winter and to the vacation dude ranch in the height of summer. She easily found the chain motel on the edge of town, but by the time she got to her room, she was freezing again. The room was like a refrigerator, so she found the thermostat and turned the heat on full blast.

She'd driven slowly because of the snow, so she only had half an hour before her appointment with the real estate agent. She changed into a warmer sweater, brushed her teeth and her hair, and put on fresh lipstick. She took off the slip-on loafers she had worn on the plane and put on black leather boots. They weren't exactly winter boots, since they had a two-inch heel and thin leather sole, but they were her go-to, all-purpose boots in DC and were definitely warmer than the loafers. She headed back out to the SUV.

She wondered how the car could have gotten cold so quickly as she moved the heat dial back to maximum. The outside temperature on the dash now read twenty-five degrees, and the wind had picked up. She drove the half-mile back to the center of town and, after locating the corner where the real estate office was, circled the block looking for parking. There was a surprising amount of traffic, but only a few people were on the sidewalks.

Leslie found a spot about a block from the real estate office and pulled in. She grabbed her purse and her tote bag with the files of information she'd been collecting about Legacy Springs real estate. As she got out of the car, she flinched when the snow stung her face. She tugged at the collar of her trench coat, trying to pull it farther up around her ears, thankful that she had at least remembered to zip in the lining before she left DC. She saw a car pull out of a parking spot up the block, directly in front of the real estate office. For a moment, she considered moving her car, but then she felt silly since it was such a short distance. *If I'm going to live here,* she thought, *I'll need to get used to the weather.*

She maneuvered over an old pile of crusted, plowed snow at the curb and made it onto the snow-covered sidewalk. Her thin leather gloves were useless against the biting cold; her fingers were already numb. She wished she had brought a warm scarf instead of the pretty, thin, silk one she had wrapped around her neck.

She took a few steps and slid a little bit. Catching her balance, she looked uneasily at the sidewalk, realizing that the new snow covered old ice. The cold and wind penetrated her clothing as if she were wearing a nightgown. She made a mental note that she'd need to shop for different boots—and a warmer coat. She scanned the signs along the street: The Outdoor Shop, the Two Whoops and a Holler Bar, the cable company, and then the real estate office on the corner. On the opposite corner was what looked to be an old-fashioned drug store with a brightly lit soda fountain inside, then a hardware store, and, directly across from her, a classic old building that she knew from the town website was the original old hotel. But now it just housed a bar and restaurant named The Pine Room.

She saw a man in front of the old hotel in a long wool topcoat, looking up and down the street. He looked familiar, but she decided it was just because he was dressed like he should be in the city, not here. A young couple in matching varsity jackets and bulky gloves passed her going the other way and offered a friendly howdy. *Nice,* she thought.

She was halfway down the block and feeling more confident about walking on the ice when she glanced back at the man in front of the hotel, who was now looking at his watch. She did know him but couldn't place him. How could she know someone in a town she'd never been to? But then it came to her.

The man was Cortez Harbinger, a contract lobbyist whose reputation as unscrupulous was well known on the Hill. He was someone who would push the envelope, or even break the rules, to get the job done, and be nasty about it in the process. Luckily, she'd never had to deal directly with him. She wondered if he was here to meet with a client or perhaps with someone from the Montana delegation. She shivered and couldn't tell if it was because of seeing Harbinger or the cold.

The parking spot in front of the real estate office was still open and Leslie wished she had taken it. Just then, a woman driving an old pickup truck with bales of hay in the back pulled in. Leslie snuck another glance over at Harbinger, not watching where she was putting her feet, and with no warning, she was flat on her back.

In an instant, the woman from the truck was beside her. "Are you all right?" she asked, her face filled with concern as she helped Leslie sit up.

Leslie slowly moved her wrist in pain. "Yes, I'm fine. It's really slippery out here. I only need to get to that office." She pointed at the door of the real estate office while starting to get up. "I'll be fine."

"I'm not sure those heels are the best thing for this weather. Here, I'll help you. Just hold on to me." The woman slipped her arm around Leslie's back and practically lifted her from the ground as they moved toward the office. Gratefully,

Leslie felt solid footing beneath her when the woman opened the door and they stepped inside.

"Come in, come in." A plump woman who was on the phone motioned to them. "Hello, Peg. Have a seat, and I'll be with you in a minute." Two large chairs and a sofa sat in front of a blazing gas fireplace with an oversized wooden coffee table between them. It looked like a ski lodge, Leslie thought, except for the four desks in the back, which were covered with computers, phones, files, and flyers.

"Thank you so much for the help," Leslie said as she moved toward the chairs. "I'm usually not such a klutz, but I sure didn't expect it to be so icy—or cold. I'm Leslie Montgomery," she said, reluctantly pulling the glove off her cold hand before extending it.

"Peg Hamilton," the woman said, not removing her thick, leather glove before engulfing Leslie's hand in hers.

The real estate agent finished her call and joined them. "You must be Leslie." She took Leslie's hand, her grip flaccid compared to Peg's. "I'm Judy Baker. Glad you found us okay." She smiled brightly, her tiny head with its bouffant pageboy poking out of her thick, turtleneck sweater. "Please, please, sit down." She motioned to the sitting area.

Leslie lowered herself gingerly into one of the overstuffed leather chairs. She could tell she was going to be sore from that fall.

Judy turned to Peg. "Can you stay for a cup of coffee? There's a fresh pot."

"No, thanks. I've got to run. I'm behind on my sewing for the grandkids, I've got bread rising that'll need to be punched down soon, and there are a million other chores. You know how it is."

Leslie examined Peg as she talked. She looked like an ad for Montana in her sheepskin coat and hand-knit wool scarf. Her blue jeans were tucked into the top of a pair of short, thick, brown boots with rubber soles. *My boots may not work well on this ice,* Leslie thought, *but at least they're not ugly.*

Peg turned back to Leslie and smiled. "Nice to meet you. Be careful out there."

"I will." Leslie looked down, embarrassed. "Thanks again. I really underestimated the weather." She rubbed her hip and could almost feel the bruise that was sure to form. "And to think that a few days ago I was running in DC in shorts and a T-shirt."

"Must be nice," Peg said. "It won't be warm enough here for that until July. That's when most of the tourists show up. You're early. But being here in April, you can see that spring is just a continuation of winter."

"Oh, I'm not a tourist," Leslie said quickly, trying to establish her credentials as a future Montanan. "I've come to look at property so we can retire here. My husband and I have been thinking about it for years." She realized her slip of the tongue—still talking as if Hugh was coming with her. Which, of course, he wasn't.

Peg frowned and looked pointedly at the real estate agent. "Maybe I will take a quick cup of coffee, Judy." She strode off toward a kitchen area that Leslie could see at the back of the long room.

"I'll get you one too," Judy said to Leslie as she turned to follow Peg. "Cream or sugar?"

"No. Black, please." Leslie was grateful to have a moment alone to collect herself.

She held her hands up to the fireplace, watching the flames curl smoothly over the fake logs, the blue tint warming her. Thinking about Hugh made her sad. She wondered if she should give it one more shot to convince him not to go through with the divorce. No, too late for that.

She had a good feeling about Legacy Springs. She wanted a life like Peg had: sewing for grandkids and baking bread in the afternoon while snow fell. Leslie imagined not caring about what kind of car she drove or what she wore to go to the store. No phones, no meetings, no stress, no worries. Although there would be no husband. And no grandkids for at least a few more years. It was bittersweet, but she could taste the contrast from her life in DC.

"I want to have a local on my land," Leslie heard Peg say in a hushed but agitated voice.

"We take what we get, Peg," the realtor answered, also in a hushed tone. Leslie realized they didn't know their voices carried to the front of the room.

"Just because these rich Easterners have been buying up the rest of Montana for their multimillion-dollar dream homes that they only live in for a few weeks, doesn't mean it has to happen here."

"Peg, we've been through this before. We've priced your property for exactly that market—if not an Easterner, then a Californian. Doesn't matter. They're the ones who can afford to pay your price, not the locals." Leslie strained to hear the rest of the sentence. "Would you rather have a drill rig on your property than a nice house? That's your other option."

Leslie slouched farther into the big chair and looked out the window, trying not to be obvious about listening.

She heard Peg answer. "You're right. That would be worse. Well, at least don't encourage that woman to buy my forty acres. It's going to be hard enough having a neighbor, let alone the kind who doesn't even know it snows in April." The rest of the conversation became muffled.

Leslie looked up as if surprised when they returned to the fireplace and gratefully took a steaming cup of coffee. "This smells wonderful. Thank you," she said to Judy.

"I really do need to get to the store," Peg said. Leslie thought she heard a coldness that was not there before. Peg gulped a few sips from the mug before setting it down on the table. "Good luck with your search," she added as she abruptly turned to leave.

"Thanks again," Leslie said, as her rescuer opened the door and Leslie felt the cold wind wrap itself around her legs.

Peg Hamilton nodded politely, thanked Judy for the coffee, and then moved easily out into the storm, her thick-soled boots providing plenty of traction.

"Whiskey," said Cortez Harbinger to the young bartender. He had deliberately chosen The Pine Room in the old hotel, the best restaurant in this godforsaken town, for the meeting with Senator Sam Curtis.

"What whiskey would you like? We have fifteen different kinds."

"Damn it. What is this state coming to, anyway?" Harbinger scowled at the bartender's earring. "Can't a man just order a whiskey anymore? Jack Daniels. Rocks."

The bartender moved quickly to pour the drink. Harbinger pulled the cuff of his starched shirt over his thin gold watch and flicked a bit of lint from his slacks. *Looking good in this new suit,* he thought, *even if I am fifty-eight and it's a size bigger. But hey, the food and booze are a part of the job, so why shouldn't I enjoy it? And fifty-eight is young these days—most of the bastards at the top are older than that. Except for Macfarlane.*

"Here you go. Enjoy."

Harbinger tapped his fingers on the bar. He wanted to have a drink before his client got there. Being able to hold your liquor was a job requirement for a lobbyist, but he knew that Andrew Macfarlane would expect him to go really slow over this dinner with Sam Curtis. Mr. Clean. Harbinger surveyed the room, eyeing the backside of a tall blonde as she slid into the booth across from him to join two other girls. One of them saw him looking and flashed a smile. He was the only man in the room in a suit and he knew she was probably just working him for a free drink, but it was worth it, he thought, as his eyes drifted from the girl's grin to the very nice cleavage displayed in the deep V of her snug T-shirt.

"Send the ladies in the booth over there a round of drinks," he told the bartender. *What the hell?* he thought. *It's the company's money.* He knew that tonight he wouldn't have time to take it any further, but every once in a while, he got lucky, and maybe they'd remember him next time he was stuck in this hellhole.

"Spending my money freely, I see," a familiar voice sounded behind him.

"Hello, Andy," Harbinger said, turning to his client. "You're early. But as long as you're here, I'll spend a little more of your money and buy you a drink too. What'll it be?"

"What do you have in the way of single malts?" Andrew asked the bartender, eyeing the bottles lined up on the shelves in front of the mirror. Not waiting for an answer and spying what he wanted, he ordered. "I'll have Laphroaig—neat."

"Coming right up." The bartender grabbed the scotch from a top shelf and poured a shot into a glass that he placed in front of Andrew.

Macfarlane really is a bastard, Harbinger thought. *Always acts like he knows some la-de-da secret code I don't, like what expensive scotch to order. He hasn't had to fight and scrape like me. Must be nice when daddy hands you the company on a silver platter.*

Andrew took off his jacket, smoothing it gently across the bar stool next to him. His starched shirt was monogrammed on the pocket: AIM.

"I don't think I ever asked you, Andy. What's the *I* stand for?"

"Ian." Andrew sniffed the scotch.

"*Aim.* I like it. Ready, aim, fire."

Andrew looked annoyed. "How are the negotiations coming on the contracts?"

"Slow and steady, but we're making progress, and so far, everything is staying quiet. Getting people to sign those confidentiality agreements up front was a brilliant idea, if I do say so myself."

"I agree. That's why I asked you to take on this assignment. You can read people and you have no scruples. You're a good lobbyist, but you're also pretty damn good with these local folks."

"Thanks, Andy. Appreciate the compliment." Harbinger puffed up his chest in spite of himself.

"When's the senator due?"

Harbinger looked at his watch. "Not for another half hour."

"Good. Let's go over the game plan again. We've got to play this one right."

"I think we've got it down, but okay. You're the boss."

"First, remember that we want him to think this is all about the eastern part of the state. No word that we're looking at development here. And the timing is important too, Cortez. Although we're getting a few of the easy claims now, next year will be the final push. We have to get legislation in place between now and then." Andrew sniffed his scotch but didn't drink. "All you need to do is get your good friend, Senator Sam Curtis, to sponsor that small change in the law, and we'll make a fortune."

"You know it's a long shot that he'll even vote for the bill, let alone sponsor it," Harbinger took a swallow of his Jack.

"That's what we're going to try to change tonight." Andrew swirled the liquid in his glass. "And if we hit a brick wall, then we move to plan B."

"Plan B. My favorite thing." Harbinger rubbed his hands together. "Finding the dirt on a politician."

"He's squeaky clean. It won't be easy."

"Everybody's got something in their closet, Andy."

21

"And I'm trusting you to find it. And don't forget." He paused. "When the senator's here, it's Andrew. Or better yet, Mr. Macfarlane. Cheers." He finally took a sip of the scotch.

Bastard, Harbinger thought. Downing the rest of his Jack, he ordered another.

CHAPTER 3

Peg fumed. She couldn't believe that bulldozers were already digging the foundation for a house. It had been less than three months since she had put the forty acres up for sale. Leslie Montgomery had flown into town, bought the property, hired the best builder, and flown back to her life in the East, all within four days. Judy Baker had told her that Leslie originally wanted a smaller parcel, but when she saw the Hamilton acreage, she said it was exactly what she had pictured and didn't even want to look at anything else.

Peg had tried working in the barn that morning, but the sound of the construction in the distance made her retreat inside the house. She paced restlessly all day, waiting for Lee to get back from moving the last of the cattle to high pasture. When he called and told her he wouldn't get there before eight, she washed her hair and let it hang loosely around her shoulders, the way Lee liked it, instead of pulling it back in her normal braid. She put on a nice sundress and earrings, hoping it would make her feel better. It didn't, but Lee's reaction when he got home helped a bit.

"You look beautiful." Lee pulled her close as soon as he came through the door and kissed her for a long time.

"Go get cleaned up and I'll put dinner on the table."

"I'll just have you for dinner."

"You must be starved. Now get going and don't take long or everything will be cold."

He was back within ten minutes, showered and changed, just as Peg was setting a bowl of mashed potatoes on the table. A large green salad was already there. "How'd your day go?" he asked.

"It made me sick, Lee. Listening to those dozers this morning, digging into my dirt to build a house for an Easterner." She turned back to the stove and moved several pieces of chicken from a large skillet onto a serving plate.

Lee struck a match on the side of the big, cast-iron stove and carefully lit the six candles in mismatched silver holders that were on the table. Peg liked that they had kept up the tradition of always putting the food in serving dishes and eating by candlelight. They'd started doing that when their three sons were young, to teach the importance of family time together and the finer points of life in contrast to the rough and tumble education of the ranch. The boys had been grown and gone for several years, and the candles now signified romance. "And why not?" Peg would say. "Why not be romantic every night after all those years of scheduling our love life around the boys?"

"I think you deserve a little shoulder rub before dinner." Lee pulled out the chair for Peg to sit down after she put the platter of chicken on the table. He kneaded her neck with his calloused hands. "Sorry I was out so late."

He gave her shoulders a final squeeze, took a roll from the basket on the table, and sat down. "How did you find time to bake bread for dinner, if you were watching them build a house all day?"

"Oh, I have my ways. Maybe these rolls are from that funny little doughboy can." She knew he would never believe that. She absentmindedly pushed the potatoes around on her plate. "I really don't feel like eating," she said. "It makes me sick to think that I've sold some of the ranch. We've always added land, not lost it." Her voice broke.

"You know there was no other way, honey," Lee said, putting his hand on hers. "Let's look at the bright side. It might be nice to have neighbors. We'll never miss those forty acres, and we still have the grazing easement." He grinned in an effort to cheer her up. "Besides, now we've got enough money to cover the bills, and we still have fifteen hundred acres left!"

"Optimist," she said as if calling him a bad name. "It'll still take me a while to get used to the idea. I wish somebody local had bought it."

"We've talked about that already, Peg," Lee said patiently. "Locals can't afford what city people are willing to pay for solitude and a slice of Montana life."

"Maybe if the economy turns around and people start eating beef again, we can buy it back."

"Maybe. But we also need to face the fact that this sale only tides us over for about a year. If things don't change, we'll need to sell more."

"I'd almost rather let the bank foreclose than sell the place off piece by piece. It's like cutting off my limbs one by one."

"We'll worry about that if and when the time comes. So back to that new house—is Mike building it?"

"Yes. He said he's fitting it in around his other work. They must be paying him extra for him to have taken it on with such short notice."

"When's it supposed to be done?" Lee poured more wine into Peg's glass.

"I guess he's supposed to have the outside stuff done by September and should have the inside finish work done by next spring."

"Any more news on whether the new owner is coming alone or bringing a husband or family?" This had been an ongoing question between them since the sale papers had been signed only by Leslie Montgomery, although Peg remembered her saying something about a husband that day in the real estate office.

"Mike said he's only been dealing with the wife. No mention of anything that the husband wants, although Mike says there's going to be a den and enough room in the garage for a workshop."

"Sounds like she's the manager of the family—like you. Maybe you'll end up being friends." Lee reached over and brushed a wisp of hair off Peg's forehead.

"Oh, Lee, you men always think everyone will get along just fine. And men usually do. But it's different with women." Peg swirled the wine in her glass and took a big drink. "I can imagine what she'll be like. A lawyer from Washington, DC, who can't even walk in the snow. What could we possibly have in common?"

"Maybe you should give her a chance, Peg," Lee said, lightly touching her arm.

"Maybe. But you know how I feel about outsiders. And it's family land she'll be living on."

Lee moved his chair over beside hers and put his arms around her, gathering her head to his shoulder and stroking her hair.

"It'll be okay," he said softly, brushing his lips against her neck. "Things will look better in the morning. Let's enjoy our dinner and the wine and forget about our problems. Because Leslie Montgomery, whatever you might think of her, has given us the gift of a year to figure it out."

⁂

"A decaf Americano, please," Leslie told the barista in the coffee shop next to the Eastern Market. It was a sunny June afternoon in DC and the outdoor tables were nearly full. She sat in one of the remaining empty chairs in full sunlight, feeling the warmth on her face—too warm for coffee really.

The cell phone vibrated in her purse. She'd already talked to the builder in Montana twice today and hoped it wasn't him again, although she had to admit that dealing with the details of building a house took her mind off the fact that her divorce was almost final. She found the phone and saw that it was her daughter, Kelly.

"I just came out of the subway and will be there in a minute."

"Okay. I've got a table outside. Want me to order for you?"

"Great idea. A skinny iced mocha, no whip."

"You got it." Leslie had jumped at the chance to leave work early on such a beautiful day when Kelly had called that morning and asked her to meet for coffee. It seemed that they never really had time to talk anymore, even though they were constantly in touch with short texts and e-mails.

Leslie got the second coffee and went back to the table. She checked her phone, but there was nothing new. She could see Kelly rushing down the street and felt proud that she had such a confident, beautiful daughter.

"Hi, Mom," Kelly said breathlessly, throwing her arms around Leslie for a quick hug. She dropped her bag on the table and sat down. "Thanks for this." She lifted the iced coffee and took a drink. "Perfect! I'm so hot. I practically ran from the subway. Sorry to be so late. Especially when you took off early to meet me." Kelly barely paused for another sip of the coffee. "But you deserve it. You should do it more often. You work too hard."

"If I don't work hard, I don't make money."

"I know, but it's time for you to kick back some."

"Thanks for the advice, Kelly, but it takes money to keep you in school. Speaking of which, have you decided which law school you want to go to? Isn't the deadline this week?"

"It is. I haven't decided yet for sure, but I'm leaning toward Georgetown. I think the pool of men might be better than in North Carolina. I'm not sure I want a Southern guy as the father of my children."

"Really? That's going to be your deciding criteria? Doesn't seem to quite match the investment." Leslie tried to keep the irritation out of her voice. *Good god,* she thought, wishing she could just shake her daughter. "You need to pick your school for the education you'll get. You need to always be able to support yourself. You can't count on anyone else. Besides, you should marry for love, not earning potential." Leslie forced herself to stop.

"You know I wouldn't get married if I wasn't in love." Kelly avoided her mother's eyes. "But there's nothing wrong with letting your husband support you for a few years while you raise a family. It's good for a mom to be there with her kids. Just because you were a wonder woman your whole life doesn't mean I have to be."

Leslie took a long sip of her coffee as she felt the sting of Kelly's words. "You're too young to be thinking of kids."

"Don't worry. I've got to get married first. But be prepared. You know I want to have them before I'm thirty. And I know you want grandchildren, so you should be encouraging me."

"There's plenty of time for grandchildren. You should have your career established first."

"Oh, Mom, that's your generation talking. I don't want to be fifty when my kids are in high school."

"You need to put your education and career first, that's all I'm saying. Look at me. Where would I be without my career now that Dad and I are getting divorced?"

"I don't want to talk about the divorce. It makes me sad."

"I know, dear, but it's going to happen whether you or I like it, so we have to get used to it."

"Well, you seem to have gotten used to it pretty quickly. You jumped right into building that house in Montana as if you didn't even care about trying to make it work with Dad."

"Kelly, your father is with someone else now and isn't interested in trying to make it work. I'm sure she's a lovely woman and it's the best thing for all of us. The house is something we were going to build together, but I've been dreaming about it since I was a kid, so I'm having a lot of fun with it. Besides, it keeps me looking forward instead of back. The facts are the facts and we've got to accept them."

"Funny, Dad says the same thing. And I'm sorry. I didn't mean to sound snippy about the house in Montana. I am happy for you since I know how much you've wanted that."

"Thanks. Maybe I'll even get some horses so when you visit you can ride and I'll feel like I got my money's worth out of all those years of riding lessons."

"That would be great. But changing the subject . . ." Kelly's voice went from serious to chatty. "I need your advice on what to wear on my date tonight."

Leslie shook her head. Kelly didn't want to hear any of Leslie's advice about life but did want an opinion about what to wear on a date.

"Who's it with, and what are the choices?" Leslie said, making her own voice light and putting her emotions on the back burner, wondering if Kelly had inherited that from her.

"The guy studying architecture. Do you think I should wear the blue V-neck top and look sexy or the black sleeveless turtleneck and look artsy?"

"Definitely the black. This is only the third date, isn't it? Go easy on the poor guy." Kelly ran through men like she shopped for dresses, trying them on for size and then putting them back on the rack.

"Fourth. If you count having coffee as a date. The turtleneck it is."

Leslie suspected that Kelly would wear the low-cut top anyway. Kelly's opinion was that men wanted sexy first and smart second. *I suppose she's right,* Leslie thought. When her divorce was final, she'd have to figure out if it was still true at her age. She thought she might be attractive to men since she stayed in shape and took care of herself, but sexy? She had no idea. She hadn't thought about that for years. She pushed the thoughts away—it was way too soon to be thinking about men. Hell, at this point, she didn't even know if she wanted another relationship.

Cortez Harbinger had had a lousy day that ended with a lousy meeting at Sam Curtis' DC office. He decided to stop for a beer on his way home from work, but when he got to the bar, he ordered his usual Jack on the rocks. It was a perfect day weather-wise—not too humid yet, but hot enough that women shed their conservative jackets and revealed those little tops they wore underneath. He decided to sit at one of the outside tables and admire the view.

Until today, he hadn't seen Senator Curtis since the dinner with Andy back in April in Montana. That had gone better than expected, with the senator agreeing to look at Xandex's concept paper for legislation to make drilling for gas easier. He even said that he would consider sponsoring a bill if it was in the best interests of the state of Montana and his constituents.

The senator had asked for more information, probing some of the key points of the proposal. Harbinger had tried to work his magic, talking about the economic hardships people in Montana were facing, especially the ranchers, and how this would help. He had charts made to show the tax revenues that would flow to the state. He even played the patriot card and talked about national security and how important it was to be free from the shackles of foreign nations when it came to our oil supply.

The senator and his staff had listened, but it wasn't good enough. Today they told him they not only couldn't support the change Xandex wanted but would actively oppose it if it were brought forward. Harbinger had pulled out all the stops and had failed. And now he had to tell Andy.

He took out his cell phone.

"Not good news," Macfarlane said when Cortez finished. "But if that's where the good Senator Curtis stands, then it's time for plan B."

Cortez smiled. Suddenly, he was in a better mood.

CHAPTER 4

Peg walked from the house to the barn, the grass thick with early morning dew and a hint of frost already in the air. This time of year was her favorite, when the chill of the morning was a disguise for the warm day that was sure to follow. The peaks in the distance weren't yet cloaked in snow, but it would happen soon enough. They needed to get the cattle down to the low pasture soon, she fretted. *But it's Labor Day weekend, and I'll be sixty tomorrow. I need to relax and celebrate.* All three of the boys were coming home for the occasion, and she loved having the whole family together, which now included two daughters-in-law and three grandchildren. *Maybe,* she thought, *the boys could ride out and help bring in at least one string. It would make it easier for Lee this coming week.* She'd talk to them this evening.

A light breeze found its way around the corners of the barn as Peg went in and pulled on a pair of worn-leather work gloves. She grabbed a shovel and went into one of the stalls to clean out the night's accumulation. Manny was already there, working in the stall next to her.

"How's yer rodeo boy doing these days?" Manny asked. "Is he comin' in for the weekend?" Will, her youngest and only unmarried son, was a professional bull rider.

"Yes, I'm so happy. It means a lot to me that he's skipping this big rodeo weekend just to be here."

"Heard he's sittin' purty to do real well down at the Vegas finals in December."

"If he doesn't get hurt first, that is. So far, the only injuries have been to his ego."

"He's too smart to get hurt. Don't you worry about him so much."

She rolled her eyes, knowing that Manny couldn't see her from where he was working. Manny, who had been a bronc rider, walked with a limp. Rodeo was a tough business on the body, and bull riding was the most dangerous event.

"Thanks, Manny. Will is smart, which is why I wish he'd go to college like his brothers. But I guess all a mother can do is hope that her kids are happy doing what they choose to do, even if I don't like it."

"The boy's got character, and he don't need to go to college to be a good man."

Peg knew Manny was right, but Will's choice still bothered her.

"You haven't said anything about the new house. What do you and the hands think?"

"I know it's a sore spot for you, so I ain't been sayin' nothin'. But now that you ask, some of the boys don't like it, but I say it'll be good to get some new blood on the land, shake things up a bit. We tend to get set in our ways sometimes, don't ya think?"

"Guess that's one way to look at it. They're city people, though, from DC, so I hope they don't get too much blood on the land!" She tried to laugh, but it sounded awkward. "To tell the truth, I'm still not used to the idea of having neighbors so close, but Lee says I'll get over it. In fact, he says maybe it will be good for me to have another woman nearby. He thinks we'll be friends." She snorted. "As if all the ones I've had for the past sixty years aren't enough." She shook her head. "I'm sure it will be fine. Worse things can happen in life now, can't they?"

They finished the chores and Peg washed her hands at the sink in the barn, feeling the irritation she always did when thinking about the new house and the new neighbors. But the feeling disappeared as soon as she heard a car in the driveway. It was her oldest son, Roy, his wife and their two children. She got to the barn door just as the kids came running to her. She knelt down and hugged them both together.

"Grammy, Grammy, can we see the horsies?" Four-year-old Jake jumped up and down. Two-year-old Emily stood there grinning.

"Of course we can, but first let me give your mommy and daddy a hug."

"Just go, Mom," Roy said as he pulled suitcases out of the trunk. "They haven't been talking about anything but you and the horses since we left Helena."

Peg scooped up Emily, took Jake's hand, and headed into the barn. *I wish they lived closer. This is heaven having them here,* she thought. Of course, she missed her sons, but she pined for her grandchildren.

"Do you remember Manny?" Peg asked when Manny came out of the stall. Emily turned her head into Peg's shoulder, but Jake ran to him.

"Howdy, pardner." Manny put his hand out to Jake. "Long time no see."

Peg realized that although she had visited Helena in the spring, the last time the kids had been here at the ranch was Christmas.

"D'ya wanna help me feed the horses?"

Jake's eyes got big with excitement and he ran to the oat bin to get started. Peg heard a truck pull into the driveway.

"Mind keeping track of him for a bit?" she asked Manny.

"My pleasure to have a real cowboy to help me." Jake beamed at Manny's remark.

"Come on, Emily. Let's go see who it is." Peg put Emily down and held her hand, but let it go when the little girl ran to greet her Uncle Will, who jumped out of the driver's seat.

"How's my favorite niece?" Will scooped Emily up in one arm, and then gave Peg a hug with the other. "Happy Birthday, Mom! And look who I brought with me." Peg's third son, Slim, came around from the other side, gave Peg a hug, then turned to help his wife get their baby from the car seat in the extended cab. They'd flown in from San Jose and Will had picked them up at the airport.

"I'm so glad everyone could make it. Was she fussy on the plane?" Peg took the baby from Slim, smothering her with kisses until the baby giggled.

"Not a bit," Slim said. "She's going to be a world traveler."

"Or a cowgirl like her Grandma," Will said. "And how about you, Emily? Are you going to be a cowgirl too?"

"Uncle Will! Uncle Will!" Jake barreled out of the barn.

"Jakie, my man. Give me five." Will set Emily down, put his hand up for the slap, and then picked up the boy and spun him in the air.

"Go in and get settled," Peg said. "I'll get lunch ready. We'll eat out on the deck."

After they finished eating, Peg watched the kids run around on the grass until they wore themselves out. Around three, the mothers ignored protests and went inside to put them down for a nap and grab some quiet adult time.

"I really wish you lived closer so I could see those kids more often," Peg said to Roy.

"Sorry, Mom. But when you work for the governor, you've got to live in Helena. It's only three hours away, you know, and you are welcome any time.

"I know, honey, but it's so hard to get away with all the work here at the ranch."

"Well, at least I'm not as bad as this guy." Roy put his arm around Slim. "Helena's a lot closer than San Jose."

"Like you said, we've got to live where the work is." Slim pulled a beer from the cooler filled with drinks.

"Speaking of work," Lee said, putting down his beer can, "I need you boys to help me with that wood." He pointed to a pile of cut logs that needed to be split and stacked. "How about we get that over with before you pop another beer?"

Slim put the beer back on ice. "Sure thing. But you sit here with Mom and we'll take care of it." The three boys went over to the wood and arranged themselves into an assembly line, working easily to get the job done.

Peg opened a beer for herself and relaxed into her chair. *Feels like only yesterday they were little like the grandkids. Where does the time go? How could I be turning sixty already?* She watched them work. *I can't believe how different they are from each other.* Roy was a big, burly man, with political ambitions. He was a Montanan through and through and would run for office soon. Slim, who was actually Lee, Jr., fit his cowboy nickname, but growing up, he spent more time in front of his computer than on his horse, not just playing computer games but inventing them. Peg was proud when he chose her alma mater, Stanford, for college, and after graduation, his career in Silicon Valley had taken off like a shot. Will resembled Lee: tall, fit, and ruggedly handsome. She worried about him the most since his job was so dangerous and he showed no sign of settling down.

"Do you think Will will ever get married?" she asked Lee.

"Only if he meets the right girl."

"He seems to run through women pretty fast. Maybe he'll always be a loner."

"You've got three grandkids already, so it wouldn't be the end of the world."

"I just want him to be happy." She and Lee sat quietly together. She looked at the aspens at the far edge of the yard and realized the leaves were starting to turn from green to gold, a tease of the saturation of colors that would dot the landscape in September. *Ought to capture that,* she thought. She could hear the boys talking as they worked.

"Hey, Casanova," Slim said to Will, "got any hot prospects? How come you didn't bring a cute cowgirl home with you?"

"Yeah, you're not getting any younger," she heard Roy add.

"You bring them home to meet mom and they think it's serious. I haven't found anybody I want to get serious with yet, so I don't bring anybody home."

"Better hurry up," Slim said. "Nobody's going to want an old, broken-down bull rider."

"When I meet the right girl, I'll know it and have a ring on her finger so fast you won't believe it. And don't forget, I'm still not as old as either of you and never will be. You guys are just jealous. And out of shape. Come on, pick up the pace."

"He's right. I'm both old and out of shape." Slim sat down on the woodpile for a break. "My arms hurt already."

"And I'm even older than you." Roy sat down next to Slim while Will kept working. "Let's let the young buck who's in shape finish this up. So what's your 401(k) invested in, Slim? We old folks need to be thinking about how to fund our retirement, you know."

Peg looked at Lee. "They're barely thirty and talking about retirement investments while we've got this whole ranch here for whichever one wants it."

"But none of them does." He smiled gently as she took a sharp breath, and opened her mouth to say something. "Wait," he said, and put his hand on her arm. "Can I get you another beer?"

Leslie smiled as she stepped from her air-conditioned car into the enveloping heat and humidity of the late DC summer.

She complained about it along with everyone else, and spent her share of time inside artificial coolness, but she secretly enjoyed the way her body was instantly covered with a moist sheen the minute she walked outside. The intensity of the humidity made her feel welcome—almost like it was a hug.

Leslie could see her best friend, Cynthia, absorbed in her BlackBerry while sitting at the window table in the bar where they usually met for drinks. They used to meet only once a month or so, but since Leslie and Hugh had split up, they'd been getting together almost every week. Most of Leslie's friends were married, but Cynthia was happily single, an interior designer who had been through two divorces.

The place was filled with the after-work crowd sipping a beer, gin and tonic, or a glass of wine before descending into the subway station for the long ride out to the suburbs of Virginia or Maryland. Leslie liked the bar for its name, Cowgirl Heaven, and its décor, which included a long, wooden bar with mirrored glass behind the shelves; thick, carved, wooden columns along the sides; and a parade of rawhide barstools. Leslie gave Cynthia a hug before settling into the chair opposite her.

"Hi, there. You two want the usual?" The waitress appeared instantly, a woman in her forties, her black hair pulled back in a ponytail. She wore the summer uniform of the place: short denim skirt, black tank top, and cowboy boots that clattered pleasantly on the wood floor when she walked.

"Nope," Cynthia said, eyeing the wine list. "Today we are going to have champagne." She pointed to an expensive one on the list. "It's a celebration."

"We don't need to do that," Leslie protested.

"Oh, yes, we do."

"What're you celebrating?" the waitress asked.

Cynthia raised her eyebrows and threw her hands out beside her. "The best thing," she answered. "A divorce. Did the final papers come through today like they were supposed to?"

"Yes, they did, but I'm not sure I feel like celebrating," Leslie said. "It actually makes me kind of sad."

"I'm with her." The waitress motioned toward Cynthia. "Whether you wanted it or not, it's a new life now and you may as well celebrate. Beats being down in the dumps about it. And believe me: I know. I've been through three of them already."

She clomped away, ponytail swaying.

"Sorry I was late," Leslie said.

"No worries. You're always late. Have been for the last fifteen years. I'm used to it. Gives me a chance to catch up on my e-mail." She clicked the button to end her session and put the BlackBerry on the table.

"I can't believe it's actually over." Leslie searched for her reading glasses in her purse. "How could it have been so easy to dissolve twenty-nine years of marriage? It barely took four months."

"It's always hardest at the beginning, but you'll get used to it. Maybe even come to like it. You know that's what happened to me after the second one. Hang in there."

"Thanks. I've been trying to ignore it all day long, and now it just feels so real. This is terrible to say, but sometimes I think it would have been easier if he had died. Then I wouldn't have to deal with the questions, the what-ifs, the things I should have done differently. I feel like I screwed up. I failed. And you know I don't like to fail." Leslie attempted a smile.

41

"You've never failed at anything in your life, and you know it. Both of you let the marriage die. It's not all your fault. Besides, you told me you weren't in love with him anymore. Being free to explore a new life is a success. Something to celebrate."

"I do feel like a weight is off my shoulders now that it's final. Maybe you're right. Thanks for trying to cheer me up."

"It's my job." Cynthia picked up the bar menu. "Let's get some appetizers to go with the champagne, and then I'm taking you out to dinner. This isn't a night to go home and wallow in self-pity."

"I would do no such thing," Leslie said, even though that was exactly what she had planned to do. "Dinner sounds like a good idea. But let's go somewhere near my house so I can park the car and walk home. If we start with champagne this early, I won't be fit to drive by the end of the night. You are so smart to take taxis everywhere."

"Less expensive than owning a car, you know. Listen, we're going to have a good time tonight. No regrets about the past; it's all about the future. I brought you a gift. Here." She handed Leslie a beautifully wrapped little package. "It's the latest Maggie Madison. If she can't cheer you up, nobody can."

"Oh, Cynthia! You're great." Leslie tore off the wrapping. "I've been meaning to get to the bookstore to buy this." She leafed through the volume. "I love the way I can randomly open her books and find a passage that speaks to me. Listen."

Darkness shattered by splits of light.
The roar of pain searing as it rumbles,
Awash with the rain of pity and self-loathing.

The thunderstorm travels on, a new beginning
in its wake.

"See! Isn't that just perfect? It blows me away that she can describe a scene from nature, but it applies to life. I feel better already. Thank you. Now my Maggie Madison collection is again complete."

"You're welcome. I knew you'd love it. You know my goal is to keep you on the positive side of this divorce." She paused when the waitress returned with the bottle of bubbly, and nodded that it was the right one. "I've got some new ideas for decorating the Montana house that I want to tell you about. A Western-chic motif. It's going to be so wonderful. I can't wait to come out and howl with the coyotes."

The waitress popped the cork on the champagne. "You enjoy this now," she said as she filled two glasses and stuck the bottle into an ice bucket next to the table. She turned to Leslie. "Are you going to have your diamonds made into a freedom ring?"

"What's a freedom ring?" Leslie asked.

"It's when you take all the precious stones your ex gave you and have them remade into a really spectacular ring. Lets you use the jewels but in a way that doesn't remind you of him. Everybody does it now." She held out her right hand, showing a large, multi-diamond ring on her finger.

"Interesting idea. I'll think about that later, but not quite yet. Right now I just need to get used to the reality of it."

The waitress left and Cynthia held her glass up high. "To you. A few years from now, you'll have a house in Montana and a new life, and I'll be coming out for vacation every year to kick back and relax. You'll be living your dream of sleeping in, and doing all sorts of creative things that you haven't had time to do for the last thirty years. So here's to Montana and cowgirls and freedom."

Leslie loved the taste of the champagne, but the taste of freedom wasn't yet sweet in her mouth.

The last bedroom door finally closed as Peg's sons and their families retired to their rooms. She sat on the big leather couch looking out to the south. The house seemed huge and quiet now. *Funny how easy it was to get used to the noise again*, Peg thought. *I guess that's why people like it when the kids are out of the house and they retire. The welcome noise of grandkids visiting, but most of the time, peace and quiet and being able to do whatever you want whenever you want.*

Retirement. How strange to hear her sons talking about that. When you run a ranch, how can you retire? It's not like you decide to just stop working one day. Have a retirement lunch, get a gold watch, and live the easy life until you died. No, cows still need to be fed, horses need to be ridden and groomed, fences mended, the garden tended. There was no such thing as a ranch retirement.

Maybe she and Lee should sell the ranch and move to Arizona. It would be warm there all year, not just for a month or two. She could get rid of her sweaters and boots and wear shorts and flip-flops all day long. Maybe she would even take up golf. Retired people played golf all the time, didn't they? She almost laughed out loud at such a crazy thought.

She cocked her head, a slight frown crossing her face. She would be sixty years old tomorrow and had never had a discussion with her husband about what happened when they got too old to work the ranch. No matter how bad the finances looked, selling out completely had never been considered. She always thought she would keep working on the ranch forever. What other option was there?

Now that the idea was in her head, she couldn't get rid of it. No, she realized, she hadn't really believed she would keep working on the ranch. She had assumed that one of her sons would take it over and that she would continue to live in the house and do light chores and her creative work until she died. The son would build his own house on some other part of the property and Peg and Lee would be helpful, but not intrusive, grandparents.

But none of her sons wanted to run the ranch or build a house. She hadn't been ignoring getting old; she'd been ignoring the fact that her kids had their own lives and dreams, and none of them included taking over the ranch.

CHAPTER 5

"All I want for my birthday today is to have a serious discussion about the future of the ranch," Peg said as the boys gathered around the table for breakfast with her and Lee. The girls had eaten earlier with the kids, and now had them outside for a walk.

"I think you ought to sell the whole thing," Slim stated bluntly. "You could get a pretty penny for it and go live somewhere warm. Maybe come to California and be closer to me."

"No way, Slim. They need to keep it," Roy countered. "It's been in the family for over a hundred years. They can't just sell it. It's bad enough that those forty acres are gone." Peg knew that Roy had never been inclined to stay on the ranch, but the Hamilton history was part of his political future.

"Are you going to run it, Roy? Mom and Dad aren't getting any younger you know," Slim persisted.

Peg wrinkled her nose. She still thought of herself as young and able.

"We're not ready to keel over yet," Lee said. "But it's a good discussion to have. Especially since the numbers haven't been penciling out for the past few years. That's the only reason we had to let that parcel go." He spooned a second serving of scrambled eggs onto his plate. "What do you think, Will?"

"I think you ought to keep going as long as you can. This is our home, where we grew up. It'd be hard to see you sell it."

Peg got up to get the pot of coffee. She was beginning to regret her birthday wish. "More coffee?" she asked to the table in general.

"I'll take some," Lee said, holding out his cup until Peg had filled it. "Truth is, boys, I don't know how much longer your Mom and I can hold on. We're trying everything we can think of."

"How bad is it, Dad?" Roy asked.

"Pretty bad." Lee pushed the eggs around without eating any. "Ever since the mad cow scare, the market price and demand have stayed down. And that report last year about the bad effects from the steroids—well, that sure didn't help." He turned around, pulled a pad of paper from the buffet drawer, and jotted down numbers as he talked. "Even though we haven't had any infected cows and we aren't using steroids, the market doesn't make a distinction. If the beef is from the US, nobody wants it."

He pushed the pad to the middle of the table. Peg could see that there was a column of numbers on it, some with plusses in front of them and others with minuses. Lee motioned to the pad. "We made a little bit of money on the beef, but it's about a third of what we've usually done. The wool from the sheep down on the Flat Forty still brings in about the same amount, but it's never been much. And then there's the money your mom makes because she's so creative, but that's for her to treat herself, even though she never does." He smiled at Peg.

"It's not enough to make a dent, anyway," Peg said. "Besides, it's not just the drop in income. The costs are also way up."

"She's right," Lee said. "Which puts us further in the hole."

"Didn't you get quite a bit when you sold the property?" Will asked.

"Yes." Lee took the pad and jotted a large number on the plus side of the sheet. "It'll allow us to keep going for about another year at the current loss rate. The problem is, once it's gone, it's gone. We can't make any more land, so if we keep selling off pieces, eventually the ranch'll be too small to make a go of it, no matter what."

"I'm not selling any more," Peg said firmly. "It's all or nothing. One of the three of you has to take it over someday, and you'll just have to decide which one."

Leslie and Cynthia spent the evening eating, drinking, and talking about life, the new house, shoes, and how to find happiness. But for once they skipped discussing the drama of men and relationships. Back home in the soft light of her bedroom, Leslie admired the ivory linens on her perfectly made bed that looked like porcelain. There was a rich red coverlet folded neatly at the bottom of the four-poster antique bedstead. Hugh never appreciated the look of their well-made bed and couldn't even be bothered to throw the covers up to make it easier for her to complete the job every morning. *At least now the house will always look the way I want it to.* The tan sisal rug scratched the bottoms of her feet as she kicked off her pumps and walked to the half-empty closet to undress. *And there's plenty of room for my clothes.* She pushed some of the hangers apart to fill the space.

She'd had a great time with Cynthia, but she still had to face this first night as a divorced woman. A single woman. Hugh had moved out over four months ago and she'd been living by herself since then, but now it was different. It was official. She put on a nightgown and crawled into bed.

She picked up a volume of Maggie Madison poetry from the stack of books beside the bed and opened it randomly.

> A kiss of light across the horizon
> Strip of turquoise, no, now pink
> Reflection of life, of grandeur, my heart
> The sky energizing me
> To face another night.

Closing the book, she felt calmer. On the cover was a watercolor of a lake with a mountain both above and within it. The title was *Reflections*.

I wish for the life that Maggie Madison writes about, she thought for the thousandth time. *I want to live in a house with a view of the mountains, with no worries and the open sky above me. I want to be content with who I am and never again take for granted who I'm with. That is, if I'm ever with another man again. And if not, I wish for the courage to live the rest of my life alone, if that's what it takes.*

She checked her BlackBerry for messages one last time before turning it off and turning out the light.

Lee was reading in bed when Peg crawled in next to him. The warmth of his body next to hers calmed her. It had been a wonderful birthday, except for the discussion after dinner about the fate of the ranch. The boys had argued, accusing each other of not caring for their heritage or their parents or both. Yet in the end, each declared his intention, and need, to live separate from the ranch. Even Will, her last hope.

"I could kick myself for not seeing that coming," she said, snuggling into him "But if they don't take it over, what will happen to the ranch? It's our legacy. And what will happen to us? Have you ever thought about it?"

"To tell you the truth, not really. I can't imagine not working on this ranch until the day I die." He ran his hand along her side and stroked her bottom. She still loved his touch, even after all these years.

"Do you think we're getting too old to run the place?"

"Don't you be listening to those boys now. We're only as old as we feel." He took her hand and placed it on his flat stomach. "Now does that feel old to you?"

"Not a bit." She could hear the baby crying at the other end of the house. Thank goodness, she was done with those days. She'd worry about the future tomorrow. Right now, she had more important things to take care of.

CHAPTER 6

It was a chilly May morning, but the sky was cloudless and the sun was warm on Leslie's face as she stood on the deck of her new house with a cup of coffee. *Thank goodness it isn't raining for moving day,* she thought. *And that there isn't still snow on the ground.* She watched the fully loaded moving van struggle up the last part of the steep gravel road. The motor growled when the low gear caught and she held her breath as the driver successfully negotiated the tight turn of the hairpin. She had arrived at the house only an hour before and had been waiting anxiously since then. Across the valley, she could see the mountains still had snow crowns, although the flanks were inky black. The van pulled into the broad driveway in front of the two-car garage facing out from the south side of the log house.

"Hello, glad you made it," Leslie said to the burly driver from the deck above the driveway. "I'll be right down."

"That's some hill." He hitched up his jeans with his thumbs. "Good thing it isn't winter or you'd never get this truck up here."

Leslie didn't care. It was a glorious spring day and winter was the farthest thing from her mind. "I know, it's a bit steep

51

at the end, but isn't the view incredible?" She spread her arms out toward the valley.

"Yes, it is, ma'am. You've got a fine piece of property here." The driver stretched from side to side to ease his back. "I've been delivering loads in Montana for years, and I've seen my share of good and bad locations."

"Did you drive all the way from DC?"

"Oh, no, I'm just the local guy. A long-haul truck brought your container from DC and dropped it about a hundred miles from here. That's where I picked it up. All I do is deliver within the state boundaries. Sometimes it's real easy, like when I'm going to the eastern flats with a decent road."

"So you don't like these hills much, do you?" Leslie said, feeling strangely at ease with the trucker.

"No, ma'am, I don't. Even though the view is great. It's tough on the truck and the roads keep getting narrower and steeper. Costs as much to build a road like this as some people pay for a house. But it seems that the farther away you come from, the steeper you want your road. Hell, in the last year I've moved people from as far away as LA, New York, and Atlanta. Then on top of it, everybody's building these houses big enough for ten people when only two or three are going to live there. You all don't realize that in the winter, steep is not good and it costs a lot to heat a big house." He looked down as if he realized he'd been talking too much. "But enough of my opinion. We'd better get started here."

Leslie smiled. *Yes, you certainly have opinions,* she thought.

"I have a pot of coffee brewed if you and your partner would like some before you start." The other man, small and wiry but with Popeye arms, was busy at the back of the truck. "The coffee pot is one of the few essentials I brought with me that I knew I'd need before you got here."

"No, but thanks anyway," the driver said, his partner already rolling the first dolly of boxes down the ramp. "We like to get a good hour's work in before taking a break. Gets the blood moving after the drive. But if you can keep it hot, I'm sure we'd appreciate some later."

"No problem." Leslie walked back into the house. *This is the last time I'll see it empty. Soon it will be filled with my things, and it will be my home. Not owned with Hugh, not shared with Kelly. Not "ours" but mine. Every decision mine alone.* Well, hers and Cynthia's. Cynthia had helped pick the furniture, and she would arrive day after tomorrow to help unpack and decorate.

She heard the men behind her as they carried a chair into the living room.

"You'll need to tell us where you want these big items," the driver said.

"That one will go on the left side of the fireplace, then the couch will be directly in front and the other chair on the other side," she said. This was it. It was finally happening.

Leslie poured herself a cup of coffee. She thought back to the fall, when it seemed like the house would never be done. There were so many decisions. At least once a week, she had talked with her builder, Mike Connelly, to check on the progress of the construction. The calls sometimes lasted an hour as she questioned details, made decisions, and listened to Mike's estimates for each new idea she had. About every two months, she'd flown in to see how it was going, and then flew back home the next day to minimize the amount of time she was away from work. When the project started, she didn't really care how long it took. After all, she had several more years to work, and without Hugh, well, she hadn't been sure about anything.

Then, in December, a large international firm wrapped up an offer to buy her law firm. The early retirement package they offered was too good to pass up. Dealing with the specter of not working every day, she felt a sudden need to be in Montana. To really start a new life.

She had called Mike. "How soon can you have it done and ready for me to move into?"

"We're still on schedule, Leslie. If everything keeps going the way it has been, and you minimize the changes you make, we'll be finished by the middle of August."

"What would it take to get it done sooner?"

"It'll take a lot of overtime and no major change orders. If you're serious, I'll work up an estimate."

"I'm serious. Get me the estimate, Mike. I want to be living there by May."

She had gulped when she saw how much it would cost, but Mike had delivered as promised and now here she was.

The movers lumbered into the room again, straining under the weight of the couch. "In front of the fireplace, right?" the driver asked.

"You've got it." She smiled as they placed it perfectly and left again.

She sat on the sofa and looked around, still not quite believing it. *Here I am, in my new house on forty acres in Montana. I did it,* she thought. She had flown in the day before, checked into a motel, and then met Mike at Judy Baker's real estate office, smiling to herself as she walked along the perfectly dry sidewalk.

"I hope you like it," Judy had said. In addition to selling her the property, Judy had facilitated the construction loan. "When you come back from the inspection with Mike, we'll do the final signing and hand you the keys."

She hadn't let Mike or Judy see her growing nervousness, using her years as a negotiator to hide what she was really feeling. It had been two months since she'd last seen the house—having had to cancel two planned trips because of last-minute work demands as she prepared to retire. She climbed into Mike's well-used, white pickup. Painted on both sides was the Connelly Construction logo, which was a bright red set of wings over the initials "CC" set in the middle of a log circle.

As they started down Main Street, a few cars went past, but most were pickup trucks, usually with a dog or two hanging a head off the side of the bed, tongue lolling and eyes sparkling. Leslie tried to relax.

They left the main road and drove along the gravel county road, a plume of dust rising behind them. About twenty minutes later, they came to a fork where Leslie's new private road took off sharply to the left. To the right, she could barely see the Hamilton family ranch house. One switchback, then two, and finally three. She didn't remember it being so far from the main road, but she knew it was only her worry and excitement. She told herself she would be gracious to Mike even if she didn't like all of the finishes. Her stomach roiled and she wondered if she would be sick. But then, suddenly, they turned a corner and there it was, in front of her, and it was beautiful.

"I need more onions, Lee. Can you bring some in from the cellar?" Peg called out the open window of her kitchen as Lee was on his way in from the barn.

The large root cellar sat adjacent to the old house, just outside the back door of the kitchen. When Peg's great, great grandparents first came across the country with everything they owned in their wagon, they dug the root cellar before even starting the house. After all, keeping their food supply safe was more important than a comfortable shelter from the high country sun.

She removed the marinating chicken from an old yellow bowl that had been on that wagon. She placed each piece on a round platter, ready to drop into the large cast-iron frying pan already filled with garlic and onion. But not enough onion, she decided. She'd need a few more to really flavor the big batch of chicken.

Peg cooked by sight and feel, the old family recipes merely a suggestion or guide. She could tell by looking how much batter was needed for fifteen pancakes or for thirty. Her nose rivaled that of a highly trained chef when it came to determining just the right spice for a dish and how much of it. Her baking was renowned throughout the county. The morning biscuits she served the ranch hands were as light and flaky as croissants; her pies won prizes at the state fair every year.

"Here you go, love," Lee said, handing her two onions as he came through the door. "Need anything else before I head out to work on the irrigation pipe on the lower section?"

"Not cooking-wise I don't. Thank you. But I'm not sure where the tack repair kit is and I want to work some on that old saddle. I looked for it yesterday but couldn't find it."

"I took it to the breaking shed last week. Guess I forgot to put it back. I'll get it before I leave." He kissed her on the cheek, squeezing her shoulder lightly.

Feeling the affection in his touch, she wished there wasn't so much to do today. During the winter, they sometimes took a break in the middle of the day to make love, but now that it was spring, there was too much work.

"The new people are supposed to be moving in today," Peg said with an affected disinterest. "Mike Connelly told me they had a moving van coming. If you see activity on the road that isn't Mike, you'll know what it is." Peg suspected that Lee already knew all this, but he had stopped bringing up the sale of the land or the newcomers unless she broached the subject first.

"Yeah, I know." Lee stopped with the door held open. "There's been no going back since we sold that land, Peg. Like I keep saying, it'll be okay. We've still got a huge ranch and our own piece of solitude and heaven. One close neighbor isn't going to hurt us. I think we're lucky they bought all forty acres and we didn't have to subdivide it and have even more neighbors. Tell you what. Let's take some of that chicken over tonight. Pack up a little care package to get them through the first few days. And why don't you make an extra loaf so they can taste the best bread on the planet." He went out and closed the door, not giving Peg any chance to argue.

She watched him go and tried to feel lucky. But that lump in her throat that came up every time she thought of the sale of her family's land got in the way. The lump that was only replaced by the bigger knot of anger in her stomach—anger directed at the buyers, the woman she had picked up from the sidewalk last year and her husband. She knew it was illogical to be angry. After all, she was the one who put the property on the market. But she couldn't help it. And now Lee was going to make her take them chicken casserole. It was, of course, the right thing to do, but she didn't have to like doing it.

All day, she tried to think of anything but what was happening down the road. She'd been able to avoid the construction most of the winter, except for a few sneak peeks here and there when she couldn't contain her curiosity. She had not wanted to see a house going up on what she still thought of as her land. By midafternoon, Peg decided she should be outside enjoying the perfect spring day. She saddled her horse and headed out to help Lee. The temperature of the air was decidedly warm, a welcome change after the long winter.

She rode through a grove of aspens on the side of the hill, their strong, white, dappled trunks a sharp contrast to the budding green leaves. As she came up over the hill, the aspens gave way to a thicker cover of pines and maples, patches of snow still hiding in the north facing pockets beneath the trees. She crested the hill and headed down the other side, appreciating the warmth from the dry southern slope that opened to a sea of sage and shrubs. The smell of the fresh spring sage was strong, and she decided to pick some to add to the chicken. She felt better already.

She picked up the pace when she got to the wide-open space of the flat lower section, spreading for miles as it eased itself into the true valley floor. About a half mile away, she could see Lee adjusting irrigation pipe along an area where they grew hay for the cattle.

Peg felt the power of the horse beneath her as it moved. She forgot about the neighbor or anything else as she concentrated on the gait of the animal. This is what made her happy. The freedom of the wind in her hair, the big sky above, and the promise of plenty from the land beneath her. This place kept her alive. She brought the horse to a walk before meeting up with Lee.

"You sure are having fun now, aren't you?" Lee said as she approached. "Did you come out to help me, or are you just joyriding?" He held the horse while she dismounted.

"Came to help, of course. That is, unless you're already done." She hoped he wasn't. She was looking forward to some hard physical labor. Now that her mind was clear from the ride, she wanted to keep that feeling.

"Fat chance. Tie the horse and grab your gloves, sweetheart." Lee lifted a piece of pipe. "We're in for a great afternoon."

It was after five when Peg and Lee finished moving the irrigation pipe, both of them stiff from the repetitive movements. "My back is killing me," Lee said, stretching his hands over his head. "I used to be able to lift pipe all day without even thinking about it. It's hell getting old."

"I know what you mean." Peg rubbed her upper arms. "I hope I can hold on to the reins on the way back."

"If you want to drive the pickup, I'll switch with you."

"Thanks, but I think a tired back on a horse is worse than tired arms. Besides, I'm looking forward to another ride. You know how much I love it."

"Okay, see you in a bit." He gave her a bear hug. "And don't dawdle. Remember we're going to welcome the new neighbors tonight."

Peg wrinkled her nose and got on the horse. *No need to hurry,* she thought. *Lee could always take the food over by himself if I'm a little late.* She gave Lee a wave as she rode off.

By the time she got back to the house, Lee had already showered and shaved and was sitting expectantly in a wooden rocker on the porch. He was sipping a glass of bourbon on ice, a content cowboy in jeans and a striped popper shirt. The only thing missing was his boots—he had on a pair of flip-flops.

She pulled the horse up in front of the porch as Manny came out of the barn. "I'll take care of her," Manny said, taking the reins as Peg dismounted.

"Shouldn't you be on your way home already?"

"I asked him to stay," Lee said from the porch. "So we can get that food over to the neighbors before dinnertime."

Peg reluctantly let Manny take the horse and came up onto the porch. "How was your drive back?" she asked as she lightly kissed Lee on the forehead and made a motion to sit in the rocker next to him.

"Oh, no, you don't." He put his arm out to block the chair. "I know you're stalling, and it's not going to work. Go get ready. I've just got to put my boots on." He motioned to the clean pair sitting beside him.

"Damn, I can't get away with anything," she said only half in jest. But she let the screen door slam behind her to make sure he knew she didn't want to go.

"And don't worry about the food!" he yelled in behind her. "I've got it all packed and ready."

Twenty minutes later, she reappeared, dressed in jeans, a lavender tank top, and a light cotton sweater. She had a leather jacket thrown over her shoulders. "It'll be cold soon." She handed Lee a jacket too. She noticed that he had already put on his boots. "Let's get this over with."

She climbed into the front seat of the blue pickup, cradling the chicken casserole on her lap and clutching a full grocery bag between her knees on the floor in front of her. It was the Western way to look out for each other, and Peg was, if nothing else, a Westerner.

It was late afternoon when the movers stacked the last of the folded blue quilted blankets in the back of the empty truck. Leslie gave them a generous tip and watched as the truck made its way down the winding road. She could hear the motor and gears playing for a long time even after she lost sight of it. A breeze lifted the new aspen leaves and turned them from side to side, reflecting the diffuse light, the rustling sound like muffled cocktail chatter.

She stood on the deck for a long time while looking at the expanse in front of her, mesmerized by the mountains and the view. A bird called in the trees beside her, and another answered from farther away. Otherwise, it was silent.

"Welcome home, Leslie," she said aloud. These were her mountains. Her birds. Her trees. It was her life and her home. It was her dream, finally come true.

She took a deep breath and became keenly aware of the silence. She noticed the jagged shape of the distant peaks. She felt the final warmth of the day's sun on her cheek and the chill of the evening breeze on her arm. A black-and-white bird with a long tail came and perched on the other end of the railing, cocking its head to and fro as it examined her before flying off. She inhaled the scent of the pine trees. She realized she could track the movement of the sun across the sky in a way she never had in the city. Time was passing and she could see it. A large bird soared into her sight, its silhouette passing in front of the sun and away, making it impossible to see any color.

I've got to get a bird book so I can find out what that black-and-white bird is, she thought. *It seems as common as a robin. And the big birds too. They might even be eagles. It would be cool to be able to identify them. But first, I've got to start unpacking.* She looked back inside at the stacks of cardboard boxes everywhere. *The view will still be here tomorrow, so I'd better get to work.*

She went through the French doors from the deck and stopped in the great room to admire the huge river-rock fireplace, the workmanship fit for an art gallery. The cast of sunlight on the raw, brown, log walls bathed the room with warmth and comfort. Cynthia had recommended heavy pieces of furniture, some with soft, tan, leather cushions and others in fabric with a bold pattern. Leslie had resisted at first (too male, she thought) but eventually gave in. Now she could see that Cynthia was right.

Off the great room, her gourmet kitchen was bigger than the first apartment she had shared with Hugh. She started unpacking, but after two boxes, she realized she needed to make too many decisions: Which cupboard should hold the plates and which the glasses? Where should the bowls go? Which drawer would be most convenient for the silverware? The kitchen was not a good place to start. She went into the bedroom, where the bed the movers had put together lay naked in the large room. Yes, this was a better place to start. For one thing, she would need to make up the bed so she could sleep in it that night.

She'd unpacked most of the boxes labeled "master bedroom" and "master bath" when she opened the box with her alarm clock. She went into the kitchen to see what the stove clock read. It was 6:28. The sun had dropped behind the peaks, but there would still be a couple of hours of daylight left. *No wonder I'm starved,* Leslie thought, realizing she had eaten nothing all day but a muffin at the motel that morning. Her plan was to order Chinese for dinner as the perfect thing to celebrate her first night in her new house. Ordering Chinese delivery when she lived in DC was standard procedure at least once a week as a quick and easy meal. Now all she needed to do was find the best place in Legacy Springs and call to place an order. She remembered that the workman from the phone company had left the local directory when he had been there earlier to connect the Internet and the landline. She pushed some boxes aside and found the smallest telephone book she'd ever seen.

She flipped to the restaurant section of the Yellow Pages. There were twelve listings, none of them Chinese. *Wonder why I never noticed that during all my trips out here,* she thought. There were four pizza/pasta places, two burger joints, one Mexican cantina, three other bars that had grills, and two restaurants that defined themselves as "fine dining" with steak and seafood. One of those was The Pine Room, where she'd usually eaten when she had flown in to check on the progress of the house.

She decided on pizza, but the first three places she called all said they didn't deliver. Finally, on the fourth try, the teenager on the other end of the phone set her straight. "No, we don't deliver. You know, nobody does. But if you come in, we'll pack it in a box for you to take."

"Thanks, but I live a good half an hour from town."

"Yeah, sure," said the girl sympathetically, "most folks do. That's why nobody delivers."

Leslie put down the phone. There was no choice. She'd have to take a shower, get dressed, and drive into town if she wanted any dinner. At least she'd already unpacked the towels and toiletries she'd need. She couldn't decide if she was more tired or hungry.

She got herself a glass of water, plopped onto the couch, and put her feet up on a nearby box. Her jeans and baggy sweatshirt were dirty, and her hands felt cracked and dry from the cardboard and packing paper. She ran her fingers through her straggled hair. *Low blood sugar,* she thought. *If I eat something, I'll feel better. So this is life in Montana.* She pulled herself off the couch and resigned herself to getting cleaned up and driving to town.

Outside, a motor broke the silence. She went to the window and looked out. A blue pickup was coming up her road. She was getting her first company.

CHAPTER 7

Leslie woke up her first morning in her new house, slightly disoriented, and not quite sure where she was. But the view of trees outside the window and the stack of boxes still in the corner gave it away quickly that she was in Montana. She looked at the numbers on the digital clock: 6:18. It was already light, but the sun was nowhere to be seen. Leslie stuck her foot outside the covers and decided it was not only too early to get up, it was too cold. She pulled the comforter over her head to block out the persistent light.

By eight, the sun had crested the mountains and shone directly onto her bed so that she couldn't ignore it. She poked her head out, feeling the stiffness in her muscles from the work of the day before. The sky was cloudless and the birds were so noisy that Leslie wondered how she had possibly fallen back to sleep. She rolled onto her side and noticed the half-empty wine glass on the bedside table. *Thank goodness for Peg and Lee Hamilton*, she thought as she remembered the night before.

Leslie certainly hadn't felt ready for visitors when the Hamiltons had shown up, but when she realized they had brought her a hot dinner—and a bottle of wine—she wanted to kiss them both. They had barely stayed long enough to get past the introductions, saying they didn't want to intrude on her first night there, and she had been grateful given how tired and hungry she was.

She propped herself up in bed, admired her new view, and thought about the interesting couple. Lee was really outgoing and friendly and Leslie immediately liked him. But Peg was giving her the same cold reception she remembered from the end of their visit in Judy Baker's office a year ago. She had tried to be sociable and offered a tour of the house, even though it was all boxes for now, but Peg turned it down. What woman does that? It had also been slightly awkward when they asked about her husband and she told them she moved there alone. They had given each other a look but didn't ask any more questions, and Leslie didn't volunteer any more information.

She thought about how it would be nice being friends with Peg and Lee and maybe even get Peg to give her some cooking tips. If the meal they brought was any indication, Peg was quite the chef. When Leslie had taken the lid off the chicken casserole, a wonderfully sweet and succulent aroma escaped with a hint of spices she couldn't identify. Another container held green beans with almonds and wonderfully pungent blue cheese. Another was filled with sliced red potatoes layered with butter and parsley (fresh snippets on top). A fourth had lettuce, croutons, and Parmesan cheese—a mini Caesar salad complete with a separate small container of salad dressing that had to be homemade. Then there was the incredible bread that Lee said Peg had baked that morning, complete with a stick of butter. Everything was fantastic, and it wasn't just because she had been hungry. The oaky California chardonnay they brought was like icing on a cake.

I guess I'd better get up and get going, Leslie thought, sticking her foot outside the covers again and deciding it was finally warm enough. She went to the window and looked at the expanse in front of her. *I can't believe I'll wake up to this every morning. It's incredible.* She put on her slippers and robe and went to the kitchen to make coffee. With a cup of it in hand, she wandered through the house, mentally noting where different things might go once they were unpacked. She looked at the walls and empty spaces begging for photographs or art to fill them. She gazed at the beams crisscrossing the high ceiling of the great room, wondering how it all held together like she always did when looking at the great cathedrals of Europe. She touched the log walls, reveling in the texture. This was her house. Her dream. She had finally done it.

She looked at the stacks of boxes and wished Cynthia was already there to help. She wandered onto the deck and cradled the warm cup of coffee in her hands to ward off the chill air. *It's so quiet,* she thought. Bird song and rustling leaves were the only sounds. She had never listened to nature in DC. She and Hugh woke to the radio, went to sleep to the TV, and had one or the other on whenever they were home—even if nobody was listening. She hadn't yet unpacked a radio, or set up the TV or the CD player, and she made a mental note to make sure she didn't fall into the habit of always having some artificial sound on. This silence was too precious.

She finished her coffee and halfheartedly opened a few boxes, pulling random items out and unwrapping them, then moving to a different box. She wanted to wait until Cynthia was there to help her decide where to put things. Today her most important job was to shop for food, and it was the perfect excuse to put off unpacking. She showered and dressed in a clean pair of jeans from her suitcase. *Maybe the clothes boxes are the next ones I need to tackle,* she thought, slipping on the same light sweater she had worn on the plane.

She poured another cup of coffee and sat down at the bar to make a list. She'd need all the staples of a kitchen as well as enough to feed herself and Cynthia for a few days. She had originally thought she and Cynthia would eat out most nights, but after her experience last night, she knew they'd be cooking in more than eating out. She looked outside at the blue morning sky. Would she ever be bored of the colors? She hoped not.

Her list completed—and several pages long—she drove down her road and felt a sense of pride, of ownership. *I'll get to know this road pretty well,* she thought, noticing one tree with a curved trunk and another so tall that it shadowed the entire road. *I live on a gravel road,* she marveled as she saw a plume of dust behind her vehicle.

In town, she went directly to the local market. She had been in it a few times on her quick visits to check on the house, but only to grab a yogurt or a piece of fruit to tide her over. It didn't take long for her to walk the aisles and realize they didn't have many of the items she considered to be essential to stock her kitchen.

"Do you have any cheese other than these prepackaged ones? And where can I find fresh ground coffee?" she asked the person stocking the dairy counter.

"You'll need to go to Stokers or the chain supermarkets over by the airport for that kind of gourmet stuff."

"But those stores are an hour away."

"That's right. There isn't enough local demand for us to keep that kind of thing in stock here."

"Even for coffee?"

"No, we have coffee. Aisle seven."

"Yes, I found that, but it's all pre-ground and not fresh beans. I like to grind my own beans."

"Sorry, but most folks just make a trip every couple of weeks to pick up what they need."

Leslie paid for the things in her shopping cart and decided she'd finish off her list tomorrow when she went to pick up Cynthia at the airport. She had enough to tide her over so she went home and tackled a few boxes before sitting down at the table to finish the leftovers from the night before. The flavors seemed even more intense, and the second half of the bottle of wine seemed to evaporate in her glass.

She carefully washed the Hamiltons' casserole dish and plastic containers and stacked them in the brown bag they had been delivered in. Maybe she would get an invitation to dinner when she returned the dishes. Or perhaps it would be better manners if she extended one to them? Maybe she could have them over while Cynthia was there? No, she wouldn't be ready yet. But Kelly was coming soon after that, so maybe then? No, she didn't want to share any of Kelly's short time there. Besides, that might be a real political clash. The Hamiltons were probably very conservative, given their backgrounds as lifelong ranchers. She wondered if they had ever really been to a city—not Helena or Butte but a *real* city like New York or Washington.

No, they probably hadn't, she decided. They were the perfect picture of an unsophisticated ranch couple, especially him in his boots and that funny striped shirt. Her life in DC had been so different with politicians and professionals dressed in suits and ties, restaurants thriving since few people cooked at home, and the length of your commute a common topic of conversation.

She looked out the window again, the stark beauty of her new surroundings a sharp contrast to the view she had from her DC townhouse. *I still can't believe I'm really here,* she thought, remembering a poem from Maggie Madison that she had read on the flight out. *I've got to find that again.* She retrieved the book from the bedside table, and it practically fell open to the page and passage she was looking for.

> Beneath the moon, Venus appeared
> In all her splendor, twinkling as the myth.
> The other goddesses, ready to pounce
> To seize her beauty, to seize her, seize her.
> In the city, I do not see the beauty.
> The lights of success cloud the reality
> That Venus is there and gorgeous
> For all to see,
> If we can dim the lights and focus
> On what is important
> And true.

She thought of all the time she had spent in the city yearning for the beauty and simplicity of life in the West. *Focus on what is important and true,* she told herself. That's what she'd do in Montana. Not be distracted. Be focused. She knew Maggie Madison lived somewhere in the West—Idaho or maybe Colorado—so perhaps she could get to one of her readings. It would be so wonderful to actually meet her.

Leslie closed the book of poetry. She thought about going out on the deck and soaking in the hot tub that Mike had so thoughtfully filled and heated for her arrival. But she was tired. It was time to go to bed, her second night in Montana.

CHAPTER 8

Two pies were in the oven, the timer was on, and Peg sat down at the kitchen table with the last cup of coffee from the morning pot. *Okay, what's next on the list?* she thought as she stared at the small notepad in front of her. Order birthday gift for Will, schedule horse shoeing, review market analysis of Japanese sales, do laundry, write a page, and do a quilt square for the baby quilt. Peg organized her day as she sipped the coffee. *With luck, I can get everything done except maybe the quilting.* That had been on the list for a month now and it always fell to the bottom. She was making the quilt for Will's first born. But since Will didn't even have a steady girlfriend, there was plenty of time.

She flipped to the second page of the notepad to start a grocery list: milk, lettuce, orange juice . . . A car pulled into the driveway. She glanced at the clock on the stove and saw it was ten thirty. Too early for the girl who came once a week to help with the household chores and the cleaning. Must be one of the cowboys running late. She wrote a few more items on the list. *Rap, rap, rap,* she heard at the front door. Nobody ever came to the front door except strangers soliciting donations.

She grumbled as she went through the living room to the front of the house, annoyed by the interruption when she had so much to do.

"Good morning," a small, well-dressed woman said as Peg opened the door.

"Yes, may I help you?" Peg peeked around the door without fully opening it.

"I'm Leslie, remember? From next door. I wanted to return your dishes and thank you for the fabulous meal. I was so famished and the food was delicious. Just what I needed. Thank you."

"Oh, my, excuse me!" Peg said stiffly, opening the door wider. "I didn't recognize you."

"No problem. I understand. I really loved the dinner. You are quite an incredible cook. Thanks again."

Peg took the brown bag that Leslie held out to her. "You're welcome," she said. Leslie did not make any move to leave. They stood and looked at each other awkwardly for a moment.

"I wonder if you might have a few minutes to chat. You know, get to know each other," Leslie said.

"I've got pies in the oven," Peg said as a sharp buzzing sound came from the back of the house. "There's the timer. Well, come in for a moment at least while I get them out of the oven." She waved Leslie in and strode to the kitchen, Leslie following. She opened the oven door, grabbed two mitts, and slid the pies onto the counter, fruit bubbling over. The aroma filled the room.

"Please have a seat," Peg said, unable to be completely rude. "Do you drink coffee? I was just getting ready to brew another pot," she lied. Her full cup still sat on the table.

"That would be great. Thanks."

"By the time it's brewed, the pie might be cool enough to have a piece," Peg said as she poured beans into the coffee grinder. *Why did I say that?* she thought. She didn't have time to sit and talk, least of all with this interloper who now owned part of her ranch. She wanted to ask the woman to leave. Instead, she sat at the table across from Leslie and made an effort. "So tell me, are you all unpacked and settled in yet? How are you enjoying Legacy Springs?"

Andrew Macfarlane sat at the bar at his club, his usual single-malt scotch in his hand. Early that morning, he'd finalized the deal to buy another copper mine in Chile. He wasn't sure which he enjoyed more: the traditional mining work his father had built the company on or the new and exciting natural gas exploration work he was leading the company into.

"Care for another, Mr. Macfarlane?" the bartender asked.

"No, thanks. I've got to drive over to Legacy Springs tonight for some meetings tomorrow, so I'd better get going."

"I grew up over there. It's all cattle ranches and a few tourists that come for the hiking in the summer. Hard to believe you'd be interested in that place."

"Sometimes the value in a place is what most people can't see. It's the secret to business, you know, finding value where others can't. If all goes as planned and my project takes off, Legacy Springs won't know what hit it."

"Well, if it means jobs, that would be good. I had to come here after high school to find work. My parents are still there, and they're struggling to make ends meet."

"Oh, there will be jobs all right, and it will definitely help the place." He was careful not to say too much. He didn't want rumors spreading about the possibility that Xandex was interested in the area. It would just drive up prices. He realized he'd probably said too much already. He finished the scotch.

"On your tab tonight, sir?"

"Yes, please. And remember one of the rules of working here is that what you hear at the club stays at the club. It'll cost you your job if I learn you've been saying anything about our conversation to your buddies back in Legacy Springs."

CHAPTER 9

Leslie turned into the airport parking lot and searched for a spot near the terminal. Although she'd only been in Montana for three days, she already missed her old friends and couldn't wait to see Cynthia. She saw an empty spot in the front row of the lot just as her cell phone rang. She reached into her purse on the passenger seat with one hand and used the other to turn into the parking space.

Crunch. She heard it before she felt it. She'd only looked down into the bag for a second, but it was enough. The front end of her car had hit the back end of the Mercedes in the spot beside her. Damn. She backed up and pulled in with both hands.

She looked at the phone she hadn't answered and saw it was Kelly who had called. *I'll call her later,* she thought as she got out of the car to inspect the damage. The front fender of her SUV was scraped pretty badly, but nothing compared to the black Mercedes, which had a broken taillight and a large dent smeared with red paint. *Well, this is a great way to start the day,* she thought as she shook her head. She looked around again.

Why couldn't I have hit one of these pickups that already has a hundred dings? Bad luck.

She rummaged through her bag, unsuccessfully looking for a piece of paper to write a note. *Damn,* she thought again, *the only paper I have is these old business cards. I've got to clean out this purse. There's everything in here except what I need.* She took two of the cards and wrote her phone number and insurance company name on the back of one and an apology note on the other. She stuck them under the windshield wiper on the driver's side and turned to go to the terminal. She had walked a few steps before she realized the person might try to call her at the law firm. She didn't need anybody to think she was still a DC lawyer and not a local. She went back and scratched out the information on the front side of the cards.

She walked toward the terminal and willed herself to get back in a good mood. *So I had an accident. That's what insurance is for,* she rationalized. *May as well get my money's worth.* She had on the cowboy boots that were still like new, even though she'd bought them a few years ago. They clicked satisfyingly on the tile floor of the terminal as she searched for a screen with arrival information. She'd consciously dressed in an outfit that she thought would make her look like a Montanan. Her new jeans were bought looking already worn. A triple-strand turquoise necklace interrupted the confluent line of her soft, black, leather jacket over a cashmere black V-neck sweater. She thought people were looking at her as she strode confidently through the building toward the gates. She was smiling until she saw the reader board. Cynthia's flight was delayed an hour.

She wandered through the few shops in the terminal before deciding to wait in the bar. Tucked into a far corner of the building, it was small and surprisingly intimate; a swath of windows provided a view of the airfield. All of the tables were taken, so she sat at the bar.

Leslie looked out the window past the airfield, focusing on the mountains in the distance. It hadn't been so long ago that she had seen them for the first time. What changes had happened since then! She looked down at her boots. Hugh had thought her foolish when she bought them a few years ago. "Where are you going to wear those?" he'd asked. Hugh, now her ex-husband, was two thousand miles away and in the arms of another woman. She sighed and looked around the room. She didn't want to think about Hugh.

"Excuse me," said a voice behind her. "Is this seat taken?" A tall, well-dressed man pointed to the stool beside her.

"No, please sit down," she said as she moved her purse from the seat. "I'm sorry. I didn't mean to spread my things all over the place when it's so crowded."

"Not a problem." The man's smile revealed perfect white teeth. "It always gets like this when one of the flights is delayed. The place is too big when nothing is happening and too small on the few occasions when something is." He laughed easily as he perched on the edge of the wide seat, his foot resting on the brass rail that ran along the bottom of the bar.

"Hi, Nick," he said to the young bartender. "What's on tap today?"

Leslie noticed the bartender's prominent nametag and wondered whether they actually knew each other.

While the men chatted about the game on the TV in the corner, Leslie surveyed the new arrival. She guessed he was in his midforties. He was thin but not skinny, and she suspected he worked out regularly. His black slacks were perfectly tailored, and his gray crewneck sweater appeared to be cashmere. She noticed an expensive watch as he reached for the pint glass in front of him. He felt familiar, like the type of man she would know in DC.

"Are you waiting to go or for someone to come?" the man asked as the bartender moved on to other customers.

"Waiting for a friend to arrive," she said. "And you?" She realized he had Paul Newman eyes. Steely blue that seemed to look right through her.

"Me too. I'm picking up a guy who's doing some work for me." He took a healthy swallow of his beer. "Do you live here or are you vacationing?"

"I just moved here from DC, so I guess, as of three days ago, I live here." She felt good saying it, but there was something about him that unnerved her a bit. She wasn't sure what it was, but he was clearly what Cynthia always called an alpha male—the kind of man who acted like he owned the world and could do whatever he wanted.

"Wow. DC to Montana is a big change. Especially if kids are involved. Any family come with you?"

"Nope. Just myself." She didn't elaborate.

"Well, Montana is much better than DC, don't you think? I spend quite a bit of time back East and I always feel better when I come home. As a native Montanan, let me officially welcome you to the wide open spaces and majestic mountains." He pretended to tip a cowboy hat as he nodded to her.

"Thank you. Cheers," she said, holding up her glass. *Shame he's so much younger than me. He's very attractive.*

A modulated voice announced the flight's arrival over the loudspeaker.

"It's about time," the man said. "Another five minutes and I would have had to order another beer." He laughed and pulled out his wallet.

Nick slid a leather folder in front of each of them. The man smoothly picked up Leslie's along with his own. "My treat," he said. "It's not every day I get to engage a beautiful woman in conversation."

Leslie tried to read his name on the platinum card he handed to the bartender.

"Thanks," she said, smiling. She couldn't remember the last time a man she didn't know had bought her a drink.

"My pleasure," he responded. "Well, there's my man." He motioned through the window where the first passengers came through the covered walkway.

Leslie slipped on her jacket and picked up her bag, watching for Cynthia but taking her time so she could walk out with him.

"Thanks, Nick," he said, shoving the signed receipt back at the bartender. "Hope your friend made it." He stepped past her and out of the bar.

Damn, why is he in such a rush? She followed and noticed how nicely his pants fit. *First time in a long time since I've thought about a man that way,* she realized.

"Don't forget we're going to the Healey's for dinner tonight, so get back early," Peg said to Lee as he left the kitchen to go out to his pickup. She dried her hands on the dishtowel hanging from the stove and followed him outside. "Wait a minute." She let the screen door slam behind her. Lee was already inside the cab. "I forgot something." She stepped on the running board and leaned into the open window. She took his face in her hands and kissed him squarely and fully on the lips.

"Well, that's a nice sendoff," he said with surprise. "What'd I do to deserve that?"

"Nothing special. Just felt like it, that's all." She turned to go back to the house.

"I love you, Peg!" he shouted after her.

"I know you do, sweetheart. I love you too." She turned to look at him sitting in the truck. She wished she was going with him, just so they could be together. "Be careful out there."

The May morning sun was yet not strong enough to have warmed the air and Peg shivered slightly as she hurried back to the warmth of her kitchen. By noon, it would be almost sixty-five degrees, but now, at eight o'clock, it was still a chilly forty-eight. Spring would hang on for a long time before succumbing to true summer in a few weeks. From her kitchen, Peg could see the peaks across the valley with wisps of cloud already beginning to build around the highest ones. The early morning chill kept the air dry, not humid. She had one of the best views in the county from her house—even better than the property she had sold to the new neighbor, she thought, although Mike Connelly had done one hell of a job positioning that house to give her a great view too. In fact, he had done a nice job overall, both inside and out, Peg had to admit, much as it pained her

81

to see the house there and have Leslie living in it. *That woman sure can talk about nothing at all,* she thought, remembering how Leslie seemed to stay forever when she had stopped by the other morning—uninvited. Pushy Easterner. And dressed to the nines just to return some dishes. She sure had money; that was clear. It only made Peg dislike her more.

Leslie led the way as she pulled one of Cynthia's three bags behind her. In the parking lot, she turned behind the first row of cars. "Can you believe this place? You don't have to pay to park and I was able to get a spot in the front row. You won't believe how fabulous the house is," Leslie said. "The pictures don't do it justice. You are brilliant for coming up with some of those things you did. Of course, everything's still in boxes. I can't thank you enough for coming out to help me unpack."

She opened the back of her SUV and hoisted the biggest bag into the car. "What on earth did you need three bags for? You're only staying a week!"

Cynthia smiled guiltily. "Oh, I know it's overkill. They even wanted to charge me extra, but I talked them out of it. One whole bag is practically all boots and shoes. I wanted to be prepared for anything."

Leslie grunted as she lifted the second bag. "This weighs a ton. They should have charged you extra."

"Oh, that one has some things I've brought for you for the house. And the last one is all clothes. If I don't have the right things, we'll have to go shopping."

"Well, that will be a short trip then. I've been telling you about the town, but you just won't believe me. If you don't have the right things, you're only option will be to borrow mine." Leslie started to open the front door when she saw the small piece of paper tucked under the windshield wiper.

"Crap." Leslie grimaced. "I forgot all about that." She opened the note. "Thank you for leaving your information. I will be in touch once I get the estimates for repairing the damage," it said.

"Forgot about what?"

"I ran into the back of a Mercedes that was parked beside me and made quite a dent. We'll see how friendly the Montanans are about this kind of stuff. But I'll worry about that later. We've got to go to the store to pick up a few more groceries, and then it'll be another hour to the house."

They got into the car and headed down the highway.

"Tell me about your neighbor. The one who brought you the food the other night."

"She's the only neighbor. Well, she and her husband. I told you they didn't stay long then, but when I took her containers back, we had a chance to chat."

"How old is she?"

"Hard to say. She doesn't color her hair and her face is weathered, but beautiful in a rugged way. She could be late fifties like me, or maybe early sixties."

"Well, how did the visit go?"

"It was a little rocky. When I got there, she was baking pies. I had a sense she didn't want to be bothered, but she invited me in anyway and I ended up staying for an hour. We talked mostly about our families. She has three boys and her family has owned the ranch since 1880. She is the fourth generation to work it and her kids will be the fifth. That is, if any of them take it over. It was clearly a sore spot for her. It sounded like they were all off doing other things, including her youngest who apparently rides bulls in the rodeo for a living. Can you believe it?"

"Well, it's interesting. Way different than anybody we know in DC, that's for sure. Do you think you'll become friends? It would be nice for you to have a friend closer at hand than me."

"I don't know. She sure fits my image of a Montana woman, and her lifestyle is what I imagine I want mine to be. The problem is I'm not sure I have anything in common with her. She's never done anything except live on this ranch here in rural Montana her whole life, right? I mean, she's a housewife. What could we possibly have in common?"

"But it sounds like you had a good conversation."

"Yes, in a 'get to know you' way, but not much else. She seems smart enough, so it's a shame she didn't do more with her life. When I talked about my career, she looked at me kind of funny. I'm sure she didn't understand anything I was talking about."

"What do you mean? What wouldn't she understand about being a lawyer?"

"Well, when I said I was relieved now not to have to work ten hours a day and that I was looking forward to having a life like hers where I could just bake and quilt and enjoy the slow, quiet pace of the days, she said something like 'Not working ten hours a day would be nice.' Like I said, she was a bit standoffish the whole time—polite but not very warm. She kept glancing at the clock too. I don't think she realized I noticed." Leslie paused. "I don't know. Maybe she felt insecure because I'm a lawyer and have been out in the world."

"Maybe. Or she might just be reserved."

"Well, that's true. In any case, she gave me one of the pies when she heard you were coming, so she can't be all bad. And if it's anything like the meal she brought me, it's going to be fantastic."

CHAPTER 10

"I just don't think the government has a right to tell us what we can or can't do with our land," Ned Healey huffed. "Private property is just that—*private*."

Ned was at the head of the table. Steaming plates of ribs and potatoes sat in front of him.

"Pass the platters, Ned, so we can eat, and then you can get back up on your soapbox," his wife, Claire, said. "Even though Ned doesn't believe in land-use laws, I do." She took the plate of ribs. "It's important for us to stay up with the times."

"I agree with you, Claire," Senator Sam Curtis said as he filled her glass with red wine from a special bottle he had brought. "Otherwise, we'll end up with sprawl like the rest of the country."

Peg and Lee sat next to each other, opposite the senator. Claire and Ned, their longtime friends and fellow ranchers, anchored the ends. Claire had removed the extra chair that normally was next to where Sam was sitting. She had been a good friend of Sam's wife, Karen, and it still pained her to think that she was dead. The removal of the empty chair was more for her sake than for Sam's, although she told herself the opposite.

"For instance," the senator continued as he placed three huge ribs on his plate, "look at this whole controversy about mineral rights under the ground on a person's property. Over on the East side, oil and gas companies have been quietly filing claims so they can drill on property where somebody else owns the surface."

"How can that be, Sam?" Claire asked. "Either you own your land or you don't."

"It's a bit arcane," Sam said, "but in 1872, Congress allowed mining claims to be made on federal land and that holds true today. Then, in 1916, they wanted to encourage ranching on land that wasn't any good for farming, so they passed the Stock Raising Homestead Act. A settler could homestead and own the land, but the government kept ownership of anything below the surface. Which means that someone else could claim the mineral rights. And that's what's happening now. The only thing that's needed from the surface owner is an easement, but if that isn't given willingly, it can be forced in court."

"We've owned our property since before 1916," Lee said confidently. "I'm sure it's not an issue for us. But I do feel for those folks over on the East side."

"Well, I'm all for private property rights," Ned said, "but that would be a hard one to judge with two parties having conflicting private property rights! Who gets to decide in a case like that Sam?"

"Well, technically, both parties have rights, but more often than not, it is the mining claim that gets the better end of the deal since development of the right often interferes with the ability to use the surface of the land. And, a word to the wise," Sam turned to Lee, "you might want to check it out anyway. It's not always clear-cut. But if you do own the subsurface rights, then the mining company would have to buy that from you before they could do anything."

Peg made a mental note to call their lawyer in the morning. Just in case. With all of their financial difficulties, they didn't need that kind of problem.

"Can anything be done about it?" Lee asked.

"Not much," Sam said. "There's a law that puts some minor hurdles in the way of contiguous development. But that only slows things down and makes it more expensive. In fact, there are some companies trying to make development easier by getting that, and other things, changed; but I don't agree with most of them."

Peg's mind wandered while the men talked. She thought about her conversation with Leslie Montgomery. Leslie had commented about how nice it was not to have to worry about things now that she was retired. Peg didn't think she would ever reach that state. At a break in the conversation, she looked around the table and asked, "Do any of you ever think about retirement?"

"Nobody's asked me that in a long time," Sam laughed. "Except maybe my colleagues on the other side of the aisle."

"Hell, Peg," Ned answered, "how can you retire if you own a ranch? And why would you want to?"

"I'd like to retire and go live in Hawaii." Claire leaned back in her chair and raised her wineglass. "I'd lounge on a deck chair next to a pool by the ocean and drink mai tais all day and never lift a snow shovel again. It would be heaven."

She laughed. "But I know I'd miss the ranch after a few weeks. And I might even miss the snow—but not those days when it doesn't get above zero and you still have to tend the animals."

"It's a good question though." Sam looked serious. "Back east, it's a major topic of conversation among folks our age—that is, retirement and what you're going to do and how you're going to pay for it. But ranchers don't think that way. It's a completely different attitude about age and work and what's important in life."

"Problem is, there's nothing in-between for us," Lee said. "It's all or nothing. There's just as much to be done when you're sixty-five as when you're forty-five. And look at us with three boys, all capable of running the place and giving us a break, but not a single one of them wants anything to do with it."

"With the state of the business today," Ned countered, "who'd buy a ranch now anyhow, except to build a fancy house like those rich movie stars or that woman who bought your place? Since the Japanese beef market tanked on us, we'll be lucky if we all don't go under within the next few years. Then the only ranchers will be the banks after they foreclose on our mortgages."

"Oh, don't be so morbid, Ned," Claire said. "Maybe the Easterners have the right idea—work hard and deal with city life for all those years, and then get your reward when you retire here. Like Peg and Lee's new neighbor. All the reward of living here but without the work."

"Without the work is right," Ned said. "I heard she's not even sixty, but she's retired. Hey, Sam, you're practically from DC now, so how come you're not retired already?"

Sam laughed. "I'm afraid your tax dollars don't pay me the kind of money she likely made as a partner in a major law firm."

"Did you know her?" Claire asked. "I can't wait to meet her."

"Yes, slightly. But I haven't seen her or worked with her in maybe twelve, thirteen years. She's a nice woman though, and smart. I'm sure you'll like her."

Peg poured herself more wine. *I don't know why everybody is so eager to like a rich outsider.*

Even though it was May, it was cold in the house when Leslie and Cynthia finished dinner. They sat at the dining room table with empty plates pushed away and full wine glasses brought close.

"I'll clean up," Cynthia said.

"Okay. I'll make a fire." Leslie went out to the woodpile that Mike had stacked on the deck and brought in a few logs. She wasn't exactly sure how to start, since the fireplace in DC had been gas, so she crumpled up sheets of the packing paper, put two logs on top, and lit a match. The paper burned before the logs caught fire, and she ended up going through a good portion of the packing paper and an entire book of matches before she finally had a blaze. *I've got to ask Mike what the trick is,* she thought. *Or buy some of those fire-starter logs they always had at the ski lodge.* She went into the kitchen to wash her hands. Cynthia was putting the last dish in the dishwasher.

"Are you ready for some of Peg's pie?" Leslie asked.

"Maybe later. Let's drink our wine and enjoy the fire." Cynthia got the wine glasses and put them on the coffee table. Leslie sat in the chair while Cynthia stretched out on the couch. "Okay, so now tell me honestly. Are you happy here? Is it all that you thought it would be?"

"It's only been four days." Leslie laughed. "I do love the house, especially waking up in the morning to the view across the valley. But the town does seem awfully small. And it's been harder than I thought to be here alone."

"What do you mean? You've been living alone for almost a year already."

"Living alone in DC where my friends and job and routine were is very different than being out here away from everything and everybody." Leslie sighed and took a big sip of her wine. "I hope I haven't made a big mistake."

"Give it some time. It's what you've always wanted."

"I know, I know," Leslie said. "Of course, you're right. If you can believe it, though, I even miss work. What do you make of that?"

"Not much. Except that you are pretty darn normal for feeling that way. Retirement always takes some adjustment. I still think you are one of the bravest people I know to have made such big changes in your life."

"Truth be told, I've actually missed Hugh more in the few days I've been here than I have in the past year. You know, I always expected him to be here with me. Being by myself wasn't in the plan. But I think I'm just feeling sorry for myself."

"Well, there have got to be some handsome cowboys in Legacy Springs, so don't worry about it." Cynthia poured more wine.

"Oh, there you go," Leslie said, laughing, "always jumping to the future instead of letting me dwell on the past—good *or* bad!"

"That's true. So let's talk about how you're going to meet Mr. Right out here in the sticks."

"Well, it's going to be hard to find anyone if I sit up here on my hill. But there probably aren't many single men my age anyway. They'll all be married. It wasn't an issue when I bought the place, remember?"

"Good point. But hypothetically, what kind of man would you like to find?"

"Who knows? It's too scary to even think about. You know, I haven't had sex with anyone except Hugh for almost thirty years. I might not know how to do it with somebody else. Besides, I'm not ready yet. I can't even imagine being attracted to anyone." *Except,* she thought, *that man in the bar at the airport.*

"What made you ask that question about retirement?" Lee asked Peg through toothpaste foam as they stood side by side at the twin sinks in their bathroom. Peg was brushing out her long hair, which had been pulled into a loose braid during dinner.

"I've just been thinking about life lately." She hesitated since she wasn't quite sure of the answer herself. "Maybe it's old age catching up to me. No, now that I think about it, it really started with that conversation I had with Leslie Montgomery. She had such a clear distinction in her mind between working and retirement, and yet what she told me she wants to do now that she's retired is all of the stuff I do every day as work. Baking, cooking, sewing, quilting. And for me, my relaxation is writing, and that's basically what a lot of her work was. It's so paradoxical, don't you think?"

Lee rinsed the toothpaste out of his mouth. "It is paradoxical, but not unusual. A lot of people think that the best part of retirement is doing something completely different than what they've been doing for the past forty years. If we sold the ranch, that would be us."

"But we don't want to do something different. And we'll never sell the ranch."

"I know you don't want to hear it, but we need to be thinking of options. The money from the sale of the property last year will take us through the fall, but that's it. Since none of the kids are interested, maybe we should sell it all off for development and take the money and kick back ourselves for awhile."

"I agree we should look at options. We haven't really talked about the long term since my birthday last year when the kids were here. But selling the ranch?"

"We're not getting any younger, Peg, and at the rate we're going, we're not getting any richer. Just the opposite, in fact. The business is bleeding away and we might want to get out while we can and before everybody else figures it out and floods the market with ranch properties they can't afford to keep anymore."

"Given what a hard time I had selling forty acres, you know that selling the whole thing might kill me. Besides, I thought you said you'd work on this ranch until you died."

"That'd be my preference, but we've got to face the facts." Lee reached over to her. "Your hair is beautiful when it's down."

93

He kissed her cheek and they made their way into bed. She spooned into him and ran her hand along his side and down the front of his thigh.

"So are you thinking we need to have more children so somebody will take it over?" Lee said.

"It's a long shot, but maybe we should try."

CHAPTER 11

"It's your first morning here, let's go for a walk," Leslie said to Cynthia after they'd had several cups of coffee and toast made from Peg's bread. "There's not a cloud in the sky."

"You've got to do this every morning," Cynthia said as they walked down the switchbacks. "What a great way to start the day and think of the exercise you'll get when you have to walk back up this road."

The sun warmed their backs while the cool air chilled their faces. "I can't decide if I'm warm or cold," Cynthia said.

"It's the altitude, I think. It's still cold, but the sun makes it feel warmer than it is."

"It smells so fresh." Cynthia took a deep, noisy breath. "And the view is spectacular. I think you made a wise choice picking this spot."

"You can thank Maggie Madison's poems for that. I knew the minute I saw it that this was the place for me. I can't wait to get out and explore the hiking trails this summer."

"It sure isn't the National Mall." Cynthia stopped to pick a small, early wildflower from beside the road. "This really is what you always talked about."

When they got back to the house, the phone was ringing. Leslie got it before it kicked to voice mail. It was her insurance company. She'd almost forgotten about the Mercedes.

"Yes, I got his insurance information. What else will you need?"

Cynthia disappeared for a minute and then came back through the living room in the terry robe Leslie had put in the guest room. "Hot tub," she mouthed to Leslie as she picked up a magazine on her way out.

Leslie put her hand over the mouth of the phone. "It's my insurance company. I'll only be a minute."

Cynthia nodded and went out to the tub.

"Yes, I understand. Okay. I'll head down there later this afternoon," Leslie said.

A few minutes later, she eased into the hot tub with Cynthia. "That's taken care of, but I have to go into town later and sign some papers. Want to come with me?"

"No, I'll hang out here and unpack some things for you. We can go into town together tomorrow."

"Okay. What are you reading?"

"There's an interesting article in this magazine about Ivy League girls who are giving up careers for marriage and kids at an early age. Who would go through all the trouble of Ivy League if that's what you intended to do?"

"Kelly, for one."

"What? I don't believe you. It sounds like something from the 1950s."

"Well, it's not quite that bad. She says she wants to work, but not while she's raising her kids. And although she picked the schools to apply to for their educational reputation, a secondary factor is where she'll meet the best husband." Leslie shook her head. "I keep hoping it's just a phase she is going through."

"Whatever happened to falling in love for love's sake instead of because of some credential?"

"I don't know, but she's been on this kick for over a year. Keeps saying there is no point in falling in love with a man who isn't able to take care of her. And by 'take care,' she means the lifestyle to which she has become accustomed after living with two affluent parents. Maybe we shouldn't' have given her so much and made her life so easy."

"You can't blame yourself. You preached independence to her since the time she was in the womb. And you've been a great role model."

Leslie remembered Kelly's remark last year about wonder woman. It still hurt that Kelly thought she was too focused on her career.

"I don't know about that. And maybe Hugh and I weren't such good role models as a couple either. We started off being in love, but she could probably tell that our marriage had become about having the nice house and nice things. She didn't see much of the love part."

"At least she's not one of those girls who marries the first guy that comes along. It might be a good thing that she's being so practical about it."

"Let's hope you are right. But that reminds me. I banged into that car in the parking lot because I was trying to answer the phone. It was Kelly and I completely forgot to call her back."

"I'm sure she managed for a day without talking to you," Cynthia said. "It's good for her to know you're not just sitting around waiting for her to call. Why don't you call her now? I wanted to read this article anyway."

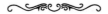

The lettered sign on the window of the insurance company was weathered and barely legible on the drab, gray storefront. Leslie drove by twice before seeing it. The building was on a side street just off Main. The glass entry door opened to a small hallway with three doors. On the right were the doors for an accountant and a massage therapist. On the left was the insurance agency. Leslie went in and found an empty room with a small service counter. Behind it were two small desks piled high with papers and manila file folders. In front, two chairs flanked an end table covered with an assortment of faded and ripped magazines. A small silver service bell sat alone on the counter.

Leslie rang the bell and waited, looking at the faded window lettering and wondering why someone didn't just get some paint and redo it. No attention to detail, she thought. It was the kind of thing that made the office seem shabby instead of charming or quaint. How much energy did it take to paint the sign? Or to put new magazines on the table? Or to have someone come to answer the bell for that matter? She really didn't want to waste her time; there was so much to do and she and Cynthia had barely made a dent in the unpacking. *Of course, it's my own fault,* she thought. *If I hadn't hit that car in the parking lot, I wouldn't be here now. But it's not my fault that nobody is coming to help me.* She pressed the bell twice more. "Hello? Hello?" she called, but nobody answered.

She watched as a teenager drove a muddy, jacked-up pickup truck down the street. It was a stark contrast to the shiny black SUV that was pulling into the empty parking spot directly in front of the building. *Now there's somebody who at least washes their car once in a while,* she mused absentmindedly, ringing the bell yet again. If someone didn't come soon, she would leave. She wasn't going to waste all day waiting here. She stared pointedly at the door between the front office and the back as if willing someone to come out to help her.

Instead, the door behind her opened. "So sorry to keep you waiting, Mrs. Montgomery," a chubby little woman with mousey, dull hair said with a broad smile. "I just ran over to the post office to get some stamps. I knew as soon as I left you would show up." She bustled about behind the counter, moving files and finally tapping on the computer keyboard, grinning the whole time. "You know I can go days without getting anybody in here, and then just when I leave, somebody comes. I'll have these papers ready for you in a minute."

"It's *Ms.* Montgomery. You knew I was coming," Leslie said, tapping her fingers on the counter. "I thought you would have them ready."

"Oh, I'm so sorry, sweetie. If you have some other errands to run, go ahead and you can get this later."

"No, that's the point. The only reason I came into town is to sign them. Oh, excuse me," Leslie stepped aside as the door opened again behind her. She didn't turn around.

"I'll be with you in a minute," the clerk said to the person behind Leslie. "Just got to get this lady on her way. She's in a hurry."

"No problem," a man said. "I'm not."

99

"Thanks," the clerk said and turned back to Leslie. "I'll go make these copies and be right back."

"Fine," Leslie said, her tone clear that it was not at all fine.

The man came up beside her at the counter. "Well, hello," he said. "It's good to see you again. We met in the airport a few days ago. Andrew Macfarlane." He smiled and put out his hand.

"Of course," she said, realizing it was the man in the bar with the Paul Newman eyes. "I'm sorry I didn't recognize you." She couldn't help but notice how suavely he was dressed in a well-cut gray suit and expensive silk tie. "You look very nice," she said, and immediately regretted it. *Why did I say that? What a lame thing to do.*

"Thanks. I'm on my way to the airport, flying out to Denver for a meeting. Hence the fancy duds. They are definitely a bit out of place here in Legacy Springs."

"I came in to sign some papers," Leslie said, still embarrassed by her comment. "I was in a bit of hurry that day at the airport and banged up somebody's car. Too bad. Nice little Mercedes. Probably belongs to some rich schmuck who will give me a hard time."

"Probably," he said seriously.

"Yes, it's my bad luck to have hit a Mercedes instead of one of the old pickup trucks that everyone seems to drive here. It'll probably cost a fortune to repair and my insurance rates will skyrocket."

"Yes, I suspect so." He looked amused.

"Most vehicles here seem to be at least ten or fifteen years old, with plenty of dings in them already." *Why do I keep talking?* she thought, but she didn't stop. "Is that your SUV out front? Much more practical." She pointed at the clean black car she'd seen pulling into the spot a moment ago.

"Yes, but it's a rental." Andrew pulled a card from his pocket and read from it. "Ms. Montgomery, I presume?" He bowed in mock greeting.

Leslie looked at the small card in his hand, the printing scribbled over on the front and a handwritten note on the back.

"Oh, you must be kidding." The pieces fell into place. "It was your car. I am so sorry. I didn't mean to call you a schmuck."

He laughed. "Not a problem, Ms. Montgomery. I had no idea the delightful woman in the bar would turn out to be a kamikaze driver bent on destroying my innocent Mercedes." He handed her his business card.

"Andrew Macfarlane," she read. "President, Xandex Exploration, Inc." She smiled awkwardly as the woman behind the counter placed several sheets of paper in front of her with "Sign here" stickers placed across the pages.

"I didn't realize when I came to sign these that the person I hit would also be here," Leslie said as she scrawled her name along the numerous lines on the page. "That wouldn't have happened in DC."

"I didn't mean to run into you either," he said. "No pun intended. I only came in to pick up my papers too." He paused for a moment before continuing. "But I'm glad you're here. I have been coming over to this part of the state fairly frequently lately, and I wonder if you would like to have dinner with me next time I'm in town? No hard feelings. Didn't you say you had just moved here yourself?"

Leslie realized she was blushing. He was asking her for a date. Her first date since the divorce. She hesitated for a moment. She looked over at the clerk who was smoothing her faded blue cardigan while studiously pretending she wasn't listening. "I'd like very much to have dinner with you," she said, a bit too loudly. "You already have my number."

"Any chance you have time for a cup of coffee now before I head to the airport?"

She signed the last paper. "Is that it?" she asked the clerk.

"That's all I need from you, Mrs. Montgomery. I know you are in a hurry, so you can go now." Turning to Andrew, the clerk continued. "I'll get your copies for you and you can be on your way too."

"Sorry I didn't realize you were in a hurry," Andrew said to Leslie. "Maybe some other time then."

"Actually, I'm not in a hurry," she said, looking pointedly at the clerk. "I'd love to have a cup of coffee." She knew Cynthia would have wanted her to.

CHAPTER 12

"This is so cute," Cynthia said as Leslie drove through Legacy Springs looking for a parking spot. "A real downtown Main Street and not a chain store in sight."

"I didn't get a chance to explore much when I was here last year, since I just flew in and out and only paid attention to the house," Leslie said. "I haven't even been in most of these stores yet."

The first stop was the hardware store. Leslie had a list: extra light bulbs, a small hammer (she realized she didn't have one when they went to hang the pictures), duct tape (never know what you might need it for), a hose for the back garden, and a bag of potting soil. As they bent to pick up a heavy bag of soil together, a thin, older man in pressed khakis and a polo shirt came up to them.

"Let me help you with that." He lifted the bag easily and put it in their cart. "Need another one?"

"Yes, please," Leslie answered. "Thanks."

"I'm Dr. Bob," he said, extending his hand after putting the second bag on top of the first. "I wanted to introduce myself and welcome you to Montana. I understand one of you is the new Easterner. Which one is Leslie?"

"I am." Leslie shook his hand. "And this is my friend Cynthia."

"Pleased to meet you both. I do hope you like it here. My son and I are the only docs in town, so I also hope I don't see too much of you." He laughed. "Enjoy your day, ladies." He went off down the aisle.

They next visited the small drug store on the corner at the main intersection. It was an old brick building with a sign over the door that looked like it had been there since the 1950s. They each carried a red wire hand basket, and went aisle by aisle so they wouldn't miss some must-have item. Band-Aids, antiseptic gel, toothpaste, aspirin. Both baskets were full when they reached the checkout counter at the same time as a man about their age. He was dressed in a plaid shirt and farmer overalls. He offered to let them check out ahead of him.

"Thank you, but we're not in a hurry," Leslie said.

"Neither am I, so please go ahead. I'm Ned Healey. Head of the county commission." He shook Cynthia's hand first and then Leslie's. "Reckon we'll be seeing you at one of the meetings—either advocating for something or complaining about something. Everybody shows up eventually."

"Thank you," Leslie said as she moved ahead of him to the counter. "I'm Leslie Montgomery."

"Pleased to meet you both. I hope you like your place up on the Hamilton ranch. I'll bet your daughter will love it when she comes out to see you. Now, you're a lawyer aren't you?"

"Retired. But yes. How did you know?"

"I'm a politician," he said. "It's my business to know what's happening in my county. I'll be asking for your vote next time around."

"This is getting a little weird," Cynthia said after they left the store. "Seems like everybody already knows who you are."

The next stop was The Outdoor Store. Cynthia insisted on going in, "just to see what's there." The front of the store displayed fishing tackle and hunting gear, but toward the back was a large space with women's clothing. "There's some good stuff here," Leslie said as she looked through the hand-tooled leather belts with silver buckles.

"Check out these hats." Cynthia modeled a straw cowboy hat.

"Forget the hats. Come look at these boots." There was a large selection of boots, short and tall. Leslie picked up a pair of alligator cowboy boots and looked at the tag on the bottom of the sole. Seven hundred and fifty dollars. Even in DC that was a lot of money for a pair of boots. *Who buys these things?* she wondered. *Surely not the local ranchers and farmers.*

A young man came up beside her. "Those Lucchese's are gorgeous, aren't they?" he said, sounding out the syllables of *loo-kay-see* and *gore-jus* as if they were honey being slathered on a warm slab of bread.

"Yes, they are," Leslie answered, wondering if he worked there. He looked to be about Kelly's age, with a wide, friendly smile that made him seem both genuine and naive. She knew Kelly would think he was really cute.

"If I were you, though, I'd be looking at these Sorels over here instead of the cowboy boots. My guess is that coming from DC, you might not have a pair yet." Another person who knew who she was. Cynthia was right. It was getting weird.

"What are Sorels?"

He laughed. "Oh, you'll know soon enough. Get the ones with the sheepskin lining is my advice. They're not only warmer, they look better on women too." He held up a pair of clunky, brown, rubber boots with a piece of sheepskin running around the top of the boot, which was just over ankle high.

"I don't think they're quite my style, but thanks for the tip."

"They may not be now, but they will be eventually." He paused for a minute and surveyed her without embarrassment. "Contrary to popular belief, I think you are going to do fine here, and it's great to get some new blood into the area."

She took the Sorel boot he handed her. "Nice to meet you, Mrs. Montgomery," he said as he turned. "Gotta run."

Leslie heard a voice from the other side of the store call to him, "Will, let's go. We're going to be late."

The young man sauntered off slowly, without a hint of urgency.

"Well, that was interesting," said Cynthia, who had been listening from behind the display. "How the hell does everyone know you?"

"Beats me. Must be either my builder or my real estate agent talking about me. It's unlikely all of these people have checked me out on the Internet."

"Why do you think it's unlikely?"

"People here don't seem to be the type to sit around and surf the web. I'll bet lots of them don't even know how to Google somebody. Besides, all they'd find on me is work-related stuff. I've tried hard to keep personal information off there."

"Yeah, you and the guy you had coffee with yesterday. When we looked him up last night, all we got is confirmation that he's a high-powered corporate guy. Not a hint of any personal details. Sometimes I wonder why we even bother."

"Well, at least it confirms that he is who he says he is and he's not a liar. Anyway, I guess I shouldn't be surprised that people know something about me, but I am surprised they recognize me in a store."

"Well, no matter what, you'd better be careful what you do and say, because everyone will know it before it even happens."

"I guess that's life in a small town," Leslie said. She wasn't sure whether she liked the familiarity of it or dreaded the lack of anonymity.

Cortez Harbinger puffed contentedly on the Cuban cigar he had purchased during his last trip to Canada. *Crazy government policies,* he thought. *Banning the importation of one of the finest pleasures on earth. As if buying Cuban tobacco would make any difference to the fate of the country. Theirs or ours. It's like banning French wine. Or Chinese silk. Or, god forbid, scotch whiskey. Yes, it's crazy how government works.*

He blew a ring of smoke toward the half-opened window of his huge SUV as he drove into Legacy Springs thinking about his last meeting. *That little old guy was easy pickings,* he thought. It would be a three-hour drive home from old man Tucker's place, and he hoped the cigar would last for a good part of it. Once he got over the pass, he'd set the cruise at eighty-five and enjoy the ride. *Better gas up before I get started,* he thought, noticing the gauge near empty. He'd stop at the place on the other side of town.

Laying the cigar carefully in the console's ashtray, he pulled into the gas station. He got out of his rig and walked around to the other side to pump the gas. *This will take a while,* he thought as he looked around at nothing in particular. He caught a whiff of the greasy fried food inside the mini-mart and thought about getting something for the drive. His mind drifted back to the meeting with Tucker. Crazy old bugger, thinking he's driving a hard bargain with me while I'm robbing him blind, and not even the common decency to offer me a sandwich. Or even a glass of water for that matter. Oh, well. Didn't matter. Tucker was ready to sign the release. One more visit ought to do it.

As he topped off the tank, a clean, red, but much smaller SUV pulled in to the pump beside him. Two babes, he observed, and good looking ones too. As the driver stepped out, Cortez surveyed her legs from between the pumps. Her skirt had been hiked up on her thighs for driving, and as she descended from the vehicle, the full length of her leg was exposed for a moment before the skirt dropped over the top of her high-heeled boots. His eyes skimmed her body from the bottom up in a practiced way, designed to take full measure of the figure before judging the face. All done with a surreptitiousness that meant the woman never even knew she was being looked at until he chose to let her know.

Not a local, he thought, looking at the heels of the boots. *Yeah, the women here don't dress up like that to come to town.* He began to feel the stirring of excitement. Lucky for him, he thought, that her gas tank was on the side where he could see her. His eyes finally flicked to her face, as she turned to put the dispenser into the tank. She was pretty for an older broad. *Yeah, I'd like to put mine in your tank*, he thought.

The woman stood at the driver's side door of her SUV while the tank filled. When she leaned in to get her purse, Cortez admired the way her skirt tightened across the back. The passenger got out and walked around the car into the mini-mart. Cortez evaluated her and heartily approved of the tight jeans with strappy sandals. Definitely not locals.

Cortez sat in his car and waited until they were finished before turning on the ignition. With any luck, he thought, they were headed to dinner somewhere in town and he would just happen to be there too. If he couldn't make it with one, perhaps with the other. They were both lookers, and he hadn't noticed any wedding rings. And worst case? Well, an evening of the hunt, watching two women who were clearly older than his normal fare, but worth the time anyway.

When they drove out of the gas station, he pulled out onto the street to follow. Yes, he reflected as he pulled into a parking spot at The Pine Room restaurant, three cars down from where they had parked, it would be better to stay here tonight and head home tomorrow in the daylight.

Andrew Macfarlane sat in a cream-colored leather chair at his private golf club. He held a short glass of single malt scotch high in the air, admiring the color. He decided he wouldn't take a drink until he heard the news. He pushed the speed dial for Cortez Harbinger.

"Hey, Andy, what's up?" Cortez answered.

"I just got in from Denver and was wondering how things went today. Where are you?"

"At The Pine Room. Two beautiful women are at a table waiting for me."

"You're dreaming again, Cortez."

"Well, they are at a table; they just don't know they're waiting for me yet."

Andrew laughed. He had to hand it to the guy. He never gave up. "Did you get Tucker to sign?"

"Nah, but he will. His old lady needs meds that they can't afford. He's only delaying so he can feel like he drove a hard bargain."

"Nice work. We'll keep picking them off one by one."

"They'll all sign eventually. And they'll all think they got the better end of the deal."

Andrew finally took a sip of the luxurious smoky liquid in his glass. He could almost taste the success. Six more months, a year at most. Then it would all be wrapped up. He didn't much care for Harbinger's tactics, but he had to admit they worked. And it allowed Andrew the luxury of staying clean and walking the high road. *That's what a man like Harbinger is for,* he thought.

"Nice job." Andrew snapped the phone closed and smiled at the waiter standing patiently next to his chair.

"Your table is ready, Mr. Macfarlane. You can go in whenever you like. Can I freshen your drink?"

"No, thanks, Robert. I've got one more call to make."

"No hurry, sir. I'll tell Chef you'll be a bit." The waiter stepped away discreetly as Andrew opened his phone again. "Forgot to ask you," he said when Harbinger answered immediately. "How are you coming with finding something on Sam Curtis? We need that bill next session to really make this deal hum."

"Sorry, boss. The guy's a real boy scout. I've been getting a few whiffs of a lady friend in DC years ago, but nothing concrete yet."

"Keep on it. We need his vote, whatever it takes." Andrew spoke quietly, since several other people had come into the bar. "When are you headed home?

"Tomorrow. It was a late one here so I decided to stay the night and drive back in the morning. I'm hoping it won't be a lonely night."

"You're never lonely, Cortez. Just make sure they're legal."

"Not to worry. These two are fifty if they are a day, but they are lookers and they are dressed to kill. Definitely tourists. Too bad you had to leave yesterday. I'd have been happy to share, of course."

"Thanks, but I don't need any more women. You behave yourself."

Andrew snapped the phone shut and followed Robert to the table, where his favorite wine was already poured and the chef's choice of shrimp appetizer was on its way.

CHAPTER 13

Leslie was excited that Kelly was due to arrive just five days after Cynthia left. *I certainly won't have time to get lonely with all these visitors*, she thought. Kelly was staying for two weeks before starting her summer job and then law school in the fall. *Well, Kelly isn't really a visitor—she's coming home. Even though she's never been here before, wherever I live will always be her home. And since she doesn't know anybody, I'll get to spend even more time with her.*

But the day after she arrived, Kelly went out for a walk and met Will Hamilton, who had been at the ranch helping Lee mend fences. Will offered to take Kelly riding, and from there, the relationship took off at a gallop. Or so it seemed to Leslie, since after that, Kelly spent time with him every day.

"Mom, would you mind if I go camping with Will for a few days?" Kelly asked one morning as they were finishing breakfast. "He wants to take me horse-packing into the mountains. Doesn't that sound incredible?"

"If that's what you're into, I guess so." It didn't sound very fun to Leslie, but mostly she was disappointed that Kelly wouldn't be here with her.

"You're the best, Mom. I can't remember the last time I had so much fun. Riding every day has been so cool, and Will is such a sweetheart."

"As long as you're back so we have some time together before you head home. When are you leaving for the camping trip?"

"Tomorrow. I'm going over to Will's now to get everything ready. I'll come back later this afternoon, and we can have dinner together tonight." Kelly gave Leslie a quick hug and then was gone.

Leslie refilled her coffee cup and went out onto the deck. The sky was crystal clear and cobalt, seeming even darker blue than normal against the white fringe atop the mountains on the other side of the valley. The birdsong was nonstop and Leslie reminded herself that she needed to learn the birds. She'd get to it once Kelly left. *Or now,* she thought. *Since she's not spending time with me anyway.* She went back inside for her phone and called Cynthia.

"Kelly has abandoned me," she complained. "She met one of the Hamilton boys when she got here and I've barely seen her since."

"Have you met him? Do you like him?"

"Yes, he's really nice. He came over for dinner one night. In fact, you met him. Remember the cute young man in the store when we were looking at boots? That's him."

"So what's the problem? Kelly's a young woman trying to have some fun. Much as we think we're interesting, we're still old people to her."

"I know. And I'm glad she's enjoying herself. But I found out he's a ladies' man and I don't want her to get hurt. The checker at the grocery store told me that Will has a reputation for 'loving and leaving,' as she put it. She said he'd broken the heart of just about every girl in the valley somewhere along the way."

"Kelly's an adult now; she can take care of herself. If what you told me about Kelly is true, you have nothing to worry about. This guy doesn't make enough money for her to be seriously interested."

"That's probably true. She'll hold out for some doctor or lawyer. Okay, you've made me feel a little better, but I still wish she hadn't met him."

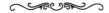

The county courthouse was built of square sandstone blocks individually hand carved and stacked upon one another over a century ago. The building stayed cool in the summer and warm in the winter, a testament to the power of the natural stone. Every other week, the county commission met around a long conference table in the large room at the back of the building.

Lee Hamilton sat at one end of the conference table, his cowboy hat hanging on the back of his chair like the other three men at the table, Ned Healey, Dr. Bob, and Cyrus Smith. The lone woman, Dory Cranshaw, was a sharp contrast as a tiny woman among four large men.

After an hour, they were nearly through with their agenda.

"Okay, so what's this final item we've got here today?' asked the chairman, Ned Healey. He shuffled through his papers. "Here it is. This is a request for a land-use exception to subdivide a ranch and carve off forty acres."

"Tucker, is this yours?" Ned looked at the old rancher sitting in the front row.

"Sure is, Ned."

"What are you wanting to do here?" Ned asked.

"I want to subdivide the way Lee and Peg did and have a forty-acre parcel sitting separately. It's the section with my house on it. That way if I want to sell the rest of the place, I can keep enough for us to live on."

"Are you thinking of selling?" Lee asked, surprised.

"Not yet," Tucker said. "Listen, I'm not supposed to talk about it, but let's just say what if some company wants to do some exploration on my property and wants me to sign an easement to let them do that. Then let's say they want to buy my property if they find something. I might want to sell the place to them. Nobody's buying any ranches these days. I don't see no harm in lettin' them look, since it won't bother the cows none. And besides . . ." He took the toothpick from his mouth where it had been hanging while he talked. "I sure do need the money. I mean hypothetically speakin', of course. It's been tough enough to buy the meds my missus needs, let alone have enough left over for a few beers when I come into town."

"What kind of company?" Dory asked.

"Like maybe a natural gas company. Hypothetically. But if they found some, I could stand to make a lot more than what they are paying me for the right to look." Tucker licked his wizened lips and stuck the toothpick back in.

Lee looked over at Peg, who sat a few seats over from Tucker. *So this is what the senator had been talking about at dinner,* he thought. He had forgotten about it, including his and Peg's intention to determine if they owned the rights under their own property.

"Say, Tuck," Lee probed, "did someone talk to you about who owned the mineral rights? Hypothetically, I mean."

"I don't rightly remember, Lee." Tucker furrowed his brow. "But you know I turned eighty-six last month so the memory ain't as good as I remember it being." He laughed at the joke he told whenever he got a chance.

"What do you mean, Lee?" asked Dr. Bob.

Before Lee could answer, Ned jumped in. "This is what the senator was talking about a while back, isn't it? A company comes in and claims that they own the mineral rights under a piece of property. And just because you own the surface rights, doesn't mean you have any claim to what's below."

Lee nodded. "Tuck, before we approve this, I think you ought to go see your lawyer and make sure you aren't literally giving away the farm if you sign that easement and that you lock up your own subsurface rights." Lee pushed his chair back from the table. "We all know that these guys are sniffing around here, so we all better pay attention."

"Well, I don't want to wait too long," said Tucker. "I'd like to get that first advance before I'm too old. Oh, wait, I guess I'm already too old!" He laughed again at his own joke.

"I'm with Lee on this one. We should wait," said Ned. "I'll need a motion."

"Move to table the item for two weeks," said Lee.

"Second," said Dory.

"Any discussion?" Ned looked at the other two. "Hearing none, all in favor?"

"*Shee-it*," Tucker said. "Then you guys better buy me a beer."

CHAPTER 14

Senator Sam Curtis threw the worn, striped blanket over the back of his favorite black mare, Abby. The leather saddle fit perfectly in its usual spot, the straps and cinches worn where they always fastened. He led the old horse out into the dusty ring. She was one of the horses Peg Hamilton had saved years ago during a wild mustang roundup, and she was his favorite. But age was getting the better of Abby and she didn't have much more time to go, so now she lived a privileged life of pasture, apples, and only an occasional ride.

He mounted the mare and walked her slowly around the perimeter of the ring, hugging the five-rail fence. She responded to his touch and his talk, two old friends out for a ride. Her head came up and she snorted as she pranced along the trodden dirt of the ring, sending little dust clouds up as each hoof touched down. Her ears pricked forward then flicked back as she listened to Sam's voice.

They left the ring and headed for the trail toward the foothills behind the house. "You're the only one that knows my secret," he whispered in Abby's ear as he bent down to adjust the rein. "So where do you want to go today?"

Sam gave the horse her head and let her go at her own pace while his mind wandered back to DC. *I wonder where she is now,* he thought. *The other Abby.*

It happened after he had been in DC for several years. He'd served a few terms in the House and had just been elected to the Senate. He knew the ropes, he knew the people, and he loved the work. Although Karen had initially moved to DC with him, she quickly became disillusioned by the city and the single focus of politics. She told Sam she felt like an appendage, and she really missed Montana. So she moved back to the ranch and he would join her on weekends whenever he could. But the travel was tedious—with no direct flight it always made for a long day. As the years passed, he realized that when he was in Montana, he spent more time at political functions around the state than at home. Although they worked to keep the marriage alive, they found themselves growing apart with their separate lives.

Sam was working on a bill that was especially important to the grain growers in Montana when he first met Abby. The grain association had hired her, a promising young lawyer from one of the prominent DC law firms, to represent them. Sam met with Abby and two staffers from the association almost every week for several months. The team had gotten a key opponent to agree to support their bill, and they were going to celebrate with dinner at a posh restaurant.

But when Sam got to the restaurant, Abby was there alone. One of the staffers wasn't feeling well and hadn't come, and the other had just left, a sick child at home cutting short the celebration.

"I'm happy to stay for dinner if you're up for it," Abby had offered while they had a drink in the bar. "Or we could reschedule for when the guys can join us."

"Of course, we should stay for dinner," he had said. "Hopefully we'll have another chance to celebrate with them when the bill actually passes."

Her jet-black hair, normally pulled back, fell softly around her shoulders and provided a sharp contrast to her business suit. He ordered a bottle of champagne.

"I have a horse named Abby," he had told her that evening. "Her mane is the same color as your hair. She's high-spirited, intelligent, and beautiful. Like you." He was thrilled when she smiled back at him.

He had known when they finished the champagne and ordered a bottle of wine that he was moving into dangerous territory.

Peg and Tucker left the commission meeting and waited outside for Lee. It was hot in the sun and Peg thought a beer sounded really good.

"Do you want to go to The Pine Room or Two Whoops and a Holler," she asked Tucker.

"Two Whoops," Tucker said. "Pine Room's too fancy for me."

When Lee joined them, they walked down the block to the small, casual bar and went inside.

"Three drafts," Lee said to the bartender as they made their way to a small table near the window. The room was cool, dark, and empty except for a few cowboys. There was a baseball game on the TV in the corner, so they talked about that until the drinks came.

"So what's this all about, Tucker," Lee asked after they'd all had a few sips. "Are you really thinking of selling?"

"I'm not making any money anymore," Tucker said. "I can barely afford to pay the hands. Nobody's buying the beef."

"I've heard they're bringing in beef from Argentina because it doesn't have the taint of disease," Peg said. "They call it 'free range' and 'organic.'"

"What's the world coming to when Americans are buying beef from somewhere else, let alone all the way from Argentina?" Tucker shook his head and took a swig of his beer.

"Look, Tuck," Lee said, "you really do need to contact Dick Henderson. Is he still doing your legal work?"

Tucker nodded.

"This business about who owns what on your property is important to check out before you make any moves or give anybody any rights."

"Hell, that property has been in my family for almost a hundred years. We were the original homesteaders. Ain't nobody else that owns any bit of it, that's for sure." Tuck drained his glass. "Thanks for the beer. I'd like to have another, but it's tough enough to drive at my age. And besides, the missus would kick my behind out to the barn if she knew I had more than one."

"Seriously, Tuck," said Peg, "even if you own the subsurface rights, you need to make sure you aren't giving anything up if you sign the easement. Promise me you'll call Dick tomorrow."

"I'll call him tonight if you think it's that important." Tuck stood up to go. "I don't much listen to anybody's advice anymore, but you two are different. If you tell me I ought to, then it won't hurt to do it. Besides, ain't nothin' else I can do until you high-falutin' commissioners meet again, now is there?" He winked at Lee and tipped his cowboy hat to Peg as he pushed in his chair, and then headed toward the door.

"I forgot to ask you," Lee said to Peg, "but did you happen to call Dick about our property after the dinner with the senator? Because I didn't."

"Sorry to say, but no, I didn't either. I'll call him tomorrow though. You don't need to do it." Peg watched Tucker get into his truck and finished her beer. "I'm worried about Tucker. I'm afraid he's going to go for the money before he checks things out. There are too many people in the valley like him who see easy salvation from a quick payout." She put her hand on Lee's arm. "I never thought I'd say it, but we were lucky we sold that property so we don't have to let those speculators near us. But the whole valley could be ruined if this becomes another drilling boomtown. I hope he doesn't do anything stupid."

"I think we may have scared him a bit, so let's not worry," Lee said. "Besides, when you talk to Dick tomorrow you can give him a warning about Tuck's situation. He'll probably call him even if Tuck doesn't take the initiative." Lee stood up. "Let's hit the road."

They walked back toward the old pickup truck. Lee decided to wait until tomorrow before telling her that the bank had called earlier in the day. The money from the sale of the property was almost gone, and the loan they needed to keep the ranch afloat for the coming year had been denied.

Sam's affair with Abby, who was thirteen years younger, lasted a little over a year. He was consumed with guilt, but he couldn't stay away from her. At first, they were careful not to be seen together socially in public, and when they were, to be strictly business. No fleeting looks, no knees touching under the table. They would wait until they were alone at her Georgetown apartment. Then they would rush to bed, fumbling to remove the suit jackets, wristwatches, belts, and nylons, eager to taste each other.

To protect Sam's reputation, they developed elaborate systems to communicate. They didn't call each other often, and had a code when they did. He never drove his car to her place but would walk when he could or, occasionally, take a taxi, although he'd always be dropped at different addresses in the area, just in case. She never came to his house.

The intrigue fueled their passion for each other and he fell in love with her. He found himself comparing Karen to Abby whenever he was back in Montana or during the few uncomfortable times when Karen would travel to DC. He still loved Karen, but Abby was so exciting and interesting. She was on track to become a partner in the firm and she was well traveled, well read, and beautiful.

Power corrupts, he thought as he turned the mare to head back to the barn. *And sex corrupts. I fell for it. And for her. But I really loved her and was lucky that we never got caught.* Sam shook his head to dispel the image of the dark-haired woman who had stolen his heart. *No. Stop rationalizing what you did. It was wrong, and you knew it.*

As the year had worn on, Sam and Abby became less cautious, familiarity taking the place of fear of discovery. He was invited as her guest to many firm functions, where the partners happily used this special access to him to request favors for their clients. Or, on one occasion, to give him advice.

The event had been a fundraiser for a fellow senator, a friend of Sam's. The crowd was well heeled and the champagne flowed freely. Sam knew many of the people at the event and moved easily through the crowd, adept at engaging in a conversation with complete attentiveness and equally adept at excusing himself when he felt the need to move on. About every third move, he and Abby intersected each other, mixing within the clusters of two and three talking about everything from the weather to politics, but mostly politics.

Sam remembered the event well because he had talked with Karen earlier that day and was still dealing with the news she delivered. She had found a lump in her breast the week before and a biopsy had immediately been taken. The results from the test had arrived. It was cancer. She would have the lump removed next week and they would do further tests to see if it had traveled to her lymph glands. The doctors were hopeful that they had caught it in time. Sam was flying back to Montana to be with her the day after tomorrow's key vote on one of his bills. Karen said she understood that he needed to stay for the vote.

He hadn't told Abby yet, but he knew he needed to be in Montana with his wife. He had married her, he had loved her, he still loved her, and he would do right by her and be by her side through this. He'd go back every weekend and would spend all of the holidays and recesses there. His constituents would understand if he missed a few votes. And Abby would understand too. She knew he was married and had never asked him to leave his wife. He would still see her whenever he was in DC.

He circled the room, blocking out his worries about Karen, and instead focusing on the people in the room. But when he would see Abby, her slender waist accentuated by the shirring of the simple black off the shoulder dress she wore, he wasn't able to block out his desire for her. He felt a combination of guilt and sexual energy that only increased with the knowledge that he was going to have less time to spend with her.

The fundraising pitch was over when a senior partner in Abby's firm, Leslie Montgomery, expertly maneuvered him to a quiet corner of the room where their conversation could not be overheard. He had worked with her on a few occasions when she did light lobbying on the Hill. He liked her and thought she was a straight shooter; a tough bird, some called her, but she was extremely competent and always able to forge compromise in the face of difficult issues. He listened to her with one ear, expecting a pitch for a client. He glanced surreptitiously at Abby moving across the room, their eyes briefly meeting.

"Look, Senator," Leslie began, "I know we don't know each other well and this may be completely out of line, but I like you and your politics."

Sam nodded, intrigued by this odd beginning.

"I also think that Abby has a great career ahead of her. That's why I'm going to warn you. You've either got to give her up or go back underground. It's becoming obvious that you two are an item. You are known as the most ethical senator in Washington and you are about to blow that wide open."

"I'm not sure what you mean," Sam said, stalling for time while he digested her comment. He tried to keep his face neutral.

She sighed. "I know you have no reason to trust me, but I admire both you and Abby and I don't want to see either of you hurt." She paused for a moment. "Personally or professionally."

"Has she said something to you?"

"Heavens, no. You two have been doing one hell of a job keeping this a secret, but your feelings are becoming obvious to anyone who is paying attention. And believe me: people are starting to pay attention, Senator. That's why I felt I had to say something. They'll bring you down, you know. It's your decision what to do with my unasked-for opinion."

Her expression told him that she was serious and sincere. She continued. "So thank you very much for your time, Senator." She looked over his shoulder. "I do appreciate any attention you can give to the matter. Well, hello, James, how have you been?" She turned to the man who had been approaching them and shook his hand, releasing the senator from her gaze.

That night, he told Abby it was over. They cried together and swore on each other's hearts never to mention the affair to anyone, no matter what. Within a year, Abby was married to another man.

CHAPTER 15

Peg returned Dick Henderson's call as soon as she listened to the message he'd left while she was in town. On her way home, she had passed Leslie going the other way and allowed herself to get into a foul mood just thinking about her and her house and her money.

"Hi, Dick," she said when he answered the phone himself. She wondered if Leslie had ever answered her own phone at the big law firm in DC. Unlikely, she thought. "Do you have good news for me?"

"Yes, I do. Because your family homesteaded your ranch before 1916, you own the subsurface rights. But that's not true for most of the property in the valley."

"Did Tucker call you? What about his place?"

"He did call, and he knew you'd ask and he told me to tell you what I said to him. He's the same as you. But he's looking at signing an easement to let the company do exploratory drilling on his land. The way it's written, he'd be giving up his negotiating power if they do find something, even though he owns the rights." Dick paused. "I advised him not to sign, but I'm afraid he's blinded by the dollar signs."

Peg hung up and immediately called Tucker's number. There was no answer. She left a message asking him to call her and said it was urgent. *Maybe that will get his attention,* she thought.

She sat in her living room on the old leather couch that she and Lee had bought when they first married, staring at the clouds in the distance. Patches of sunlight poked through a few holes in a white and gray mass of afternoon thunderclouds billowing up to their anvil tops. This was the time of year when she usually got to splurge a bit. The money from the annual operating loan would have been in their bank account by now. But this year, for the first time ever, they'd been denied the loan. Lee had told her it would be okay, that they would figure something out. But she wasn't so sure.

Without the loan and without any profits, things would be even tighter than they'd been the year before. Ranching was always a tough business to be in, but she and Lee had been successful most years and certainly could stand to have a bad year here and there. But these past three years were the worst she had ever seen. That whole mad cow debacle started it. In fact, was this even the fourth bad year and not the third? She counted backward using the events of her children's lives as markers.

Yes, she confirmed, *this is the fourth year running that we've been in the red. Maybe I'm getting used to it,* she mused with a touch of anguish. She pulled her sweater closer, as if to ward off the chill of financial trouble. It didn't help. She got up to close the window in case it rained and then sat back down on the couch. *Maybe if I stare at the clouds long enough, I'll come up with an answer.*

The sound of the back door broke the silence. Peg glanced at her watch and realized she had been sitting there for over an hour. Will sauntered into the room, his boots making a satisfying sound on the wood floor.

"Well, this a surprise." He laughed as he sat down next to her and gave her a hug. "Mom just sitting and staring instead of doing. I don't think I've ever seen it before—not even a pad and pencil in front of you to capture the thoughts."

"You're right." Peg stood up quickly. "I need to be getting dinner ready. I guess I lost track of the time."

"Sit for a minute, Mom, and talk to me." Will grabbed her hand and gently tugged. "I'll help you with dinner in a minute. What were you so lost in thought about?"

Peg smiled and sat next to him. "Oh, I was thinking about the future, I guess. What's going to happen with the ranch. And how we're going to get through yet another year with no profit to speak of." She tried to sound nonchalant. She didn't want Will to know how much worse it had gotten, and she certainly didn't want him to be worrying about it. He was twenty-six now and had his own life to lead with his own problems. Not that he shared them with her, but she knew. A mother knew.

"It'll all work out," he said, patting her hand. "You've always said you'd seen a lot of tough times over the years and always came through it. This will be the same."

"Of course, you're right," she agreed, knowing that this time it was different; it was worse. Much worse. "So what have you been up to? It seems like ages since we've talked about something other than sick cows or money trouble."

"Well, Mom, I've been thinking about the future too," he said hesitantly.

Peg's heart skipped involuntarily. Against her will, she found herself hoping that he was about to tell her that he wanted to take over the ranch after all. That he would give up the rodeo and settle down. She let herself, for just a moment, think about how it would feel to not be in charge or worry about the day-to-day chores. To kick back and plan days of leisure. That dinner at Ned's had really gotten to her. "So what are you thinking?"

Will stammered a bit. "I, uh, well, you know, these last few months have made me realize I don't want to be on the rodeo circuit my whole life. You know, it's a short career. And I'm not getting any younger."

Peg smiled at his words and waited patiently. She realized that Will had actually come to say something specific and hadn't just stopped by. As he fumbled for words, she was sure he was trying to ask her about taking over the ranch without seeming like he was trying to run her and Lee off. She could see that he was growing up, finally willing to take on responsibility, find a solution to the financial troubles, and make the ranch profitable again. She would be able to spend the next decades playing with grandchildren—when she wasn't in Hawaii, far from the cold of the Montana winters.

"Are you okay, Mom?" Will said. "You're smiling and you don't even know what I'm going to say yet."

"Sorry, dear," she said, snapping back to the present. "I was thinking of Hawaii." She stopped abruptly, aware of the absurdity of her remark. Here she was, a woman who had never dreamed of beaches before and who loved Montana in her soul, suddenly talking to her son about Hawaii. "I mean, Claire and Ned had been talking about Hawaii. But I'm smiling because I'm anticipating what you are about to say and yes, sometimes a mother knows, even before she's told, what her children are thinking."

Will sat up and smiled. "This is so great, Mom. I knew you would understand and support my decision. And I promise you I'll call so often you won't even know I'm gone."

The smile left Peg's face. "Maybe you'd better spell it out for me after all—just in case I got it wrong."

"I'm going back East to visit Kelly for a few weeks. You know she's in law school in Georgetown. I think I might be in love with her."

CHAPTER 16

The Montana summer days had been exactly what Leslie had imagined. The air was crisp and cool in the mornings and evenings yet delightfully warm during the day. She relished the contrast to summer in DC, especially when she talked to Cynthia and heard the temperature and humidity numbers.

Every morning she got up early, savoring how the light filled her bedroom since she didn't have to draw the curtains at night for privacy. After breakfast, she'd jog down her road and walk back up. She loved the idea of having nothing in particular to do and, at first, had no trouble filling her days. But as summer wore on, she found herself fidgeting from one thing to the next, sometimes even missing the routine and stress of going to the office. And definitely missing the feeling of doing something useful.

She tried exploring the hiking trails in the area, but felt uncomfortable being alone if she got very far from a trailhead. She started taking riding lessons at a local stable, but that was only an hour or so twice a week. She found herself making excuses to drive over the pass to buy something she couldn't find in Legacy Springs. She was having a hard time meeting people and wondered if she'd made a mistake not settling in one of the tourist towns where there would be more going on. Every night, she'd pour herself a glass of wine and sit in the rocking chair on the deck to watch the sun set.

I can't believe the summer is almost over, Leslie thought one night as she settled into the rocking chair with a book. *One thing about this new life is that I have plenty of time to read.* She opened Maggie Madison's *Life on the Land* and started at the beginning. Maggie described living with nature and beauty, exploring creativity, and being blessed with family and friends. *It's the lifestyle that I wanted and now have,* she thought. *At least partly. The nature and beauty are here for sure, but I spend more time reading than doing anything creative. I haven't made any friends yet, and the only family I have left is Kelly, who is never going to live nearby. But really, I'm not lonely. Just getting used to a new place and a new way of life.*

It was too bad Peg always seemed so busy. Twice Leslie had stopped by, thinking it would be nice to get to know each other even if she and Peg were so different. But each time, Peg had some reason why she couldn't talk for more than ten minutes. Leslie could tell that Peg didn't like her, but she didn't know why. Oh, well, it didn't matter. She'd try to find someone else to be friends with, someone who was more educated, who had experienced life outside of Legacy Springs. Someone she could talk to about the huge difference between the hectic lifestyle she'd had in DC for so many years and this self-imposed quiet that she wasn't sure was really her cup of tea.

The only person she'd met so far that fit that description was Andrew Macfarlane. He had come to town shortly after Kelly left and had followed up on the dinner invitation. They'd gone to The Pine Room. She found him to be charming and interesting, and very handsome. She watched him for signals that he might be interested in her but didn't want to appear foolish, so she'd acted very businesslike. She wasn't sure she even knew how to flirt anymore. Especially with a man who was ten years younger. She decided that he probably realized during dinner that she wasn't as young as he thought, especially when she talked about being "retired," which was why at the end of the night they shook hands and there had been no indication that he wanted to see her again.

The wind rustled the leaves of the aspen trees that surrounded the house. The brilliant blue day-sky was morphing into a serene aquamarine over the distant mountains. Soon, the stars would explode from their cloaks and dot the night sky. First, just a few, then so many that there was more light than dark. The fading warmth of the late August day gave way to the mountain chill. Leslie went inside to put on her pile jacket and wool headband so she could stay sitting outside comfortably.

It couldn't be more different from August in DC, she thought again, with its stifling heat and humidity, unceasing, making the whole city lethargic. Nobody ventured outside unless they had to. Women wore loose linen clothing and sandals and carried light sweaters in their big handbags for when they went into the heavily air-conditioned buildings. Men suffered in khakis and seersucker. The thought of wearing a jacket and hat to sit outside in August was ludicrous.

The final birdcalls stopped abruptly as darkness fell. Leslie loved the quiet. No sound at all, she used to think when she first began rocking on the deck after dinner. But as her ears became accustomed to the place, she gradually heard more and more.

She heard the trees almost constantly chattering, the sounds of the aspen different from those of the pines. Then the whisper of small animals scurrying through the scrub. And, as the evening deepened, the hooting and calling of the night birds, usually far in the distance and sporadic, sounded as lonely as her heart.

Leslie started when the phone rang. It happened infrequently these days. When she first moved, it seemed that everyone from her old life wanted to hear how she was doing and fill her in on the latest gossip. But now she'd go two or even three days without talking to anyone.

She went inside in search of the ringing. She wasn't even sure where the phone was. *Gosh, I've come a long way from being tied to the thing constantly,* she thought as she fished the phone out from beneath a pile of newspapers in the kitchen. Glancing at the caller ID before opening it, she saw that it was Kelly.

"Hi, sweetheart. How are you?"

"I'm great, Mom. I went to orientation today and it was really cool." Kelly had finally decided on law school at Georgetown. She told Leslie the details of her day. "I can hardly wait until we start. And there are some good looking men in my class."

"You're going there for the education, remember?" Leslie said in her mother voice. "The men are secondary, and you won't have time for them anyway, especially during the first year. It's the most grueling of the three."

"I know, I know. You've been telling me that for years. But it doesn't hurt to look, does it? In fact, it might do you some good to start looking too, you know."

"It's slim pickins' out here in Legacy Springs, darlin'," Leslie said with an exaggerated Western twang. "You met the only eligible bachelor for miles around."

"Speaking of which, Will's been calling me a lot all summer. I thought it was only a fling, but now he's talking about coming to visit. Wouldn't that be interesting? Cowboy meets Georgetown. It should be fun. Do you ever see him?"

"Not a bit since you left. Although I did pass him on the road one day as he was driving to his parents. He waved."

"Well, if you see him, give him a hug for me. I've got to run now. I just called to say a quick hi."

"Call me after the first day of classes," she said, trying to keep Kelly on a little bit longer.

"Sure. You should be happy, Mom. I'm finally following in your footsteps. Love you. Bye." Kelly hung up.

My footsteps, Leslie thought as she went back outside. *Hardly. My footsteps were all about success and career. I wouldn't even have Kelly if Hugh hadn't insisted on having a child. Thank god he did.* He had been the real parent, even if it pained Leslie to admit it. She loved Kelly more than life itself, but her priority had been her career, which meant putting in the long hours required to be a successful lawyer. The hours that had paid for their nice house in DC, the trips to Europe, and Kelly's education. The money that had bought this land and built this house that she now lived in all alone.

Make your own footsteps, Kelly, she was thinking when the phone rang again. *Kelly must have forgotten something,* Leslie thought, flipping open the phone without looking at it. "Hello, dear, what did you forget?"

"What a nice greeting after such a long time," a male voice said. "I forgot, I forgot, what? Uh, to call you sooner?" The voice went up at the end of the question.

"I'm sorry," Leslie said. "I thought it was my daughter. Can I help you?" *Somebody trying to sell me something,* she thought. *Maybe I should just hang up.*

"Now there's another interesting question," the man said. "You most certainly can help me. You don't recognize my voice, do you?"

"I'm sorry, I don't."

"It's Andrew. Andrew Macfarlane. I'm going to be over your way next week and hoped you'd have dinner with me again. I do apologize for not calling sooner, but we had a bit of an emergency with the company and I had to go to South America for several weeks to straighten it out. I just got back last week."

"Oh, Andrew. Of course. Sorry. I thought you were a telemarketer." Leslie felt her heart start to beat faster in spite of the fact that she had told herself she didn't care about him, didn't care that he hadn't called.

"I've been called worse, but no offense taken. Well, how about it? Dinner. Next Wednesday or Thursday. Will you be in town?"

"Yes, I'd love to. Either day is fine." *God, I hope I don't sound desperate,* she thought.

"Great. Let's make it Wednesday. Shall I pick you up, or do you want to meet me in town?"

"I'll meet you," she said, remembering Cynthia's admonitions about not telling men where you lived too soon—especially when you lived out in the middle of nowhere. Can't trust anybody these days, she had said.

"Okay. Seven o'clock at The Pine Room on Wednesday. It'll be good to see you again. I'm looking forward to it."

"See you then." Leslie closed the phone.

She let her face melt into a huge grin, and she actually danced a little jig. She wasn't undesirable, too old, not interesting, or whatever else she had told herself. He wanted to see her again. She had a date. She felt a little ping when she went over the conversation and realized he hadn't asked her how she was doing or how she liked the house or anything. It had been almost six weeks since she had last seen him. *Oh, well, I guess I'm out of practice with the dating game,* she thought, tamping down the uneasiness. *Maybe that's just the way it's done these days.*

CHAPTER 17

It was dark by the time Sam put the horse in her stall and stowed the gear. The smell of the barn reminded him of his childhood on the ranch, cleaning the stalls after school each day. Luckily, he now could depend on Alice and Stan, the couple who lived in the caretaker's house and ran the place for him. Another piece of luck, he thought, that they'd stayed with him, especially after Karen died.

He walked down the center aisle of the barn, holding his palm flat to feel the warm muzzle of each horse delicately nibble the piece of carrot he offered. He turned out the light at the end of the row and went outside into the Montana darkness. A great horned owl hooted in the distance. He walked toward the beckoning lights of the house and saw Lee Hamilton sitting on the porch.

"It's a beauty tonight, isn't it, Sam?" Lee nodded at the half moon that was rising above the ridge behind the house.

"You should have come out to the barn, Lee. How long have you been waiting?"

"Not long. I enjoyed sitting here. Sorry I didn't call. I stopped by on the off chance that you were home."

"I'm glad you did. It's good to see you," Sam said as they shook hands. "I was just going to pour myself a much-deserved whiskey. Will you join me?"

"Don't mind if I do. But I'll warn you: with that good stuff you pour, it may end up being more than one!"

They went inside the sprawling old family ranch house, a mixture of homey small rooms and comfortable large spaces, each filled with big leather furniture and original Western art. Since Karen's death, Sam's home had taken on the patina of a Montana bachelor with less flower and frill and more leather and wood. But many of his wife's feminine touches still softened the room.

"I'm worried about old Tucker," Lee said as Sam poured two tumblers of whiskey. "He's been approached about an easement to look for natural gas under his property and then to sell his subsurface rights if they find anything. You know it can't be easy to keep up a place like his, and his wife's medical problems don't help."

Sam's eyebrows shot up. "What do you mean selling the subsurface rights? That's an issue on the east side, not here."

"Not anymore. Seems some oil and gas company is interested in looking at Tuck's place."

"Has he signed anything yet?"

"I don't think so. He did talk to Dick, and Dick told him the risks, but you know how stubborn Tuck is." Lee leaned over with his elbows on his knees and swirled the whiskey in his glass.

"Do you think I should call Tuck?" Sam asked.

"Wouldn't hurt. He told Peg he hasn't made up his mind yet. Are you home for a while now?"

"Yes. It's a welcome break to get out of DC in the summer. So tell me, how's Peg getting on with Leslie Hamilton. Have they become best friends yet?"

"Unfortunately not. Peg has a grudge against the poor woman. She can't get past the idea that a stranger is living on her land. And she's got a prejudice against lawyers from the East. Thinks they're all pushy and rude."

"Well, a lot of them are." Sam laughed and held up his empty glass. "Care for another?"

"Just a short one, then I've got to get going." Lee gave his glass to Sam, who poured more whiskey into both it and his own glass.

"From what I remember, Leslie's a really nice woman. It's got to be pretty hard for her, moving here and not knowing anybody. I'm surprised at Peg."

"Me too. But Peg thinks Leslie can't possibly have anything to offer, so she's keeping her at arm's length. I'm trying to get Peg to have an open mind and give her a chance, but you know Peg."

"Yes. But if anybody can convince Peg to change her mind, you can." Sam sipped his whiskey. "Say, if you don't mind my asking, how are things on the financial front?"

"Not good." Lee downed his drink. "But that's a conversation for another night." He stood to go. "There are dark clouds on the horizon. I only hope we can weather the storm."

The small votive candle on the table flickered and finally went out as Leslie and Andrew finished dinner at The Pine

Room. The restaurant had been full earlier but now was mostly empty. Their conversation had been easy and interesting and, Leslie thought, flirtatious. But she wasn't about to assume anything after her last dinner with him; she wasn't so sure that he wasn't just a charming man, no matter whom he was with.

He told her some of his history and that he had been divorced for almost five years. She did the math and decided he was definitely at least ten years younger, as she had suspected, which made her feel even more cautious about assumptions. He said he liked being single and living alone. She told him that she and Hugh had "grown apart" and she was living her dream by moving to Montana. She consciously didn't say anything that might reveal her age and avoided the word *retirement*.

She felt his knee lightly touching her own and wasn't sure if it was intentional or not. She moved her leg away slightly. His knee followed. Their waitress appeared with a tray of desserts that she balanced on the edge of the table.

"We have huckleberry pie, chocolate sin cake, fudge brownie sundaes, and ice cream." She pointed at each one with her free hand. "I recommend the pie. We only have it in August when the berries are ripe, so if you don't get it now, you'll have to wait until next year."

"Nothing for me," Leslie said. "After that steak, I'm stuffed."

"Not even sin cake?" Andrew said, lightly touching her arm and grinning. "Or maybe a coffee?"

"No, thanks." Leslie noticed that her skin tingled at his touch. *He really is handsome and intelligent and easy to be with,* she thought. *And sexy.*

"Just the check please," he said to the waitress. He picked up Leslie's hand and held it in his. "I've really enjoyed our evening. Can I convince you to have a nightcap in the bar?"

"I shouldn't," she said, even though she didn't want the evening to end. "I've got to drive home."

"Good point," Andrew said. "If we drive home first and then have a drink, that would be better."

Was it her imagination or was the pressure of his knee against hers more intense? He still held her hand and looked at her with those wonderful steely blue eyes. She felt giddy.

"And exactly what are you suggesting, Mr. Macfarlane?" Leslie wondered if she was pushing too far.

"I'm suggesting a nightcap at your place. You've been talking about the house all night, and I'd love to see it. I have a bottle of old port in the car that I've been wanting to try."

"Old port? Is that something you usually carry around with you?" Leslie stalled for time, wondering if having him come to her house meant that she was inviting him to have sex. She barely knew him. What would Cynthia tell her do?

"No, I brought it tonight in case we had the opportunity to share it." Andrew slowly ran his index finger from her wrist to her elbow and back again.

Leslie shivered slightly and crossed her legs, feeling a pleasure in pushing her thighs together. *Why not?* If he wanted to have sex and she didn't, she would just say no. She was a lawyer, after all, and knew how to handle things. "Sure, let's go back to my place and try it. That is, if you don't mind having to drive all the way back into town," she added, thinking it was a good idea to set the expectation straight from the beginning.

"Not a problem." Andrew signed the slip the waitress had brought. "I'll follow you."

As soon as Leslie was alone in her car, she called Cynthia but was immediately kicked to voice mail. *Of course,* she thought. *It's almost two in the morning in DC.*

"Leave me a message," she heard Cynthia's chipper voice say.

"I just had dinner with Andrew—you know, the car crash guy—and now he's following me back to my house for a nightcap. I really like him. I'm sure it's fine, but just in case, if I don't call you in the morning and something happens to me, his name is Andrew Macfarlane and he's the president of Xandex Explorations, Inc. Talk to you tomorrow."

Leslie hung up. For years, Cynthia had left similar messages with Leslie, the theory being that if, during a date or a one-night stand, she ended up with a pervert or murderer, there would be a trail to follow to catch the guy. This was Leslie's first time.

She looked in the rear-view mirror, half hoping Andrew wasn't still following her. The headlights were still there. She hit the redial on her phone.

"Leave a message," she heard again.

"He's ten years younger than me. If we go to bed together, I'm worried that he might be turned off by my body," Leslie said to the machine. "Okay, Cynthia, I know you tried to prepare me for this, but I haven't had sex with anyone but Hugh for thirty years. It's kind of scary. Talk to you tomorrow."

Leslie pressed the off button and concentrated on the dark road as it wound farther and farther away from town. Maybe it was nerves, but the darkness felt almost ominous. Two deer ran across the road and she had to hit the brakes, her hands shaking.

Finally, she came to the switchbacks leading to the house and was glad she had turned on most of the lights before leaving. Their glow in the sea of darkness reassured her and made her happy to be home. *It will be fine,* she thought. She would have one drink with Andrew then politely send him on his way. Maybe the next time she saw him, if the attraction was still there, she would think about having sex with him, she told herself. *After all, he's still a virtual stranger.*

She pulled into the garage and, even though it was designed for two cars, parked in the middle. He could park outside. It seemed too suggestive to have him park inside her garage. She was out of her car and waiting for him with the garage door up when he pulled into the driveway. "Do you mind coming in through the garage? It's not as dramatic as through the front door, but it is late," she said as he got out of his car with a brown bag in hand.

"Suits me just fine," he said. "Grand entries are usually overrated."

She led him through the garage and up the stairs to the kitchen and could feel him close behind her, maybe a little too close. "Well, here it is," she said, opening the door and wondering if her nerves were obvious. The great room beyond looked cozy and inviting in the soft lights she had left on. "Let me get some glasses for the port and then we can sit by the fireplace."

He pulled the bottle out of the bag and set it on the counter. She dropped her purse onto a bar stool next to the island and went to get two glasses from the cupboard. As she reached to the upper shelf, she felt his arms around her waist. He spun her around to face him and pressed her against the counter, one arm holding the back of her head as he kissed her, first softly, then more aggressively, his tongue sliding around the outside of her lips before slipping into her mouth.

She could feel his hardness as he pressed against her and felt the thrill of knowing that he wanted her. She returned the kiss and instinctively ran her hands up and down his back. He slid one hand under her shirt and cupped her breast. The word *melting* kept running through her mind, as if she had never truly known its meaning before. She felt as if she couldn't breathe, didn't want to stop. His mouth never left hers as he turned her away from the counter. She let him unzip her skirt and it fell to the floor.

Suddenly, he lifted her and sat her on the island. He stripped her shirt over her head as she voluntarily lifted her arms. His mouth covered hers again as she felt his hand stroke the side of her waist and then move along her thigh. He pulled back briefly as she unbuttoned his shirt, exposing his perfectly tanned chest. She giggled self-consciously as she realized she was sitting on the counter in her panties and bra. *Thank goodness, I had the good sense to wear the black lace*, she thought, although she had never anticipated this type of scene.

"What are you laughing at?" He unsnapped her bra and lowered his lips to a nipple.

"It's crazy," she said with a slight moan. "I can't believe I'm sitting on my kitchen island half-naked." She ran her fingers through his hair, holding him to her.

He pulled back again. "You're right," he said. "That is crazy. You should be completely naked."

He tugged at her panties as she lifted herself to let him pull them off. She wasn't sure how it happened, but his shirt was on the floor and his pants were down around his ankles. She had just enough time to notice that he wore tight black briefs before he was spreading her legs, his mouth on her, the feel of the cold hard granite a stark contrast to the soft heat she felt through her whole body. Never taking his mouth from her, he removed his underwear and stepped out of his pants. She tilted back her head, feeling long-forgotten sensations. She didn't think she had ever felt so sensual, so desired, so excited—-except maybe in the beginning with Hugh. She pushed the thought out of her mind. Hugh was history. And she didn't remember the sex ever being like this. She sighed with pleasure.

"Tell me you want it," he commanded, running his tongue up her torso. Her legs wrapped around his back.

"I want it now," she replied honestly and breathlessly.

He lifted her off the counter and went to the floor with her. His weight pressed her spine uncomfortably into the hard floor. She turned her head from his kiss and mumbled, "Maybe we should go to the bedroom."

"You said you wanted it, so you're going to get it," he said gruffly. He entered her with a quick thrust and she gasped.

She had a fleeting thought of a condom, but this man wanted her so badly, and she him, so she didn't say anything. Surely she didn't have to worry about disease with a man like him, and she realized with relief that she didn't have to worry about pregnancy anymore.

Andrew moved atop her and she forgot about the discomfort of the floor in the frenzied pushing. Within a few minutes, he grunted and finished and lay, sweating, on top of her. She breathed heavily, still full of desire. She moved her hips against him, but he got up and pulled her to her feet. "Now let's try a glass of that port and then I'll take you to the bedroom and we'll start all over again."

She stood naked beside him and became self-conscious about her too round stomach and her sagging breasts. He wanted her when she was fully dressed, but naked? Well, that was a different matter. "I'll just go get my robe." She stooped to gather her clothes. "I'll get you one of the hot tub robes too."

He lightly slapped her butt. "No need, but if you're cold, then go get your robe."

"I am kind of cold," she said, holding her bundle of clothes in front of her to shield her body from his view. "I'll be right back."

She returned fully wrapped in her robe and carrying one for him. He was completely naked except for his black socks, and he was standing by the counter with two glasses of port in front of him. She tried not to stare at him but could see that he was just as attractive with his clothes off as on. He seemed completely comfortable.

"Don't you look warm and cozy?" He handed her one of the glasses and then put on the robe but didn't tie it. "I prefer you naked." He pulled at the front of her robe, spreading it to reveal more of her neck and cleavage. "That's better."

They sipped the port and talked for a while, although when Cynthia asked her later what they had talked about, Leslie couldn't remember a thing. She did remember, though, that once they got into bed and he made love to her again, he did make sure that she was fully satisfied.

CHAPTER 18

Winter had settled silently onto the valley. The snow had begun in November, quiet and easy at first, politely elbowing the dried brown grasses aside or sitting prettily on the green arms of the pine trees—there one minute but gone the next. By December, the snow had become like a moody teenager: sometimes light-hearted and carefree but often sullen and with disdain for anything in its path. In January, the snow came in full force, bullying the trees into submission and eliminating, with a wave of an imperious hand, any trace of manmade or natural objects less than four feet high.

Leslie watched the white dust gather in the corners of the windows, only to be blown off abruptly until it became too thick for the wind to budge. Outside, the air was a jumble of snowflakes being tossed upward and sideways. Sometimes the wind blew so hard Leslie felt as if it were moving the thick walls of the house.

Mike Connelly did a good job building this place, she thought, remembering how often she had talked with him while the house was being built. *Funny how people move in and out of our lives. I haven't talked to him in ages. I should call and invite him and his wife to dinner. Yes, that's what I need to do. Reach out more and be the one who initiates invitations instead of waiting for them to come to me.*

She padded into the kitchen in the sheepskin slippers that had become her most frequent footwear. Most days, she didn't even venture outside of the house unless she had to buy food. Going to town meant navigating down the switchbacks of the steep, curving, snow-covered road. She tried to save the trips for those days between storms, when the sky was so clear and blue that it looked like you could run your hand along it and crystals formed in the air in front of your eyes and hung there, floating then disappearing. Those days were magic to her, and the beauty of it all raised her spirits. Maggie Madison had captured the feeling in one of Leslie's favorite poems with the phrase "the universe of stars has come to visit in daylight, and has enveloped me in infinity."

On the days when she stayed home, she followed a routine that was different from in the summer with its early light and temptation to get outside. She didn't awaken until the sun came up, then she'd stay in bed under the warm covers watching the colors of the sunrise, in no hurry to get up. When the desire for coffee won out, she'd wrap a warm terry robe around her flannel pajamas and shuffle into the kitchen to make it. Then she would head back to the bathroom to shower, run through the regimen of lotions for her face, and finally get dressed. Even though she wasn't going anywhere, she never felt the day could start unless she got out of her pajamas.

With her first cup of coffee in hand, she always read one of Maggie Madison's poems to remind herself why she was here in Montana in the middle of the winter. Sometimes the poem would suggest to her an activity for the day. If it was about the joy of freshly baked bread, she might try baking. If it was about a grandmother's heirloom-embroidered tablecloth, she might try embroidery. If it was about something that she had not yet attempted, like making jam or tatting lace, she might spend the day researching the topic on the Internet and ordering supplies or books. She bought a lot of things via the Internet these days and had come to know the two UPS delivery people, a young man and a middle-aged woman, as well as she knew anyone else in the community. They could never stay to talk, but they did break the monotony of the days.

She read the *New York Times* on her computer and picked up the local weekly newspaper when she was in town. Most days, she spent an hour in the basement workout room, watching mindless TV as she ran on the treadmill. As darkness fell in late afternoon, she would haul logs in from the pile on the side of the deck and make a fire. She'd read and eat dinner in front of the fire, ready to go to bed by 8:30 or 9:00. It was only when she curled up in bed under the thick down comforter with yet another novel that she would admit to herself that she was bored and quite lonely. Except when Andrew was there.

"Can't you come more often?" she asked after yet another of the three-week hiatuses.

"Come on, Leslie," he said. "You know I've got business all over the world. The small development project here doesn't need my attention very often. Mostly I come just to see you."

Leslie had to admit that, despite her initial self-consciousness, Andrew did not seem concerned with either the condition of her body or her age and, in fact, made her feel young and sexy.

His body was fit and muscular and a sharp contrast to the soft pudginess of Hugh. When they made love, he took charge, as if he owned her, and she let him. It was something Hugh had never done. When she was with Andrew, she felt connected to the world again and alive in her sexuality. They sometimes went out to dinner and they talked about books and current events, but the relationship was mostly about the sex. If they started to have a disagreement, one of them would initiate lovemaking, putting a quick end to the discussion.

"I do love my house and it's what I've always wanted," she said to Andrew one morning as they drank coffee in bed. "But I'm starting to feel a bit claustrophobic. For years I dreamed of having time to do all the creative things I never had time to do when I was working, but now, I'm not sure it's enough. I'm starting to feel like I'm not doing anything of value, or maybe I just don't have enough stimulation."

"You're adding a lot of value to this guy." He opened his robe and stroked himself. "And as for stimulation, well, I can take care of that." He reached toward the tie on her robe.

"That's not what I mean," she said, pulling back and gathering the robe more closely around her. "It's not all about sex, you know. I'm talking about intellectual stimulation. For example, what's this project you're working on? You never tell me anything about it."

"Okay, okay." He crossed his legs and pulled the robe over them demurely. "I can't really say much about the project. It's a development that's in its early stages, and I'm sure you can appreciate how important it is to keep development projects confidential. Otherwise, speculation can drive the prices sky high and make the return on an investment evaporate. But I can tell you that, if it works, the company will make a boatload of profit. And that's very stimulating to me."

"Be serious, Andrew. What about the environmental impacts of your mining operations? I don't think I ever told you that I used to represent an environmental group, pro bono of course, that opposed mining operations in the Appalachians. Some of their practices were pretty bad. How do you do it?"

Andrew looked mildly irritated. "We follow the law when we can, and we have a voluntary environmental restoration fund. But I believe that gas and oil and hard rock were put here for man to use. The environmentalists forget that we need to heat our homes and fuel our factories. The cars they drive are made from metal, not to mention their coffee pots and wedding bands. Mining helps us live the good life. The tree huggers want us to go back to the Stone Age."

"That's not true at all," Leslie bristled. "Protection of the environment is really important. If we deplete the resources or harm the environment to get them, there won't be anything left for the next generation. It's why we have environmental laws."

"There you go being an Eastern environmental liberal again," Andrew said as he laughed and got out of bed and went into the bathroom.

Irritated, Leslie pushed herself up and was sitting propped against the headboard when he walked back into the room. He came and sat down beside her, taking her hands in his.

"Look, it's my business to get resources from the ground and make money while I do it. It's a good thing, and I'm not going to be apologetic about it. We follow the law, but there's nothing wrong with making sure we interpret it to our advantage whenever possible. You're a lawyer; you know there's more than one way to look at everything. It's what kept you in business for all those years, isn't it?"

"You're right," she said, hoping to avoid an argument. "But I happen to think that it's possible for businesses to make a profit while doing the right thing. It's a concept called sustainability. You might think about looking into it."

"I'll do that," he said. "But as president of Xandex, my obligation is to my stockholders, and they don't really give a damn about how I make money as long as their share price keeps going up. Speaking of which, something else is going up that needs to be taken care of." He climbed back into bed.

"Why don't you invite Leslie to join your book group?" Lee asked Peg one morning while he was reading the newspaper. "She's over there all alone."

"She is sort of pathetic, isn't she? But my book group? I don't even know if she likes to read. Besides, I don't know that she'd fit in. She's always so uppity. I get the impression she thinks we're a bunch of hicks."

"Peg," he said sternly, putting aside the paper and looking over the top of his reading glasses, "you are being ridiculous. You've seen all the books in her house, so of course she likes to read. And she doesn't think you or the other people around here are hicks." He sighed. "I think you're the one who is being uppity. What would it hurt to invite her?"

"The hurt would be if she came and everyone hated her and we couldn't get rid of her. The others would never forgive me."

Peg made a face. She'd started the book group years ago with five of her friends and they met every other month without fail. Mary Gaylord was a teacher at the elementary school and Claire Healy, her friend since childhood, was a rancher like her. Emma Patterson and Edith Applegate were in their late seventies, both widows, strong pioneer women who made their way through life on guts and determination. Dory Cranshaw, the newest member, had joined them when she moved to the area about ten years ago as high school principal.

"Why don't you ask them about it?" Lee went back to the newspaper. "If they agree with you, then you shouldn't invite her."

"Oh, for heaven's sake. All right. I'll do it." Peg picked up a section of the newspaper. "Shouldn't we be hearing from the bank this week? They've got to know we need some relief since we haven't made a mortgage payment yet this year."

"I'll call again today," Lee said. "Don't worry, I've got it under control. We'll work it out."

"I hope you're right. I can't be losing sleep over the mortgage *and* whether the club will like Leslie." Peg smiled, but her heart was heavy on both counts.

After breakfast, Peg called each of the club members, hoping at least one of them would object to inviting Leslie. But they all thought it was a great idea.

"Give us some new perspective," Mary said.

"I've been wanting to see what our new city lawyer was like," Emma said.

"I was so grateful when you asked me to join, I'm sure she'll feel the same way," Dory said.

"I hope she's an expert in Russian literature," Edith said. "I could use some help."

This year, they were reading Tolstoy, Chekhov, and Dostoevsky. Last year, they had focused on the Greek classics. The year before was American twentieth century. They didn't shy away from reading difficult books. As Peg reflected on the upcoming choices—*Anna Karenina, The Cherry Tree, and Crime and Punishment*—she decided that the list was daunting enough to scare off most people. Including Leslie. The risk that she would accept the invitation was low.

CHAPTER 19

It was the middle of February and a major storm was forecast. Leslie watched the high, white clouds that looked like horsetails give way the next day to a heavy, gray mass that blocked out the sun. That night, it started snowing, and by the next morning, almost two feet had fallen without any end in sight. She paced between the kitchen and the living room, restless. None of her half-done projects held her interest. She picked up a book, only to realize that she had read for ten minutes and hadn't comprehended a thing. She pulled at a quilted square, sliding the needle up and down through the fabric, but quickly put it aside. What was wrong? She felt like the walls of the house were creeping closer and closer together, making each room smaller as the day went on.

I've got to talk to somebody, she thought. She called Cynthia.

"Leave me a message."

"Damn it, where are you when I need to talk to you? Call me back when you get this. It's snowing again and I'm going stir crazy." Leslie snapped shut the lid of the phone, then opened it and called Kelly.

"How are you, sweetie?" Thank goodness, Kelly had actually answered.

"Great, Mom, but I can't talk for long. I was just on my way out to a movie. How are you?"

"I'm fine," Leslie lied. She didn't want her daughter to know that she was lonely; she only wanted somebody to talk to. "Who are you going with?"

"A guy from school who's in his second year. He had an interview with your old firm last week, so he's definitely got some earning potential."

Leslie sighed. "How about spending time worrying about your own earning potential?"

"I do. I just said it to bug you. I'm doing fine and classes are good."

"Have you worn that sweater yet that I bought you for Christmas?"

"I love the sweater. I've worn it a lot. Are you okay? You sound funny."

"Oh, I'm a little lonely, I guess. Maybe next year we can spend Christmas together. I miss you."

"You really should have come back to DC. It was nice to be with Dad, but Christmas wasn't the same without you."

"It was important for me to be alone and in Montana this year. It just turned out to be harder than I thought." Leslie had expected to spend some time with Andrew, but by the time she talked to him about it, Christmas was two weeks away, and he looked at her with surprise. He was spending the holidays in Mexico. He apologized that he neglected to tell her that, but it hadn't occurred to him that they would spend it together. He told her he had assumed she would be with Kelly.

So she spent the holiday alone. "No cooking, no tree, no family arguments, no cleanup. What could possibly be better than a holiday with no hassle?" she said if anyone asked, almost believing it herself.

"Listen, Mom, I'd love to talk, but I've got to run. I'll call you tomorrow." Leslie hung up and looked at the phone again, wondering who else she could call. Instead, it rang while she still held it. To her surprise, it was Peg Hamilton.

"I just had a call from Max who plows our road. One of their trucks broke down and they aren't sure they'll be able to keep the road open during the storm. But they promised to clear it as soon as they can after the initial hit is over. You don't have any reason to go out, do you?"

"No, I don't. I managed to get stocked up earlier in the week." She laughed. "I might finally be getting the hang of this, knowing that I can't go to the store any old time I please and buying enough to tide me over through these storms. I'll be fine." She felt a touch of panic at the idea of being stranded.

"If there's anything you need, please feel free to call," Peg offered, although Leslie could hear the stiffness in her voice.

"There is one thing you can help me with," Leslie said, hesitating slightly. "I'm wondering if you have any tips for not going crazy when you can't get outside for all this time. How do you do it? What do you do all day?"

"It's just cabin fever, Leslie, and everyone gets it. The best thing is to go outside and do something, anything. Chop wood or shovel the deck, even though it'll fill right back in behind you. It's the exercise that makes the difference. The other technique is the exact opposite. You make a crackling fire and use the time to read or write or watch old movies. Whatever it is that will absorb you and take your mind off it."

"I've been reading and baking and quilting and doing all of those things that I never had time to do before, but now I have too much time." Leslie knew she was only talking to keep the conversation going. "When will we see bare ground again? The white is driving me crazy."

"Welcome to Montana. Don't worry. The ground is still there. But don't get your hopes up. It'll be April before you see any brown, unless you go out with a shovel and find it yourself. We've got a ways to go before then. Call us if you need anything. It's been nice chatting with you."

Peg hung up the phone and realized she had forgotten to ask Leslie about joining the book club. *Maybe I forgot on purpose. Oh well, I can call her tomorrow.* She went into the living room where Lee lay on the couch in front of an exceptionally large and roaring fire. He had put several extra logs on to warm the room. The daylight was muted by the storm, making the space feel like a cocoon.

"It's lovely in here," she said as she snuggled beside him.

He pulled her close and stroked her arm. "What's up with the neighbor?"

"Having a little trouble adjusting to the Montana winter." Peg tried not to sound pleased at Leslie's unhappiness. "She wanted to know how we manage being housebound during these storms, but since she lives by herself, I didn't have the heart to tell her." She kissed her husband deeply and tenderly, ready for the time to fly by.

Cortez Harbinger was the only person left in Two Whoops. Every half hour, the bartender had shoveled the snow away from the door, and one by one the other patrons had left.

"I'm afraid I'm going to have to close up soon, Cortez," the bartender said. "The roads aren't getting any better and I don't want to have to spend the night in the bar with you when my beautiful wife is at home waiting for me in a warm, cozy bed. I hope you have somebody to go home to."

"No. I'm a lucky man. No woman owns me." Cortez downed the remainder of his whiskey. "I'm in the motel down the street, so the roads aren't a problem for me. Although it would be nice to have a woman in bed with me. If you know of any likely candidates, send them my way."

"Not in my job description." The bartender laughed. "You're on your own for that one."

"Okay, well then, since you are closing early, can you at least sell me a pint of whiskey so I can have some solace as I lay alone watching junk TV?"

"That I can do, yes. That I can do." The bartender placed the bottle on the counter. "If this storm lets up, I guess I'll see you again tomorrow."

"I suppose you will. I was hoping to finish my business and get back home, but that's not likely given this storm. Hell, I'm starting to like this little town. You just need to get more babes coming into the bar. Maybe I can help you with some marketing."

"Sure thing." The bartender ushered Cortez out the door and into the snowstorm.

Cortez put on his gloves and stuck his hands in his pockets. The hotel was only a block away, but the wind in his face made the walk feel much longer.

When he let himself into the room, he took off his coat and poured two fingers of whiskey into the plastic hotel glass. He called Andrew, expecting to leave a message on voicemail, and was surprised when Andrew answered. "Sorry, boss, but I'm not going to be able to get back to your office for that meeting day after tomorrow," Cortez said as he held his phone to his ear with one hand and the glass with the other. He took a sip. The whiskey just didn't taste as good out of plastic.

"Is the storm as bad there as it is here?" Andrew asked.

"Probably worse. Even the bars have closed here. The whole town shut down early." Cortez took a sip and frowned. "Jesus, Andy, sometimes this job sucks. Can you believe I'm drinking whiskey out of a plastic glass? Worse, I'm alone with a big hotel bed."

"Well, that is truly a disaster."

"Tell me about it." Cortez ignored the sarcasm. "I probably won't be able to get to my appointment tomorrow, so I'll have to stay an extra day. That's why I'll miss the meeting."

"We'll manage without you. Remind me who you were supposed to meet with?"

"The Pinkertons. They're the couple in their seventies. They live fifteen miles up a steep, dead-end dirt road, and it's hell to get there on a good day. Last time the potholes nearly ate my rig."

"Too bad about the weather. Are they ready to close?"

"Yeah, they're ready," Cortez said, draining his glass and pouring another. "Hell, they're planning to buy a house in the

161

tropics with the windfall they think they are going to get. And with the weather here tonight, I wouldn't blame anybody for dreaming about sunshine."

"If you can't get up there tomorrow, then see if you can close it the next day. We only need a few more after the Pinkertons to make this deal profitable. Who's our next most likely prospect?"

"There are three that I've been working. The most likely is Emma Patterson. She's a widow. Kids all live in other parts of the state. They seem to take good care of her, but they aren't around here. I haven't called her, but I may just drop in. My guess is that if I show up, she'll be happy to have some company, especially with this storm." Cortez parted the curtain and looked out at the snow he could see swirling in front of the hotel's bright red vacancy sign. "Worst case, Andy, we have to buy some rights from the pre-1916ers."

"That'll cost more," Andrew said. "Buying an easement where we've got the claim filed is a lot cheaper than buying the right that somebody else already owns. We only need a few more and we're there. Who else do you have after Patterson?"

"I've got another widow lined up, Edith Applegate. I think both of them will fall like bowling pins."

"I want to get this sewn up, Cortez. Let's pick up the pace."

"Don't forget I have dinner lined up with Sam Curtis to see if I can get him to change his mind."

"All the more reason to finish up sooner rather than later. If we can't make this deal fly financially, we won't need the senator."

"Right." Cortez took another swig and, emboldened by the whiskey, asked a question he wouldn't normally have dared to ask. "You hearing anything from your lady friend here? About whether people are talking?" Cortez knew about the affair since Andrew stopped staying at the hotel when he came to town and Cortez had seen him and Leslie together at dinner one night, holding hands across the table.

"You know I don't talk about my private life." Andrew's tone was ice and Cortez knew that he had crossed the line, but he plunged ahead anyway.

"I know, boss. I just thought it might be good to know what you're hearing. It could help me. But never mind. Sorry I asked."

"She hasn't said a word, nor asked a question. But she's too new to be connected into the community, so that isn't a surprise. Your job is to assume the word is getting around, and get your butt in gear to close the deals."

Cortez tried to appease Andrew. "My prediction is that I'll have them done within the next two weeks. And if I don't, you can make me stay here until I do." He took another drink. "But if I do put a bow on it in two weeks, then I'll expect a nice little bonus." Andrew snorted and Cortez heard a dial tone. He put the phone down and turned on the TV. He poured two more fingers of whiskey in the glass and turned the heat up to seventy-eight degrees.

He stripped to his jockey shorts and spread out on the bed, beginning the long and endless search through the cable channels for something to watch. *Hell, I'm not getting out anytime early in the morning*, he thought. He reached over and poured four fingers into the glass.

163

"How are you faring today?" Peg started the conversation when she called Leslie the day after the storm.

"Better," Leslie said. "I did go out and shovel my way to the mailbox, and you were right. It did help. Did you know they plowed the road? The mail truck was here a few minutes ago. I can't believe they deliver the mail on a day like today. I can barely get out to the box to pick it up, and they've driven all the way out here to deliver a bunch of flyers and junk mail."

"It may seem strange to you, but we believe that stuff about 'neither rain nor snow.'"

"Well, it's a mystery to me how they do it. But I'm glad they made it through, because right behind them was UPS with my latest shipment of books. Thank god. I was running low on new things to read."

"You like to read?" Peg hoped against hope that Leslie would say no.

"Yes, I do. It's one of my favorite ways to pass the time. I miss having someone to talk to about what I'm reading though. Do you like to read?"

"Yes, I do. In fact, I actually called to ask you if you would be interested in joining a book group I'm in with five other women. I've checked with them and they've agreed we could use some new blood. We meet every other month and have a theme for each year. This year, we are reading Russian literature, which can be pretty heavy, so if you aren't interested, we would understand."

"It sounds fabulous. I would love to join you."

Peg's heart sank. "Our next session is on Thursday and we're reading *Anna Karenina*, so it's probably too soon for you to get through it. Maybe you want to wait until the April meeting to start. We're going to read Chekhov's *The Cherry Tree*—a bit more manageable. Then, in June, we're tackling *Crime and Punishment,* so if you want to reconsider, no hard feelings."

"I'd love to come on Thursday. This is the most exciting thing that's happened to me in months. I wouldn't miss the meeting for anything. I read *Anna Karenina* years ago and I know exactly where my copy is, so rereading it should go pretty quickly. I'll be ready."

"We rotate location and the hostess provides the food and wine. The meeting next week is at my house."

"Sounds fun, Peg. Thanks so much for thinking of me. I really do appreciate it."

Peg hung up the phone and then reluctantly called the club members one by one to let them know the "outsider" was going to join them.

CHAPTER 20

The snow caught the early morning sunlight and reflected brightly into Leslie's bedroom. She could tell it was later than usual when she woke up. *Funny how I'm so in tune with the rhythms of the days and the seasons since I moved to Montana,* she thought. In DC, she would have been hard pressed to say what time the sun came up or went down, and she knew the seasons mostly by weather on a weekend after spending all week in controlled heat or cold. She rolled over to see that the clock radio read quarter past nine. As she rolled, something fell off the bed.

Anna Karenina. She leaned over to get the book from the floor, and then sat up, pulling the down comforter around her shoulders. She decided to read at least one chapter before getting out of the warm bed. *I've got to get through this,* she thought, paging through to find the place where she had dozed off the night before. *I won't be the one who hasn't finished the book.*

She hoped the group wasn't like some she had heard about, where some people didn't even read the book and the conversation veered instead into a gabfest about life, men, children, or work. But even if it did turn out to be that kind of group, it was a chance to meet women from the community. Peg had said the members included a teacher, the high school principal, a rancher, and two women she said were "older."

Leslie was distracted by a small flock of crossbills that flittered in front of the window and landed in the snow-laden branches of the huge fir tree that grew closest to the house. She was proud of herself for recognizing the little birds; she'd been studying the bird book, trying to distinguish one type from another. She thought they looked like ornaments, the red males and yellowish-olive females together, hopping and trading positions among the branches.

Pay attention, she told herself. *Get back to the book.* She read slowly, marking passages she particularly liked so they would be easier to find during the discussion. Anna Karenina had just fallen for the handsome Prince Vronsky and their ill-fated love affair was about to begin. Leslie knew that throughout the book, Anna would struggle with her intense attraction to Vronsky and her inability to say 'no' to him. Leslie was deep into another tension-filled scene between the two lovers when the phone rang.

"Hi, gorgeous, did I wake you up?" Leslie heard Andrew's voice. It had been over a week since she had talked to him.

"No, I've been up for hours," she lied. She still thought of herself as a working woman, not somebody who spent the morning in bed.

"I'm planning to head over your way later this week and was hoping we could get together. I found an interesting little French wine that I thought you would enjoy."

"Great. It'll be nice to see you. What day will you be here?"

"Thursday. I can't get there until the evening, and I've got an early meeting Friday morning, but at least we can steal a few hours together. How'd you do with the storm?"

"I survived. I called you and left a message a few days ago. I was having quite a bout of cabin fever."

"I'm sorry I didn't get a chance to call you back. I heard it was a bad one. One of my consultants got caught over there for a few extra days because of the road conditions. But everything will be clear by Thursday. I should be at your place by seven." Leslie noticed that he didn't give an explanation for not returning her call.

"Oh, no." She looked at *Anna Karenina* in her lap. "Thursday won't work for me. I'm sorry." It was the first time since they began seeing each other that she was not available. Including the times he called with less than a few hours notice.

"Just cancel whatever it is you have. I can only be there for one night. I'll call you if the plane's late."

"No, I can't cancel. I've been invited to join Peg Hamilton's book group and this will be my first meeting. We're reading *Anna Karenina*."

"You can go next month. The biddies won't mind if you don't show up. Besides, who wants to read something like that anyway?" His tone was dismissive.

"I do," she said, becoming annoyed. "I've been looking forward to this, and I'm not going to cancel."

"Come on. It might be another couple weeks before I get over there again. Go to the book club for an hour or two and come home early. Leave me a key and I'll wait for you—in bed. If I'm asleep, you can slip in beside me and wake me up with a little hand job. If your hands are warm, that is," he added.

Usually, Leslie liked his frank sex talk, but she didn't feel sexy with this conversation; she felt like he expected her to adjust to his schedule without regard to hers. She knew he was a man who was used to getting his way, but she had never needed to push back on him about anything until now.

"Look, I already said I am going to the book club. I intend to stay until it's done. I don't know how late that will be, and," she said, surprising even herself, "if you have an early morning meeting, maybe you should just stay in town and save yourself the inconvenience of driving all the way out here."

"I'm sorry. I've clearly upset you." He sounded conciliatory. "I would really like to see you, and Thursday is the only day I'll be there. I'll wait up for you and we can enjoy a quiet glass of wine together."

"Okay." She felt better that he had apologized. "But I'm staying until book club is over. Being invited to this group means a lot to me. There's a key under the mat at the back door."

"Great. I'll see you Thursday. Gotta run."

She closed the phone and looked out the window. The crossbills had left and were replaced by a flock of black-capped chickadees, another bird she recognized. The sound of their call—*chick-a-dee-dee-dee*—made her feel at home as she watched them flying among the branches of the big tree. *I wonder about this relationship with Andrew,* she thought. *If it even is a relationship. Maybe it's just sex to him. Is it just sex to me, too? Do I even want it to be something more? Am I seeing him because it's good for my ego to have a man—and a younger man at that—interested in me? Or, do I just not want to be alone?*

She didn't have answers, but knew that she didn't like the Andrew she'd heard on this call. So controlling. But it wasn't only this time. He always had to call the shots. When he would see her, what they would do, when they would make love. Yet, even so, she was still incredibly attracted to him. In bed, when he took command, she had to admit there was something sexy about it. *And he's so charming and interesting. So what, he likes to get his own way. All men do. It's really not that big a deal. And anyway, I'm certainly not ready to give him up just yet.*

She picked up *Anna Karenina* and tried not to think about the parallels to her own life.

CHAPTER 21

The freshly plowed snow was so high on the sides of the road that it was like driving in a tunnel. Sam Curtis had allowed extra time to get to the dinner meeting with Cortez Harbinger, but the pavement was clear. He slowed down. *Don't need to spend any more time than necessary with the man. I wonder what he wants this time. Nothing good for sure, if it's coming from him and his cronies.*

Sam parked a few blocks away from the restaurant to kill more time, but he was still fifteen minutes early. When he walked into The Pine Room, Harbinger was already at the bar, a glass of whiskey in hand, dressed casually in jeans and a crew-neck sweater. Sam wondered if he was trying to pass for a local, but the diamond pinky ring and expensive thin watch gave him away.

"Glad you could make it, Senator." Harbinger stood up when Sam approached. "I really do appreciate your time. And the fact that you were willing to drive into town."

"It's not far, and the road was clear."

"Please, sit down. Let's have a drink before dinner. What would you like?"

"No, thanks. I'll have some wine with dinner."

"Well, let's head in to our table and you can tell me what's been keeping you busy these days. I'm interested in your opinion on a couple of different matters."

Much as Sam disliked him, he had to admit that Harbinger knew his business and never missed a beat. He reminded himself that this was serious and often dirty politics. He needed to be on his guard all night.

"She let them get to her. That was the problem," Edith Applegate stated firmly. "It's no different today. Women get stuck in a rut with some husband they can't stand, but when they finally meet the love of their life, they can't deal with the guilt and shame, which is just pressure from people on the outside."

"I don't know that her guilt and shame wasn't more imposed from within," Mary Gaylord said. "They had gone to live in Italy and could have been perfectly happy there, but they chose to go back to Russia."

"Right," Dory said, taking a bite of the chocolate raspberry cake that Peg had made.

"No, it was all about her son," Emma Patterson chimed in. "She couldn't deal with being away from him. I remember when my youngest left home. I was devastated. Wondered what I would do with the rest of my life. And poor Anna lost hers when he was so young. I can't imagine having to choose between my lover and my son."

Leslie looked at her with a small smile. Emma's weathered face showed the many years of hard work, indoors and out, running a ranch and raising her seven children. It was funny to hear a woman Emma's age talk about "her lover" as if it were a current event.

Leslie had finished the book that afternoon and had not had time to look at the critiques and analyses of scholars as she'd planned. Sitting in Peg's living room, listening to the commentary, she was glad she had run out of time. This conversation was so much deeper and more personal. These women didn't need a stuffy objective analysis; they shared their own life experiences and views as a way to make real their understanding of Anna Karenina's actions and motives. Leslie felt a twinge of shame for thinking that the women might not have been educated enough to appreciate *Anna Karenina*.

As the evening wore on, she realized that, although the women all freely offered their opinions, they would subtly defer to Peg to synthesize the points, add her own analysis, and deftly state a conclusion that encapsulated each of their thoughts. She would then introduce a new point and open the door with a probing question that stimulated an entirely new train of discussion. She was clearly the leader of the group.

"Well, ladies," Peg finally announced as she began stacking empty dishes onto a tray, "I think we have dissected poor Anna enough for one night." It was almost midnight. They had been at it practically nonstop for five hours. Leslie couldn't remember the last time she was engaged in such fascinating conversation, and all about one book. She felt the best part was that she had gotten to know each of the women.

"At least the next book is shorter," Edith said. "We'll have more time to catch up on the gossip." Leslie enjoyed Edith's irreverent manner. She wondered just how old Edith and Emma were.

"That's right," Emma said. "I wanted to tell you all about the nice man who's been coming to visit me and who is going to make me rich."

"You have a rich lover you've been hiding from us?" Edith cried. "Details, dearie. We want details." Leslie laughed along with the others. *These two really are characters.*

"He's the sweetest thing," Emma said with a wink. "He's with some small company. They're going to pay me to let them wander over my property. Looking for natural gas, he says. If they find it, I'll be like Jed Clampett and the Beverly Hillbillies—sitting pretty on a wad of money."

"Wait a minute," Edith said. "He's been over to see me too. Is his name Cortez Harbinger?"

This is no longer amusing, Leslie thought, her neck prickling at the mention of Harbinger.

"Yes," Emma said. "He said his mama was from Mexico although he grew up here in Montana."

"I haven't signed anything yet, have you?" Edith asked. "Why didn't you tell me he was talking to you?"

Peg stopped loading the tray. "Please don't tell me you've got a contract with him, Emma. It never occurred to me that they would be over on your side of the valley."

"I have signed, Peg, but it's a fair deal. I'm not as senile as the man thought I was. I got double what he originally offered me. And what do you mean my side of the valley?"

Emma and Edith both turned to Peg.

She told them about Tucker and what she knew about the problem with the subsurface rights. They all listened attentively.

"Hell's bells, Peg, why didn't you tell us before this?" Emma said. "He led me to believe that my property was the only one that had any potential for gas under it. That's why I wasn't worried. It seemed like such a wild goose chase that if they wanted to pay me a bunch of money to go looking for something that probably wasn't there, or if it was, wouldn't be much of it, then what's the harm?" Emma screwed up her face. "I did sign something that said I wouldn't tell anybody about my payment, but of course that kind of legal mumbo-jumbo doesn't apply to friends. He told me it was so other people wouldn't get worked up and expect to be paid for nothing. What a little weasel. He was probably lying, too, when he said my pumpkin bread was the best he ever had."

"It's too late now to do anything." Edith started adding glasses to Peg's tray. "I mean, it's too late tonight. Let's talk tomorrow and compare notes."

"Good idea," Emma said. "I'll read that document again tomorrow more closely."

"I'd be willing to help if you like," Leslie found herself saying. "You know, to look at the documents." She thought about telling them what she knew about Harbinger but decided to wait. No reason to get them more upset.

They all looked at her. Emma spoke first. "That's very sweet of you, but how could you help, dear?"

"You silly goose," Edith chimed in. "Remember, she's a big-city lawyer. She knows how to read these things." Turning to Leslie, she said, "I think that's a great idea. Why don't you come over to my place tomorrow and pick me up and we'll drive on over to Emma's?"

"I'm not licensed to practice here in Montana." Leslie remembered her ethical duties. "But I'd be happy to help you informally. Shall I pick you up at two?"

On the short drive home from Peg's, she thought about how ironic it was that she'd be so far from DC and still have to deal with sleazy lobbyists. Cortez Harbinger. Shit.

She decided to ask Andrew whether he had heard anything about this. She doubted he would know Harbinger, but he might recognize the name of the company Harbinger worked for. He might even know some of the senior people there and could help. She would ask him about it the next time she saw him, she thought. As she approached her house, her heartbeat quickened.

I don't remember leaving on that many lights when I left. But her fear quickly subsided when she saw Andrew's car in the driveway. She had completely forgotten that he was arriving that night.

Sam Curtis wondered when Cortez Harbinger would finally get down to business. The dinner plates had been cleared and he still hadn't make the pitch Sam knew was coming. "You know, Senator," Harbinger finally said once there was a glass of brandy in front of him, "I asked you here to talk about the subsurface mining rights issue."

"I told you last year I wouldn't support your concept. Have you changed it in any way?"

"No. But let me be straight with you, Senator. Xandex is considering expanding from hard rock mining into oil and gas exploration. My client thinks it's important to save America by not having to rely on foreign sources of oil and gas. And the economy of this state could sure use some help right now, what with all of the restrictions on the timber industry and the debacle of the foreign boycotts of our beef. There are reserves in the eastern part of the state that are ripe for development; Xandex just needs some incentive to go after them. Development would help the economy of the whole state by bringing jobs and tax revenues."

Sam had to agree that the economy could use a boost. But everyone knew that timber and ranching were cyclical businesses. The ups and downs were part of it. But Sam also knew that the rebounds were harder since the globalization of the markets.

Harbinger leaned on the table. "We just need that minor change in the law that will let us develop these gas reserves profitably."

"I'm sorry, but my position hasn't changed."

"Look, Senator, I understand where you are coming from, but Montana needs this change to happen. Not to mention that it is vital to national security."

"Playing the national security card isn't going to cut it on this one, Cortez. Save it for the DC folks. You know I'm on record as supporting American independence from foreign energy sources. But that doesn't mean I support drilling in places that are sensitive. Your proposal not only ignores that, but would encourage drilling in those areas."

"Senator, you know we'll find a way to get this through, either with you or without you, and I'd rather have it be with you. What's it going to take?"

"It's not going to take anything because you and I both know it's not going to happen." Sam knew the stakes of the game were rising. This must be worth a fortune to Xandex or Harbinger wouldn't have jumped to that question.

"What I do know is that positions change and everything is a negotiation." Harbinger leaned back in his chair and held the brandy glass out in front of him, slowly turning it. "So if it's a large donation that's needed to—what was it? Breast cancer research?—then that could happen."

"I don't respond to bribes, Cortez."

"Never suggested a bribe, Senator. You know me better than that. But if it's not a donation, well, I'd hate to have to go down that other path."

"And what path would that be?"

"The mudslinging one. It has ruined more than one career, and for some pretty minor things."

"I don't like the tone of this conversation. I've got nothing to hide and you know it."

"Yes, I'm well aware that your reputation is squeaky clean. But everyone's got something if you look hard enough. And these days, it doesn't even have to be true to get the press and the public all riled up."

Sam struggled to keep both his composure and his poker face. He assumed Harbinger was bluffing, but in the back of his mind he always wondered if the affair with Abby would ever come out. Now that Karen was dead, at least she wouldn't be hurt by it, but Sam's reputation—and probably his political future—would be. He still trusted Abby not to talk, although a lot of time had passed. He leaned back in his chair, matching Harbinger's posture. "You don't worry me, Cortez. But if this is so important to you, why don't you have your client give me a call and I'll meet with him to make sure I understand what his concerns are."

"Great idea, Senator. I'm sure Andrew would welcome the opportunity to meet with you again. He likes you, you know. Always been a big supporter."

"His campaign contributions do not go unnoticed, if that's what you're angling at," Sam said with some sarcasm. "I'm only suggesting the meeting because I want to tell him that if he wants anything from me, then he had better call me directly and not send you to do his business." Sam stood and offered his hand. "Thank you for the invitation to dinner. I'll be paying for my half of the bill on the way out."

Andrew Macfarlane lay on his back sprawled across the sofa, feet up, shoes off, one arm dangling to the floor. The fire in the fireplace was nearly spent, an empty wine glass sat on the table beside him, and a full bottle, still corked, sat on the edge of the bar, a big gold ribbon tied around its neck. He was snoring, his mouth wide open.

Leslie quietly took off her boots and left them in the entryway. Tiptoeing toward the kitchen, she glanced at the clock. It was 12:25. She wondered how long he had been there and debated whether to wake him or not.

She decided to let him sleep until she had changed out of her clothes and was ready for bed. As she slipped out of her jeans in the bedroom, she could hear him stirring.

"Are you home?" A groggy voice came from the other room.

"Just got here. I'm changing. Be right out," she answered, slipping into her robe.

He came into the bedroom. "I didn't think you'd be so late," he said, giving her a hug.

"Neither did I," she answered honestly. "Remember, it was my first one. I had no idea what to expect."

"Did you like it?"

"Andrew, it was so much fun, I can't even begin to tell you." She started describing the evening to him, bubbling over with excitement.

"Wait a minute. Wait a minute," he said. "Why don't we get into bed and you can tell me all about it? Or would you like a glass of wine?"

"No wine, thanks. I've had plenty. These women know how to drink *and* how to critique a novel. It was incredible."

She continued talking nonstop as he took off his clothes and they got into bed. She was still talking as they snuggled under the sheets.

He let her talk for a while, his hands gently stroking her back and her sides, curling up around her breasts and back again. She continued talking as she felt him grow hard. They made love quickly and easily.

Just before she fell asleep, Leslie reminded herself to ask him about Cortez Harbinger in the morning.

CHAPTER 22

Leslie woke up to the sound of the shower. "You're up early," she said as Andrew came out of the bathroom, a towel wrapped around his waist.

"Remember I told you I had an early meeting."

"I forgot. What's the meeting about?" she asked absentmindedly, looking out the window at a flock of chickadees playing around the deck.

"It's a meeting with one of my consultants. We're about to close on an important deal. The one that's been bringing me here so often. I'm hoping today is the clincher, so I want to make sure everything is set up to go just right." He opened the small suitcase he had brought with him and put on a pressed plaid flannel shirt and a pair of dark brown corduroy pants. Even in casual clothes, he looked like money, each garment impeccable in its cut and fabric.

"Oh, that reminds me," she said as he walked back into the bathroom, "Do you know anything about the issue of subsurface mineral rights? I don't know if natural gas drilling is different than the hard rock mining that you do, but the word on the street is that people are being asked to sign contracts for natural gas exploration that may not be very fair for them. And some small company is pushing it."

He didn't say anything.

"Can you hear me in there?"

"Yes," he answered as he walked back into the bedroom, fully dressed, the blue in his shirt accenting his eyes. "I wouldn't worry about it if I were you. Probably just small-town gossip." He kissed her lightly on both cheeks and then again on the top of her head. "I've got to run."

"I didn't say I was worried about it. I asked you if you knew anything about it."

"Yes, I do know a bit about it. It can be complicated. I don't have time to explain it now. I'm already late."

"Do you know a man by the name of Cortez Harbinger?"

He took his Rolex from the bedside table and strapped it on. "Next time we get together, we can talk about it. But for now," he said as he picked up his suitcase and headed for the door, "don't you worry your pretty little head about it."

She seethed at the remark as he closed the door. Could her charming Andrew really be such an arrogant ass?

"He's such a nice man, it's hard to believe that he would be trying to take advantage of us," Emma said as she, Edith, and Leslie sat around her kitchen table. The kitchen in the small ranch house was cozy and warm.

"Shush," Edith said. "She's trying to read."

Leslie had each of their contracts in front of her.

"Let's go in the other room until she's done." Emma picked up her cup of coffee and Edith followed her.

Half an hour later, Leslie called them back into the kitchen. In front of her was the yellow legal pad she'd brought with her, several pages filled with notes.

"Emma's deal is better than yours, Edith," Leslie started, "but they are both far too favorable to the company to be a good deal for either of you."

"Mine's better because I negotiated," Emma said, sitting up straighter and snickering slightly at her old friend.

"Yes, but I haven't signed yet," Edith retorted.

"No lawyer would have let either of you sign," Leslie said. "Mr. Cortez Harbinger is a shifty character no matter how you look at it. Emma, I can't tell you what to do, but I think you should get legal help to see if you can get out of this contract. You should be able to renege if you act within three days. And Edith, you shouldn't sign under any circumstances. But if you really want to sign, then I strongly advise you to get legal advice before doing so." Leslie was polite and matter of fact, acting the way she always did with clients, hopeful that the women would listen.

"You are just in the nick of time," Edith said. "Mr. Harbinger is due at my house tomorrow to pick up my signed papers. What am I going to tell him?"

"I'll go with you and tell him a thing or two," Emma said. "He's taken advantage of me and I'd like to tell him where to go. Then I'll tell him that he can't fool both of us and to be on his way. Hell, I might even take the broom after him and shoo him out. It would help cement his stereotype of us as crazy but gullible little old ladies."

"Edith, you don't even let him in the door," Leslie advised. "You politely tell him that you've changed your mind and are not interested in talking with him anymore. If he persists, you can tell him to leave your property. And if he doesn't, you should have your cell phone in your hand and start dialing the police. I really don't think it will come to that, but you do have a cell phone, don't you?"

"You bet we have them," Emma piped up. "We don't go anywhere without them anymore, including to the bathroom." She and Edith both pulled cell phones out of the pockets on their long cardigans. "That way, if we fall or feel bad, we can call somebody. These things are the reason we can still live alone and not have our kids go completely crazy with worry."

"That's great," Leslie said, liking the women even more than she had the night before. "Edith, do you want someone to be there with you when he shows up? To be sure there isn't any trouble?"

"No, I'll be fine. I want him to think he's still dealing with an innocent old widow—just to see how he handles it. Although Emma, you might want to be there to hear the fireworks. You've got me all riled up so I'm looking forward to telling him where to shove it." She reached over for Emma's hand. "We haven't had this much fun in years, have we?"

"I wouldn't miss it for the world. Leslie, you need to be there too. We'll stay in the other room and listen. He won't even know we're there."

Peg reluctantly left the comfort of the barn and horses to change her clothes. She had to clean up and get changed for the appointment she and Lee had with the bank manager in town. Since last August when the loan was denied, they'd been working to improve the balance sheet. It was worth one more try, Lee had said, to see if they could convince the bank to loan them enough to cover expenses for the next year.

Lee was sitting in the kitchen and paging through the accounts book when Peg came in. "If the bank says no, are you sure there's no other option besides selling more land?" Peg asked.

"Sorry, Peg. I can't think of anything else to do. It's not so bad having a neighbor close by now, is it? Leslie's quiet and keeps to herself. What did the book club think of her?"

"They all seemed to like her," Peg admitted with reluctance. "Acted as if she'd been with us forever."

"So she isn't so bad then, after all."

"She's smart. And she was kind of fun. But that aside, I don't like the way she is carrying on with that man from out of town. Who is he anyway?"

"She's a grown woman, Peg. If I wasn't in the picture, I'd expect you to find yourself another man too."

"He spends the night a lot. I see him leaving in the mornings."

"There's nothing wrong with that and you know it," Lee scolded. "It's winter here. For all you know, he sleeps in the spare room. Or he's related to her."

"No, I heard he's the president of a mining company. You ought to know who he is."

"I probably do know who he is, but I don't concern myself with it because it is none of my business."

"I think she might be in on this whole thing about bilking people out of their mineral rights. It's a plot they've schemed up together."

"You ought to go write this stuff down. It would make a great fantasy novel. Besides, I thought you said she was helping Edith and Emma on that, not trying to bilk them."

"Yes, I guess you're right." She'd forgotten that fact in her rush to find fault with Leslie.

"That's better. Now just give it up, Peg, and go back to being your lovely, accepting self."

"We'll see. I still feel like she's looking down at me somehow. And she's trying so hard to fit in and be a Montanan. But she's just so, so . . . Eastern."

"The only reason you don't like her is because she's not from here. It's got to be hard for her. Give her a chance. And go get in the shower or we're going to be late."

Peg quickly showered and pulled on a pair of clean jeans, a nice black sweater, and a pair of earrings. She rubbed some lotion on her face and hands and ran a brush through her hair before pulling it back into a loose bun. She barely glanced at herself in the mirror before going out to the car where Lee sat waiting for her.

They drove in silence as if going to a funeral. Which they kind of were, Peg thought.

They got to the intersection with the main highway as Leslie was turning onto the side road, going in the opposite direction. Peg could see Leslie's white turtleneck sweater under a leather jacket, a turquoise necklace around her neck. *She always looks like she's just stepped from a magazine*, Peg thought. *What a luxury to have hours to spend getting dressed to go into town.* Lee waved, but Peg pretended not to see Leslie, and peered down the road as if looking for traffic coming the other way.

Edith slammed the door on Cortez Harbinger and watched out the window as he drove away from her house. "You showed him," Emma said, putting her hand up in a high-five.

"Nice job, Edith," Leslie said. "He couldn't believe his ears. I don't think I've heard such fast-talking from someone in a long time. And believe me: in my profession, you hear a lot of fast talking."

"Honey, you have saved my bacon." Edith patted Leslie on the arm. "How am I going to thank you?"

"Don't worry about thanking me until we see if we can get Emma out of her contract. It's great that your lawyer can see you this afternoon. I was afraid it might take several days to get an appointment. Let's get down there."

"You may know about contracts and stuff like that, but you don't know anything about living in a small town, do you?" Edith said. "Dick Henderson would find time even if he had to stay half the night to get to everybody. And if he couldn't, Sam Curtis would step back in to help even though he doesn't have time to practice law anymore since he went to Congress."

"That's right," Emma said. "We all take care of each other. It's the way folks are around here."

"I guess I haven't seen that kind of welcome." The words slipped out before Leslie realized what she was saying.

"What are you talking about? Haven't people been nice to you since you've been here?" Emma asked.

187

"I didn't mean to sound like people aren't nice," Leslie hastily added, "just that it's been difficult to make friends."

"I can't believe that," said Edith. "Why, everyone in town knows who you are and where you came from, and that Will Hamilton is sweet on your daughter, and—"

Emma cut her off. "That's enough, Edith. It's clear that people think they know Leslie because of gossip, not because they've become friends with her." She smiled at Leslie. "Well, that's all about to change. We'll make sure you meet people around town. Hell, Edith and I have lived here so long, I don't think there's anyone we don't know, is there, Edith?"

"Leslie is about the only one, and now we've gone and fixed that." She put her hand on Leslie's arm. "And honey, as long as you don't mind the fact that we are both cranky old ladies, we are happy to be your new best friends." Edith smiled broadly, the lines of her old face creasing so much that her eyes nearly disappeared.

"I'm thrilled by the idea," Leslie said. She was starting to feel at home.

Leslie drove along the straight stretch of the main road out of town and marveled yet again at the endless white blanket that covered everything as far as she could see. Even the green boughs of the pine trees were flocked with white like an artificial Christmas tree. She now kept a pair of sunglasses on the dashboard because of the glare from the snow even on cloudy days. As she turned off the highway and onto the county road, she saw Peg and Lee going out.

Lee smiled and waved when he saw her, but Peg was looking the other way.

I hope the book club helps break the ice between us, she thought, wondering again why it was that Peg didn't seem to like her. *I may have underestimated her, thinking she wasn't smart because she spends her time baking and sewing. But now I have to wait two months before another meeting. I wish the club met every month.*

She pulled into the garage and unloaded the groceries from her car. She put everything away, made a fire, poured herself a glass of wine, and then sat down with a book. As often happened, she found herself staring out the window at the view or the birds or the snow instead of reading. *I can't believe I live here,* she thought, *but it sure isn't what I expected.*

She got up and pulled a volume of poetry from the shelf.

The red of blood and cherries,
The ochre of clay pots with yellow tulips,
The greens of a depth unknown,
Distant memories during the time of endless white,
When life becomes a waiting game.

Maggie Madison had done it again—written exactly the right words to describe how she felt. Waiting. But for what? For the white to be gone? Or something else?

She flipped randomly through the small volume, feeling isolated and alone. Emma and Edith held true to their word and had become her new best friends, calling often to chat, but she hadn't seen them since the day she had looked at their contracts. For the past two weeks, a pattern of storms rolled into the valley: three days of snow followed by two days of sunshine that melted the snow on the roads, which promptly froze into an ice sheet again every night, only to be covered again by new snowfall. Leslie tried not to drive anywhere if she didn't have to, but she needed food and had braved the weather to stock up.

The trip hadn't alleviated the feeling that this winter was going on far too long. And it was only the end of February. There was at least another month yet of endless white. She hadn't talked to Cynthia in over two weeks, so she picked up the phone, and called.

"Do you have time to talk?" Leslie asked when Cynthia answered.

"Plenty of time. How are you doing?"

"Surviving. I didn't expect the winter to be so hard. The snow and the drifts and the power outages all seemed so romantic at first, but now I'm ready for it to be over."

"So, what do you do all day?" Cynthia asked.

"Well, I probably have the cleanest house in Montana. I read. I'm trying to quilt, but I'm not good at it. I shop."

"Wait a minute," Cynthia interrupted. "You shop? What do you mean? Are you skiing to the hardware store for kicks now?'

Leslie laughed. "No, I've been shopping on the Internet. It's my lifeline to the real world—just like talking to you."

"I thought you said Montana was the real world."

"You know what I mean," Leslie protested. "The Internet is amazing. I found a site where I can order that beef from Argentina that I used to love in DC.

"My god, Leslie, that stuff was outrageously expensive when you bought it at the local market here. I can't imagine what you're paying to have it shipped to Montana. You're in the middle of cattle country. Surely there's some good local beef."

"The local beef is all corn-fattened and shot up by steroids. The natural, grass-fed stuff is much better, and better for you, even if it does cost a lot more."

"Okay. So what else have you been doing besides shopping?"

"I've started going for walks outside, even when the temperature is ten degrees. Can you believe it? I bundle up, and you know, the interesting thing is that it isn't half-bad if you are dressed for it. And I've got a new project."

"What kind of project?"

"I'm starting a movement to oppose natural gas drilling here in the county. There's a small company that isn't playing fair, and local people are being taken in by the scheme. I'm starting to do some research on oil and gas law."

"That sounds interesting. But why do you want to do that? I thought you said when you retired that you didn't want to even think about the law anymore."

"I know, but I feel useful again, and I can help these people."

"How did you get into it?"

"I offered to help these two wonderful old ladies who are in the book club I told you about. They got conned, but I got them out of it, then they got mad, and the other day we started talking about organizing against the project. I'm sure they have no idea where to start, but that's where I come in."

"Have you ever done anything like that before?"

"No, but I'll be able to figure it out. How hard can it be?"

"What are you going to do? Are you going to become one of those tree sitters or people who chain themselves to fences?"

"No." Leslie laughed. "I'm thinking maybe a petition or something. And we'll need by-laws and a charter for the group so we can get people in the area to join. And eventually we may want to raise money. I haven't really decided what should happen first."

"Well, good luck, Leslie. This is the most enthusiasm I've heard in your voice in a long time."

Peg was stoic when the bank manager told them there was nothing he could do; the revised financials still weren't good enough to justify any more loans.

"But what I can do," he said, "is go to bat for you with the head office in Helena. I'll see if I can find some way to get you the money."

"Thanks," Lee and Peg said in unison.

"I can't promise anything though. You know how it is. There are bank rules and regulations, and sometimes, there isn't anything that can be done. If I can't get you the loan, I'll see what I can do about giving you some leeway on the mortgage payments to give you time to raise some money. You know, if it was up to me alone, I'd bet on the Hamiltons any day of the week and you'd have whatever you needed to tide you over until the market rebounds."

"We understand the tough spot you are in," Lee said. "We appreciate anything you can do for us."

Peg held her head high and her face was expressionless during the conversation. *I will not break down,* she thought. *I will figure this out. The boys will find a way to help. Lee will have an idea. And worst case, there might be a golf course on the lower forty.*

CHAPTER 23

Sam Curtis took another letter from the pile stacked in front of him and began to read. He welcomed these winter storm cycles as a time to catch up on the letters, e-mails, and requests for favors. The kink in his back told him he had been at it long enough for today. *One more,* he thought. *Just one more letter, and then I'll stop.* He picked up the one on the top of the pile in front of him. It was handwritten, more of a scrawl than anything else.

Dear Senator,

I'm writing about the buying up of mineral rights that is going on in this valley. There are some in town who are saying that it shouldn't be allowed and that you agree with them. I sincerely hope you do not. This is a free country and it was made great by allowing industry to do what they need to do to make a profit. That provides jobs and that helps the economy.

Sam knew this line of reasoning well. Many of his constituents were very conservative in their political views, but they still voted for him even though he was clearly middle-of-the-road. He always believed it was his integrity and transparency that they appreciated, even if they didn't agree with all of his views.

He stopped reading and stared out at the jumble of snowflakes being tossed wildly by the wind. Integrity and transparency. What a sham he was, he thought. *I cheated on my wife and fell in love with another woman. If they only knew.*

The memory of his exchange with Cortez Harbinger burned in his gut. Sam knew he had messed up and that was a fact. *Ethics are sometimes a slippery thing,* he thought. If Harbinger went digging, what would he find? Who knew anything? Or more importantly, who would talk? For years, he'd been able to push it to the back of his mind; the odds of anything coming out were very slim.

But now it was all here in front of him again. Harbinger digging, and Leslie Montgomery, the woman who had warned him those many years ago, living here in Legacy Springs. What would she remember if Harbinger got to her? What might she say?

The voters would forgive me, he thought. *They would recognize the good I've done for the state.* Integrity and transparency—that's what he stood for. But even if the voters forgave him, he couldn't forgive himself. Damn, it was hard enough to live the lie in secret. He took a deep breath.

He had to trust Leslie. She could have destroyed him back then and didn't. But it was a long time ago and he had no idea what her views were now. He needed to talk to her and make sure she understood the importance of continuing to keep quiet. Maybe, if he was lucky, she had forgotten all about it.

He gave up on reading the rest of the last letter and eased out of the chair. He stood with his arms over his head, stretching his tired back muscles into movement again. The snow continued to flutter randomly in the wind, a mirror of the thoughts arranging and rearranging themselves in his mind. Whenever he landed on a plan, just like the snowflake that landed on the railing, something came along and swept it back into the air.

He poured himself a glass of scotch. He had lost both Karen and Abby. Perhaps the price was loneliness. He hoped it wouldn't be more than that.

Best to let things be, he decided. No reason to say anything to Leslie. No reason to dredge up the past. Harbinger might never find out. No reason why he would even be talking to Leslie. No reason to worry about it. No reason at all.

Leslie brushed her hair and looked in the mirror with a critical eye. *A little lipstick,* she decided, picking out a tube from the makeup bag. *No, too dark,* she thought, wiping the first choice from her lips. *More subtle.* Something that didn't look like she'd actually gone to the trouble to make up her face. Three choices later, she was satisfied with the result.

Light mascara. Simple earrings. The image in the mirror stared back at her. *I look different,* she thought. *My eyes don't have dark circles under them anymore. And my mouth isn't as pursed up as it used to be. It's softer.* Smiling slightly, she noticed that the perennial crease between her eyebrows was also nearly gone. When had that happened?

Nine months ago, she had left Washington, DC, for her new life. She hadn't been back to the city since then. She hadn't gone to work since then. She hadn't had a regular schedule of any kind since then. She had little to worry about except how to fill her days. The change showed clearly on her face.

She went into the large walk-in closet and surveyed the choices. Nothing seemed right. *Why am I so indecisive about this? It's just a meeting. What I wear isn't going to make any difference.* She shook her head as if to erase the thoughts. She put on black jeans, a crisp white shirt, and the little, black leather vest she had found in New York the month before moving. Classic but Western, businesslike yet casual, and not looking too studied. That's what she wanted to convey. *Yes, that looks fine,* she thought with a final look in the mirror.

She had scheduled the appointment with Senator Sam Curtis a few days earlier at Edith's suggestion. "He's been talking about legislation on this issue," Edith had said. "We need to know what he's thinking before we go too far with our idea about a grass-roots opposition group."

Leslie had readily agreed. "Do you think he's on our side?"

"Oh, yes," Edith had confirmed. "I'd be happy to come with you, if you want. It can sometimes be intimidating to meet with a senator, but I've known him since he was a little boy."

"No, no need for you to come along," Leslie said a bit too hastily. She was anxious to renew her acquaintance with Sam Curtis. He would understand the contrast between her life before and now better than anyone. She thought they might become friends. "I actually knew him in DC. Not well, but I'm pretty sure he'll remember me."

"Oh, of course, honey," Edith had quickly apologized. "I do keep forgetting that you were an important Washington attorney."

Leslie chuckled as she thought of the older woman's concept of people in power and that she might be afraid of them. Leslie had dealt with senators on a daily basis—some of them much more powerful than Senator Curtis. *Then why am I so worried about how I look?*

For now, she needed to get on the road or she'd be late. She checked her hair one more time and smiled into the mirror. She looked good, but on a whim, she undid one more button on the white shirt. *No reason to be frumpy just because it's cold out.*

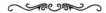

"I think the best course of action is legislation that would resolve the issue once and for all, but it will be difficult to write and difficult to pass," Sam explained to Leslie when she told him why she was there. "Even here in the valley, there are mixed feelings about the drilling project. My mail on the topic is evenly divided."

"Senator, you and I have each worked on some pretty tough things in the past. There's no reason why we can't figure out a way to stop this project." She leaned forward earnestly. She didn't remember him being so handsome. "Especially if there is strong community opposition."

She had walked into Sam's office with the self-confidence and assurance she had always had when dealing with other lawyers or legislators. He was gracious and easy-going. The activity of strategizing, maneuvering, and thinking through options energized her. Twenty minutes into the meeting, she was completely engrossed in the topic, back in her element and enjoying it. She felt an extra zip, an extra energy that was almost sensual.

"Would you like some coffee, Leslie? I can ask Brenda to make some."

"Coffee sounds great, thanks."

"Let me guess. I'll bet you drink it black."

"I do." Leslie felt an unexpected rush when he met her eyes and smiled at her before leaving the room.

You are involved with someone else, she told herself, *so don't even think about it. You can get excited about the work, but that's it.* But she couldn't help wondering if he was still single.

He came back in and sat on the couch beside her instead of returning to the leather wingback chair where he was before. The office was dark and comfortable, with law books lining the shelves behind the desk. Heavy red draperies, pulled back as far as possible to let in the low winter light, framed the long, tall windows. The room was a reflection of a man comfortable with authority.

"I haven't been able to figure out who's behind this," Leslie said. "I'm not very good at research. I used to have a slew of associates and legal assistants to do that for me." She wondered if he did his own research or if that was also part of Brenda's job.

"What do you mean, 'who's behind this'?"

"The corporate name on the documents Edith and Emma had doesn't even show up on an Internet search, which leads me to believe it's a shell subsidiary of some other company. But without access to the sources I used to have at the law firm, I haven't been able to find anything."

Brenda came in and placed a black lacquer tray on the table. A small plate of biscuits sat between two cups.

"Thank you, Brenda." Sam turned back to Leslie. "You are completely right. Of course, the parent company couldn't risk letting its name out during the early stages. Otherwise, it might drive prices up. I hadn't really paid attention to that before, but it makes perfect sense."

"So how do we figure out who the parent is? You know how hard it is to find out a secret if somebody wants to keep it hidden."

"Yes." Sam paused, took a deep breath, and then continued. "And some secrets are best kept hidden."

Leslie remembered his affair with Abby. She felt embarrassed by the insensitivity of her remark but wasn't sure if he was even referring to that. She took a chance. "I'm sorry, Senator, I hope I haven't inadvertently opened old wounds."

"Of course not," he said, looking uncomfortable. "Look, we're not in the capital now, so please call me Sam. We don't need the formalities. Where were we?"

"Finding out which company is behind all this so we can determine the best way to attack and bring them to their knees." She gestured with a clenched fist and a smile.

"I'll have Brenda make a few calls. There's got to be some record with the secretary of state or the contracts would be voidable. Give me a few days."

Brenda tapped lightly on the door. "Your next appointment is here, Senator."

"Sorry to have to cut this short. We haven't even had a chance to catch up on old times. Let's get together for dinner sometime."

"That would be lovely." She was excited by the idea and wished he had said "soon."

CHAPTER 24

Leslie gathered the notes she had been keeping about the new drilling opposition group and stuck them into a file folder. She was meeting with Edith and Emma later today to begin planning their strategy. She knew she would have to do all of the work, of course, since Edith and Emma were both old and not computer savvy. Not to mention that they had lived their entire lives in Legacy Springs, so they wouldn't know the first thing about organizing an environmental opposition group. Not that she did either. But Sam's endorsement of the idea made her confident it was the right thing to do.

"Looks like it's going to be a party," Edith said as Leslie and Emma came up the stairs onto the porch of the big old ranch house. "Get yourselves in here out of the cold. I've got some goodies to warm us up."

"I have a few things here too," Emma said, offering a small canvas tote bag. "Can't start a revolution without some gunpowder." The two older women giggled and set off immediately for the kitchen.

"Throw your coat there on the bench!" Edith called over her shoulder to Leslie. "And grab some slippers from that basket there after you take your boots off. They'll keep your feet from getting cold."

Leslie sat on the wooden bench and unlaced the bulky boots she had taken to wearing whenever there was fresh snow. They were the same kind she had thought were so ugly when Peg had them on the first time they met at the realtor's office. Now they were indispensable and she was even starting to like the look. She chose a pair of sheepskin-lined moccasins from Edith's basket. Emma returned from the kitchen, took off her boots, and fished a small pair of fuzzy black slippers from the basket.

"I like to hide mine at the bottom so nobody else wears them," she said. "Wait until you see what Edith's got lined up for us!"

In contrast to Emma's small and cozy kitchen, Edith's was enormous with windows all along one wall. In front of the windows, a table was covered with a bright red tablecloth with embroidery on the edges. On the table sat a bowl of nuts, a plate of thinly sliced sausage, a wooden board with cheese and crackers, and a plate with bite-sized squares of quiche. There was also a tray of cookies that smelled like they had just come out of the oven. On the sideboard were two bottles of wine and a tray containing a cocktail shaker, three martini glasses, and assorted liquor.

"Edith, you shouldn't have gone to so much trouble," Leslie said.

"Oh, don't worry, honey," Edith answered. "Emma helped. She's the one who brought the sausage and the cheese and crackers."

"Well, knowing you, Edith, we'd have had plenty to drink, but nothing healthy to eat." Emma turned to Leslie and whispered conspiratorially, "Edith doesn't believe in protein."

"So, what'll it be, ladies," Edith said with the swagger of a bartender, poised with the shot glass in hand. "I'm suggesting Manhattans because the bourbon always warms the soul on these cold winter days."

"Perfect," said Emma. "I love the red tablecloth—red for the revolution. This is going to be so much fun." Edith and Emma giggled again.

Leslie thought they sounded like schoolgirls ready to play a prank on the teacher.

"Okay, I guess I can't be the spoilsport here," Leslie said. "I'll have a Manhattan too."

Edith expertly mixed and poured the drinks. "Where did you learn to do that so well?" Leslie asked.

"Oh, my husband loved a good cocktail, so I learned early on how to make them. You know back in the fifties when we were first married, people drank cocktails a lot more than they do today. My husband's daddy was governor for many years, so there was a lot of entertaining. But today everybody wants to drink wine. Not that there's anything wrong with wine, of course." She grinned mischievously. "You see, I have some here if you'd prefer it."

"No, thanks. The Manhattan is fine," Leslie said.

"It's so nice having some new energy in town," Edith said when they finally sat at the table with drinks and plates of food in front of them.

"And somebody new to tell our stories to," Emma added with a laugh. "But let's get down to business."

"Yes," Edith said. "Tell us what Sam said when you talked to him." She looked at Leslie. "I hope he doesn't think we are crazy."

"No, he doesn't," Leslie said. "He says that influencing federal legislation will be difficult, but the idea of a grass-roots opposition group would be tremendously beneficial. Even if only for the educational value. To let people know what's going on."

"Yes, if I had known, I wouldn't have signed that contract," Emma said. "You sure saved me on that one, Leslie, especially telling me I had three days to get out of it. Dick Henderson said that is what made it easy."

"You were lucky," Leslie said, reaching into her bag and pulling out her file. "Listen, I put together a list of ideas for how we should start. Getting something like this going isn't easy and it might take a long time, so I want to warn you both to not get discouraged."

She caught Edith and Emma raising eyebrows at each other, their thin, wrinkled lips upturned at the corners. She thought they might be feeling the alcohol already. "Go on, honey," Edith said. "We'd like to hear what you came up with."

"Well, we'll need a name, of course. And a mission statement describing what it is that we are for and against. And a desired outcome. Then we'll need to figure out how to recruit other members to our group. And get our message out." She paused.

Edith and Emma nodded, both still smiling sweetly. "Yes, yes, go on," Emma encouraged.

"I think if we could get twenty-five people to sign a petition, that would be a good start. Then when we confirm who is behind this, we'll try to meet with them to present our opposition and make our demands."

"Oh, yes, very good," Edith murmured.

"Next on my list is to raise money. We'll need it for some of the activities we'll want to do. I think our first order of business will be to find a few young people who agree with our position and convince them to do the grunt work of calling on people and getting the word out. If we can get some kids on board in the next two weeks, I think that in another month or so we should be able to get this up and running. I just hope it isn't too late."

Edith and Emma looked at each other. "You start," Emma said to Edith.

"Sounds very good, Leslie," Edith began. "Tell me, have you ever organized something like this before?"

"No, I really haven't," she admitted. "So the three of us will have to make it up as we go. But to get things started, I did come up with a possible name. What do you think of Against Bad Contracts—ABC?" She watched them both grimace.

Edith went over to the sideboard and picked up a well-used manila file folder. She sat at the table and opened it. "I do hope you won't be offended, Leslie," Edith started, "but we came up with a name without you. We may have gotten ahead of ourselves."

"No problem," Leslie said, surprised but curious. "We can bat it around and see if we like it. Nothing is set in stone yet, so let's hear it."

Edith and Emma exchanged glances. "It's the Legacy Springs Preservation Project. I do hope you like it because it might be set in stone."

Leslie saw that it was already written on the tab of the folder. "It's very nice, but perhaps we need something with more pizzazz or a better acronym. Why do you say it might be set in stone?"

Edith pulled two sheets from the file folder and handed one each to Emma and Leslie. At the top, in capital letters, were the words LEGACY SPRINGS PRESERVATION PROJECT. Below was a spreadsheet with a series of columns labeled Name, Address, Phone Number, E-mail, and Amount. There were twenty-five lines, each filled in.

"We kind of got started already," Emma said as Leslie looked with slow comprehension at the sheet.

"Here are the other three pages." Edith sheepishly handed her additional pieces of paper. In all, there were ninety-two names listed. The subtotal at the bottom of the final page for the amount column was $1,480.

"There's a lot of support for what we are doing," Emma said. "We only had a few folks turn us down, and mostly they are the ones who have already signed contracts and are counting their profits. We got a bit of a slow start because of the storm, so there are lots more people we haven't even talked to yet."

"E-mail makes organizing so much easier than it ever was in the past," Edith said. "In the old days, we would never have been able to get this much done so quickly."

Leslie was stunned. She had totally underestimated these women. How foolish she felt sitting there with her plan. "What else have you two done—in the old days?"

Edith spoke up first. "Oh, we've rabble roused on lots of issues. I don't know. Emma, what do you think was the first one?" She looked at Emma. "I know we really got rolling when we decided to protest the Vietnam War, but then that was easy because it was happening all over the country."

"Yes," Emma agreed, "I think the harder ones were some of the local issues—like the time the school district was going to try to consolidate with two others down valley and have the kids riding school busses for an hour or more each morning to get to school. We got that squelched even though a lot of people at first thought it would be a good idea to save money."

"And then there was the fluoride in the water issue, and the expansion of the library," Edith added.

"And the migrant worker issue. Trying to get health care for the migrants, you see," Emma explained.

"But the first one was probably that time back in sixty-five, remember? We were so young and idealistic back then," Edith reminisced. "Nobody thought that girls should be playing sports in school, but we both had strong, athletic daughters who loved baseball. And they wanted to play in the Little League. Remember, Emma?"

"Oh, yes," Emma agreed. "I think that was the first thing. We were the talk of the state, letting girls play in the Little League with the boys. Took the rest of the country a while to catch up with us, didn't it? But Edith's granddaughter went to college on a softball scholarship, so it must have been in the genes."

"I feel really stupid," Leslie said.

"Don't be silly, honey," Edith comforted her. "Your ideas are all really good. You're our ace-in-the-hole lawyer."

Leslie had to laugh. She had always thought that one of her best skills was to be able to read people and see them for who they really were. She was coming to the realization that she had no skill in that whatsoever.

CHAPTER 25

"What looks good to you?" Andrew asked Leslie as they sat in the restaurant, looking at the menu. "I'm starved and thinking about the steak." He had called earlier that day and said he was at the airport. He wanted her to drive over to meet him for dinner. "Bring a bag and stay at the hotel with me," he had said. "I have a surprise for you."

"I think the salmon looks good."

"It's not as good as the steak," Andrew said. "Sure you don't want some good, old-fashioned American beef?" He smiled and took her hand across the table. "It's good to see you again, Leslie. I've missed you."

"You know I don't like the corn-fattened stuff," she said, ignoring his attempt to make nice. She was still miffed at him from their last meeting and wasn't going to give in so easily. "If it's not from Argentina, I don't eat it."

"A very unusual woman you are," he said, stroking her arm lightly. "And a beautiful one, too."

Leslie's mood softened. It still annoyed her that Andrew thought he could call at any time and she'd come running. Yet, she did want to see him so had driven the hour over the pass to the restaurant. She hadn't seen him in over three weeks, and he had called only once.

"You've been busy," she said, as much a statement as a question.

"Yes, it's been crazy for the past few weeks. I had to go to Chile again and then to New York. But you remember how that is. One thing leads to another, and pretty soon, the month is shot." He looked up at the waiter who had stopped at their table.

"Would you like something to drink?" the waiter asked.

"Laphroaig, please, neat." Andrew nodded toward Leslie. "Would you like your usual martini: Stoli dry and with a twist?"

"Yes, please," she answered, feeling a strange pleasure that he knew her "usual" drink. She knew she was being inconsistent, simultaneously liking and chafing at his old-fashioned chivalry.

"Tell me about your trips," she said, hungry for conversation.

He talked of his travels and the business deals he was doing. She felt like she was living vicariously through him now that she spent her days at home alone.

By the time they finished dinner and the waiter had poured the last of a bottle of wine into their glasses, she decided to broach the topic of Cortez Harbinger and the exploration company. He'd been doing most of the talking and she hadn't mentioned the new Legacy Springs Preservation Project.

"Andrew, the last time we were together, I asked you about the natural gas exploration that everybody's talking about in Legacy Springs. Do you know what's going on or who is involved?"

"Not really. I've heard some rumors when I've been there, but nothing solid. Why are you interested in that anyway?"

"Just curious." She wasn't sure why she didn't want to tell him about her project. "Do you know Cortez Harbinger?"

"Never heard of him."

"Have you heard the name of the company that is doing the exploration?"

"Nope. Sorry if you had your hopes up. What do you want for dessert?"

"Nothing for me. You go ahead." Leslie had been so sure that Andrew would know something. She felt let down.

"Having you in bed with me will be dessert enough." He paid the bill and they got up to leave. He put his hand on her back as she walked in front of him. "Don't forget, I have a surprise for you."

"I did forget. What is it?"

"Just a little present."

"A present? What for?"

"Because you're so special and because I haven't seen you for a while and because you deserve it. Now no more questions, or it won't be a surprise."

"Tell me again," Andrew said as they lay entwined on the bed, their bodies glistening with the moisture of sweat and sex. "You had such a successful practice back in DC. Why did you give that all up and move out here to the wilds of Montana?"

"I'd been fascinated with the West since I was a teenager, but I really fell in love in my thirties when I started reading poetry about it and vowed I'd live here some day. I love the mountains, the scent of the air in the morning, the views, the whole feel of it. And yes, even though I complain, I have even come to love the harshness of the winter and the interminable snow. I've told you that before."

"I know, but it doesn't seem to fit. Giving up a glamorous career with a life on the Hill, hobnobbing with the powerful people."

"It sounds glamorous, but it was very stressful. I'm glad to be away from it, even if sometimes I am a bit lonely and bored."

"Don't you ever miss it?"

"What I miss is the feeling of being in the game, being useful. People asking my opinion. I must admit that sometimes I wonder if looking out the window at the fantastic view is going to be enough for me in the long run." She snuggled her face into the crook of his neck, nibbling at his lower ear lobe.

"Tell me about your work on the Hill. Wasn't it exciting?"

"Yes, it was. But it's like anything else. At first, it's exciting, and then it becomes routine, and then it just becomes part of the job." She felt Andrew's legs wrap snugly around her own.

"You must have run into our own senator, Sam Curtis, at some time during those years. Did you ever get a chance to know him?"

"Yes, I knew him years ago. We worked on a few projects together, but not closely. Do you know him?"

"I've met him. He isn't always in tune with me politically, but I do contribute to his campaigns. Got to keep the options open in a state like this, but he's often taken positions that are actually hostile to my business interests."

Leslie pulled back and looked at him. There was something different about his tone of voice. "I've always found him to be a very thoughtful legislator."

"Thoughtful, yes. And they say very ethical, but everybody's got a skeleton in the closet. I'd like to know what his is." Andrew had been slowly stroking her back and now his hand circled around to the front of her thighs. Leslie liked the way it felt and wanted to stop talking.

"Well, I hope his never comes out. He's a good man and doesn't deserve that."

"I thought you'd know something." Andrew stopped stroking her and sat up. "I got you a little present so you'd share it with me."

"What?" She wasn't sure she had heard him correctly. Or rather, that she had understood him correctly. She had heard him just fine.

He reached to the bedside table and pulled open the drawer. He took out a flat, blue box wrapped with a white, satin ribbon.

"Tiffany?" She recognized the signature color.

"Nothing but the best," Andrew said. "I picked it up when I was in New York last week. And all you need to do to get it is let Sam Curtis's skeleton out of the closet." He held the box away from her.

"You must be joking. You'll give me a present so you can get dirt on a politician I might have worked with years ago?" She couldn't believe that he was serious. "Like a bribe?"

"Not a bribe, exactly," he said easily. "That sounds so, well, so harsh. Let's try it a different way. I bought you a present, and as a thank-you, you can tell me something that I'd like to know."

"Why would you care? Why do you want to know about Sam?"

"Oh, it would just be handy to know. In case something came up that was really threatening to the business. You know, a bit of insurance. Surely you advised your clients to have something on key politicians so they could play that card if they needed to."

"I did no such thing," she said indignantly, although she knew that some of her partners had advised exactly that.

"Of course, you didn't," he said sarcastically. He held the box in the palm of his hand. "You'll like it, I'm sure. It will look great on you."

"I don't care if it's the Hope diamond. I am not about to accept a present in exchange for gossip about a decent, caring man who is a damn good senator." She unwrapped her legs from his and moved away from him as she tried to sit up amidst the tangle of sheets.

"Oh, Leslie, don't get huffy, now." She felt him pull at the sheets to free her while at the same time he tried to pull her closer to him. "I was just joking, of course. I bought you the present because I wanted to. Forget I ever said anything about Sam Curtis."

"I don't want your present, thank you." She sat up on the edge of the bed.

"I said I was joking. I'm sorry. I didn't think you would take it so personally. Calm down, and let's get back to where we were a minute ago. Come here. Snuggle up against me, and we'll start over." He slid his arms around her waist and kissed her neck lightly, the box still in his hand.

"It wasn't very funny."

"I know. I'm sorry. Please, forgive me." He continued kissing her neck. "I am so sorry that I bought you a present to make it up to you." He turned her around to face him and looked at her with a sad, puppy-dog look.

"Good recovery." Those blue eyes always got to her. "Okay, I'll forgive you. But I never want to hear about it again."

"Deal." Andrew opened the box and she gasped at the white gold bangle studded with small diamonds that gracefully curled on the blue cushion.

She wore the bracelet while they made love again. She didn't realize that Andrew had found out what he needed to know. There was dirt to be had on Senator Curtis.

CHAPTER 26

The melody of "Moonlight Sonata" ran through Leslie's head. She rolled over on the couch and realized it was her cell phone ringing. It was a lazy Sunday afternoon and she had fallen asleep, her book on her lap. Outside, it was getting dark, and she realized she must have been asleep for a couple of hours.

"Hello," she mumbled.

"Hi, Mom," Kelly said in her perky voice. "Did I catch you at a bad time?"

"Oh, no, dear." Leslie sat up, shaking the cobwebs from her head. "I was just taking a nap. How are you? It seems like ages since we talked."

"I know. I'm sorry. I get so busy with school and all. My constitutional law class is killer and I've had lots going on lately. But I called to tell you some good news."

"Wonderful, sweetie. Did you get that internship with the Department of Justice?" Leslie asked hopefully.

"No. But don't worry. I still have a few other irons in the fire. That's not what my news is about."

"Okay, what is it?"

"Before I tell you, I want you to promise to be supportive. Don't immediately go negative. Promise."

Uh-oh, Leslie thought. "I promise to be supportive, because you know I always am. But I can't promise to be positive about something if I don't think it's a good idea. Just tell me what it is."

"Well, you know Will and I have been seeing each other quite a bit." Although Kelly meant it as a statement, her intonation at the end implied a question. She waited for a response.

"I know he's been there to see you a few times. And you know I think you should be concentrating on school, not entertaining visitors."

"I know, Mom. That's why I haven't talked to you much about him. But he really is quite wonderful, and he is so funny and attentive and smart. We have a great time together. You'll like him when you get to know him better."

"If he's so smart, what's he doing riding bulls instead of going to college? I don't think his mother is very thrilled with his choice either." She had heard Peg say so at the book club meeting.

"It's a good way to make a living for a while. He makes good money, and it's exciting."

"The medical bills will be exciting when he breaks his back or gets stomped on the head."

"He's a professional. And bull-riding isn't any more dangerous than a lot of other jobs."

"It's a lot more dangerous than being a lawyer. So, get to the news that I'm not going to like. What is it?"

"Well, you know Will travels all over the country to compete, which means he could live just about anywhere. So, he's going to move here and make this his home base."

"He's moving to DC?"

"He's moving in with me. In fact, we're thinking about getting married. I really love him, Mom. I want you to be happy for me and supportive."

Leslie was stunned. She had no idea the relationship had gotten so serious.

"Kelly, you are in law school. You can't get married now. You've got to concentrate on your studies." Leslie tried hard to keep her voice even. This was much worse than anything she had imagined.

"I seem to recall that you met Dad while you were in law school, and you got married after your first year."

"That's true, but he had a good job and was settled in his career." Hugh had been one of her professors in college and his status was part of the reason she was attracted to him in the first place.

"I knew you wouldn't approve, but I'm pretty sure this is a forever thing. I've never felt like this about anyone else. It might sound like a fairy tale, but this is true love. Nobody is more surprised than me, but I finally realize that you were right all those times you told me not to marry for money or position or all those other things. You always told me to marry for love, and that's what I'm going to do. Please don't be mad at me, Mom."

"I'm not mad, Kelly, but this is really quite a shock. I want you to be happy, but please give it some time. You barely know him. Don't rush into anything." *I'll find a way to talk her out of it later,* she thought.

"We're not rushing. We're going to wait until after I graduate next year. So there is plenty of time to be sure we know what we're doing."

After Leslie hung up, she felt like her world was imploding. Kelly and Will. Getting married. It wasn't right. He was going to ruin Kelly's life. What if she dropped out of law school? What if he broke her heart? Married. What was Kelly thinking? She was too young and had her whole life ahead of her. *She isn't nearly as mature as I was when I got married at her age.*

Her head hurt thinking about it. She got up and took two aspirin. It was only a little after six, but she thought about going to bed. *I'll just pull the covers over my head and when I wake up in the morning, it will all be a bad dream*, she thought. But the bed would have to wait. She saw Peg's car pull into the driveway. *Damn. The last thing I need right now is to talk to her.*

Leslie opened the door before Peg had a chance to knock. The look on Peg's face was as grim as Leslie felt. "Hi, Peg. Come on in."

"We need to talk." Peg stepped in and Leslie closed the door. "Will just called me."

"And I hung up with Kelly a few minutes ago. Looks like the kids wanted to make sure we heard the news at the same time. Let's go have some wine. I don't know about you, but I could use a glass."

"Did you know this was happening?" Peg said as Leslie ushered her into the kitchen. "What is your daughter thinking?"

"My daughter?" Leslie looked at her with surprise. "How about your son? I didn't even know they were serious about each other."

"He's been going out there every month to see her. How could you not think it was serious?"

"Look, I'm not any happier about this than you are, but the truth is that they are old enough to make decisions for themselves and neither of us could have done anything about it even we knew it was happening—which I, for one, didn't."

"You're right. I'm sorry. I just can't believe it." Peg paced back and forth in the kitchen. "I was so upset when Will told me, and Lee isn't home, so I came right over here."

Leslie poured two glasses of wine, and handed one to Peg. "To our children, and to being supportive of them even when they are making choices we may not agree with." They clinked glasses and each took a long drink. Peg sat on a bar stool on the other side of the counter from Leslie.

"You know, Peg, my parents weren't at all happy with my choice of husband at first. But then they got to know Hugh and I think my mother ended up liking him better than I did. What did your parents think of Lee?"

"My parents were fine. Whatever their daughter wanted, they wanted. On the other hand, Lee's parents were a different story. They did not think our marriage was a good idea at all. I was too cerebral, they said. Not grounded enough."

"That's hard to believe. You seem like one of the most grounded people I've ever met."

"I'll take that as a compliment. Look, Leslie, I don't have anything against your daughter. I only met her a few times last summer when she was out here and she's very nice. But she's not right for Will. You know he's a top money winner on the bull-riding circuit. He isn't a city kind of person. He belongs in the West."

"I certainly agree that they aren't right for each other. Kelly has always had aspirations for her life—and for who she married. I can't see her settling down with a man who hasn't even gone to college. Kelly's not going to be interested in wasting away her life on some ranch, watching the cows eat grass every day."

Leslie saw Peg stiffen. "There's nothing wasted about a life on a ranch. It's very rewarding. And it's a lot better than spending your life getting rich off other people's problems. The world would be a better place if there were fewer lawyers in it."

"Being a lawyer is a noble profession. It's financially rewarding because it takes smarts to do it."

"It takes smarts to run a ranch, too. You Easterners don't understand that if it weren't for us, you wouldn't have meat on your table or shoes on your feet or all of this expensive leather furniture. But we don't do it for money, we do it because we love the land and the way of life."

Leslie knew she should just be quiet and let them both calm down, but she couldn't help herself. "I wouldn't have bought this property if I didn't love the land and want this way of life. But, I will not apologize for having money and sophistication, even if it offends you."

"Money and sophistication?" Peg snorted like a bull in a pasture. "You really do think you are better than us, don't you? I wish I had never sold you this property." She stood up, the rest of her wine untouched.

"Well, I'm glad you did, because I love it here and I'm staying. Besides, it's probably good for the kids of Legacy Springs to have some educated role models that have done something with their lives."

Peg was at the door. She turned back to Leslie. "I don't know what that's supposed to mean, but you're like every other snob from the East. Too full of yourself to see that the rest of the world doesn't care about you or your uppity attitude. If your daughter is anything like you, I hope Will finds out before it's too late." She turned and stormed out.

Leslie finished her wine and poured the rest of Peg's into her glass. She carried the bottle into the living room and pulled a Maggie Madison book off the shelf. She needed the wine and Maggie's wisdom to ease the ache in her heart.

CHAPTER 27

Peg's mind drifted as she stood at the kitchen sink, wiping the sponge over the already clean plate again and again. March signaled spring in many parts of the world, but it was still winter in Montana. The days were getting longer and the constant cold was giving way to temperatures above freezing. The dark-blue, crystalline sky was a sharp contrast to the blinding white of the new snow that had fallen the day before. Peg loved the way the snow sparkled in the sunlight like stars on the ground. She finally rinsed the plate and picked up another one when she saw Lee pull into the driveway and come toward the house with the mail in his hand.

Despite the still snowy landscape, March was the time for calving and lambing, and Lee had been out checking on the animals. It was always an exhausting time of year, since the cows and sheep often needed human help with the process at all times of the day or night, and Peg was tired.

She'd been out late with Lee the night before, coaxing a reluctant calf from its exhausted mother. Not that she would have slept anyway. She'd been tossing and turning ever since the argument with Leslie a few days ago. Will, Kelly, Leslie—

they all rambled through her sleepless brain, interrupted only by worry about the ranch and the bank and the lack of money. They had missed yet another mortgage payment.

Lee tossed the mail on the counter. Out of the corner of her eye, Peg could see a stark white envelope with the bank's logo on the corner amid the flyers and catalogs. "I'm going to clean up and then we can head into town," Lee said. "I don't want to be late for the commission meeting. Are you ready?"

"Just need to change my shoes," she said, wiping her hands on a towel and following him into the bedroom. "I talked to Will again this morning. I can't seem to knock any sense into him."

"You need to let him live his own life. Like you wanted our parents to do when we were first together. Remember, they weren't too thrilled and look how well we've done." Lee patted Peg's bottom affectionately.

"I know, I know," she reluctantly agreed. "I think the argument I had with Leslie bugs me almost as much as the fact that Will and Kelly are getting married. I've played it over and over in my mind. I can't believe it, but she thinks that I never went to college. How could she think that? Especially after book club?" She followed him into the bathroom.

"Does she know about your writing?" Lee undressed and got into the shower.

"Well, I doubt it." Peg put the toilet seat lid down and sat next to the shower. She raised her voice so Lee could hear her. "You know I never talk about it. Doesn't matter, though. I don't think she'd get it."

"You might be surprised. Why don't you make up with her by taking her a pie or a book or something? It seems a shame to be on bad terms not only with our closest neighbor but our son's future mother-in-law."

"Don't remind me. I hope this is just a phase that Will's going through. He'll miss the West so much that he'll be back within six months. And that will be that. Maybe he'll even come home and run the ranch."

"Come on, Peg. You know he has said for years that running the ranch isn't for him—not for a long time to come at least and maybe never. He wants to make his fortune in the world, not do the same thing as his old man." Peg handed Lee a towel as he got out of the shower. "Now how about making up with Leslie? Let's invite her to dinner."

"No. I'm not ready for that."

"Okay, not dinner. Not yet, but sometime soon. In the meantime, you've got to clear the air with her. Why don't you give her one of the books by my favorite poet?"

"A Maggie Madison book? I doubt if she'd respond to that. But if she does, then there might be hope for her. If not, then I'll write her off forever."

"Good plan—except for the last part. Remember: whether she's our son's mother-in-law or just our neighbor, we need to be on good terms. Who knows? We might need to count on her someday. Don't put it off. You know the longer you wait, the harder it will be."

"How come you are always so logical and persuasive? I promise I'll do something tomorrow." She heaved a heavy sigh. "In the meantime, are you almost ready?"

"Almost done," Lee said, running a comb through his hair.

"What's on the agenda today?"

"The usual stuff, nothing major. You don't have to come if you don't want to. I hope it doesn't go too long. I'm bushed."

"I'll come along. I'll do the grocery shopping while you're in the meeting."

"I don't know what I'd do without you." Lee put his arm around her shoulders and gave her a quick kiss on the cheek.

"You'd do the same thing you do now. You'd work all the time. I'm the one that should worry—if you weren't around, I'd actually have to figure out all of the financial stuff. So don't you get any bright ideas to run off with somebody else and leave me here alone."

"Fat chance, baby. I don't think anyone else will have me."

"Probably true." She laughed as he kissed her lightly. "We're going to be late. Let's get a move on."

"Peg," Lee said, taking her by the shoulders and looking at her squarely in the eyes, "don't worry about the finances so much. We'll figure out a way to make it work."

"Maybe if I understood it a little better I wouldn't be so damned worried about it," she said as she walked out of the room. "Let's go."

Peg put a carton of milk into her cart and moved to the yogurt section, peering intently at the labels, her reading glasses perched on the end of her nose.

"Hello, Peg." She knew before turning around that it was Leslie Montgomery.

"Hello, Leslie," she responded coolly.

"I'm glad I ran into you." Leslie touched her arm lightly. "I'd like to apologize for my comments the last time we met. I was very angry with Kelly and I shouldn't have taken it out on you. I said some things I shouldn't have and I regret it. I'm sorry. I'd like for us to be friends again."

How could we be friends again, Peg thought, *if we were never friends before?* She sighed and remembered her promise to Lee. "Apology accepted. And I'd like to apologize to you too. My hands aren't clean either." She awkwardly stuck out her hands with the palms up, as if to show the dirt.

Leslie took Peg's hands and held them. "No problem. We've got some kids we need to deal with, so there's no point in the two of us not getting along."

"No point," Peg said, pulling her hands back. "No point, indeed."

"Let's get together for coffee and talk sometime soon."

"That would be fine," Peg lied. "I'm sorry, but I've got to run now." She tossed a few yogurt containers into her cart and hurried off down the aisle.

Peg loved the way the house looked as they drove up the driveway in the early evening after the commission meeting. It reminded her of a Christmas card: snow surrounding the log house and yellow lights in the windows. Once inside, Peg set about making dinner. Lee sat at the table, separating the mail into piles.

"Anything other than junk mail?" Peg asked.

"Here's a letter from the bank. Maybe it's good news about the loan."

He unfolded the sheet of paper and began to read. "I can't believe they are actually doing this," he said. "I guess having a local advocate didn't help us after all." He put his head in his hands. "I'm sorry, Peg. I thought I could find a way out."

Peg took the letter from his hands. There, in capital letters at the top of the page, were four words: FINAL NOTICE BEFORE FORECLOSURE.

CHAPTER 28

The night was long and Peg barely slept. She tossed in bed, alternately clutching Lee and pushing him away, the night sweats she thought were long gone returning in full force. She was helpless, unable to make her brain stay quiet enough to have a coherent or logical thought, the swirling of fears and obligations sucking her down like a strong eddy. But then Lee would pull her back, hug her quietly, and tell her it would be all right. She loved him for being the proverbial pillar of strength, even when he shared with her his own fear and sense of inadequacy at letting it come to this.

Sell, sell, sell, her subconscious said. *Fight, fight, fight,* her waking mind countered. She knew her ancestors would not have given up so easily. They would have fought. Surely they had faced worse situations than this in all those early years of homesteading. Clearing the land and planting crops that froze out in a freak August snowstorm. Switching to cattle and battling with the government to get the grazing rights needed to sustain the herd. Building the first ranch house only to have it burn to the ground when a whiff of wind blew the curtain into the candle flame.

"We're just going to have to sell more property," Lee said at some point in the middle of the night. "We can't risk losing the whole thing because we are too stubborn to give up part of it. The lower pastures would make a great golf course, if we could find a developer. More people like Leslie Montgomery want to move here every day. We could cash in on that in a bigger way."

Peg listened to each of the ideas, the grim reality of the situation settling into her bones. She knew she was to blame. If she had agreed to sell more land earlier, they would have had enough cash to ride out another year. By then maybe things would be turned around. Japan might lift the beef embargo and rejuvenate the market. Eating steak might be popular again. She had gotten them into this mess, and now she was going to have to pay even more dearly to get them out of it. They would sell more property, and instead of one neighbor, there would be many. The ranch would slowly be devoured, until it was a mere shell of itself, a cannibal eating its own flesh.

"Maybe it would be best if we sold the whole thing and moved away." Peg said to Lee at some point. "We won't be able to hold our heads up around here anymore, so we may as well run away." Then later, she said, "There's got to be a way we can save the ranch. If we just think hard enough, the answer will come."

"Don't be unrealistic, Peg." Lee hugged her tightly. "We've been thinking hard about this for the past year. I don't think there's any other answer than to start selling."

By 4:30 a.m., Peg felt as if she had been through labor. She was exhausted and spent. She began to cry and Lee held her close, the tears dampening his chest and combining with her sweat. They lay together quietly.

Finally, at 5 a.m., she fell asleep.

The midmorning light broke over the peaks as Peg scuttled to the barn, head down, oblivious to the splendor of the day. Normally, she would have reveled in a day like this, taking time to smell the air and taste the cold. Normally, she would have composed some verses of a love song to the experience, singing the words in her head until a later time when she might or might not remember them enough to write them down.

She pulled the bucket from the oat bin and set about refilling the horses' feedbags. Most days, she had time to stop and pet the soft snout of each animal, talking with them as if they were gossipy neighbors, sharing the news of the day and the night before, checking to make sure each was okay. But today, she went through the chores robotically.

Lee came into the barn and began saddling his horse. "The road to the shepherd's cabin is mostly melted out, so I'm going to take a ride out that way and see if any of those cows in the canyon have calved yet."

"I think I'm going to take a nap." Peg yawned. "Sure you don't want to take one of the snowmobiles? There's still enough snow beside the road for that, and it would be quicker."

"No, the ride will do me good," he said as he saddled up. "Maybe you ought to head out for a ride too. Clear the mind."

"I'll think about it. One thing is for sure: it couldn't hurt. I'm feeling about as low as you can go right now."

"I've already scheduled a meeting at the bank for next week, so there isn't anything else we can do until then. Try not to worry. I'll be back by three or I'll call you. Unless I'm in the canyon without reception, that is."

"I love you, Lee," Peg said as he kissed her lightly on the forehead.

"I love you too, Peg." Lee threw his long, muscular legs over the back of the horse and rode away.

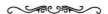

"Everything is a big mess, Cynthia," Leslie said. "Maybe you should have lunch with Kelly and try to talk some sense into her."

"Maybe she's making sense," Cynthia said.

"What do you mean?"

"Well, weren't you upset that she was going to end up not working after law school and being a stay-at-home mom?"

"Yes."

"And that she was expecting some man to give her the affluent lifestyle she wants instead of working for it herself?"

"Yes."

"Well, if she marries Will, she'll definitely have to work to make ends meet. And it's likely that she would be the primary breadwinner, right?"

"I don't want her to have to support him. That's no different than her being at home and being supported."

"Listen to yourself, Leslie. You're letting your emotions get in the way of your ideals. You've always said that both men and women should have the option of working or staying home with the kids. You just didn't want Kelly to be dependent on someone else. If they're in love, they'll figure it out."

"Love. She's too young to know if she's in love. Or if she's ready for marriage."

"Might I gently remind you that she is already a year older than you were when you got married?"

"You know too much." Leslie paced around her living room as she talked to Cynthia. "But you're right. I guess I need to give them a chance."

"Maybe your daughter has finally grown up and figured out what's important for her to be happy. You should be thrilled that she's found somebody she loves instead of hanging on to that idea of marrying for money and position. Better to be with a man who treats you right than one whose work always comes first."

"That's true. And the good news is that if children learn about relationships from their parents, Will has some pretty good role models. I'd have to say that I've never been around Lee and Peg when they didn't treat each other with complete respect and even affection. And I've never heard Peg say a bad thing about him, even when I complained about my life with Hugh."

"Well, that's saying something for a marriage of—what?— over thirty years?"

"At least. I think their oldest son is over thirty. I know you can never really know about another person's marriage, but from what I can tell, they pretty much have the best one I've ever seen."

CHAPTER 29

It was 4 p.m. Peg had spent a good portion of the day pacing between the barn and the house. She knew they needed to sell at least another eighty acres, if not twice that much, to satisfy the bank's crazy demand to pay an exorbitant amount of money within the next sixty days or lose the whole thing. She called Lee several times on the cell phone but never got an answer. She knew he must be in the canyon or he would have called her back.

Peg put some potatoes on the stove to boil and pulled two steaks from the freezer. *We've got plenty of meat,* she thought, *and I'll be damned if the bank is going to get any of it.* She went into the cold cellar and scanned the wine shelf, looking for something special. Something that would signify that the bank hadn't gotten the better of them. She found an old bottle of cabernet. *May as well drink it now,* she thought. *We might not be able to have such fine things soon.*

By five thirty, the sun was below the peaks and the evening dusk washed the landscape in muted colors. She tried again to raise Lee on the phone. It was unlike him to not come out of the canyon at some point to call her and give her an update.

Especially when he said he'd be back by three. There must be a problem with one of the births, she thought, knowing how unpredictable pregnant cows could be. She went out to the barn to catch Manny before he left for the day. "Do you know anything about how the calving is going? Lee was due back hours ago and still isn't here. Were there lots of cows left in the canyon?"

"I was up there yesterday, and yeah, there were maybe eight or ten. So I wouldn't worry about him. You know how it is when those cows get going. If it gets too late, he'll ride over to the shepherd's cabin for the night. I'll go out first thing in the morning to give him a hand." The shepherd's cabin was fully equipped with supplies so any cowboy could spend a few nights there if need be.

"Thanks, Manny," she said. "You're probably right, of course. Stop by here in the morning before you head out. I'll probably go with you."

She went back inside and ate her half of the meal in silence and went to bed when the wine was almost gone.

Cortez Harbinger applauded politely when Andrew Macfarlane went to the stage to accept an award at the annual mining industry dinner. He was a veteran of these types of events and knew that the speeches were just beginning. He made sure he had a full glass of whiskey before they started, since it was impolite to get up to get another drink while some brass in a monkey suit was talking, especially his own client. Seated between him and Andrew at the table of ten was a young, up-and-coming congresswoman who was skeptical about mining. She had been invited as their guest so she could see what an environmentally sensitive company Xandex was. Cortez liked that her dress was a little too big and gaped invitingly at him whenever she moved.

He barely listened to what Andrew was saying and instead surveyed the room. He didn't mind the black-tie affairs—after all, it was just another uniform he had to wear—but mostly he enjoyed the skin so many women showed in their formal dresses. Sure, the skin wasn't all good. There were the matronly types in strapless numbers with fat spilling over the top and competing with their massive cleavage, and the anorexic trophy wives who had no breasts and no business wearing a dress that needed them. And then there were the Washington women who thought they had to cover it all up to be taken seriously. But the rest of them—the ones who were comfortable showing off the goods—were definitely worth looking at. Like the congresswoman next to him.

He noticed another lobbyist a few tables away and made a note to go over and chat when the speeches were done. He'd already made sure he spent time during the cocktail hour with all of the politicos who were there, but it wouldn't hurt to loop back with them as well. He plotted his map in his head to maximize his exposure at the dinner. *Some people might think of events like this as leisure,* Cortez thought, *but I know it's work and it's got to be done in a way that nobody thinks it is.*

Andrew returned to the table and showed off the plaque he had received.

"Congratulations, Mr. Macfarlane," Cortez said, playing along with the script that Andrew had talked to him about before the dinner. "Tell us how you got an award for environmental restoration while you're running a successful mining company."

"Well, as you all know," Andrew gestured around the table, "my grandfather founded Xandex Exploration, and he always said that we can't just take, we have to give back. He was ahead of his time and always made sure the people who worked for him were treated fairly. Then, when my father took over, he decided to take it even further. Like a lot of geologists, he was an avid fisherman and hunter and loved the outdoors, so to him it was a natural thing to be interested in the environment. It was 1978 when he created the restoration-funding program that won this award. All I've done is keep it alive."

Cortez was pleased when the congresswoman nodded appreciatively. Mission accomplished if they could start turning around her opinion, he thought. *We're going to need every vote in Congress to get that legislative change through. Especially since that damn Sam Curtis is really digging in.*

The congresswoman leaned forward on the table. Cortez did too to improve his view. She put her hand on Andrew's arm to get his attention. "I've been hearing rumors that you're considering getting into natural gas development in addition to hard rock mining. Is it true?"

"Xandex is always on the lookout for new business opportunities," Andrew said. "Natural gas exploration and development is very expensive, you know. And there are some hurdles that make it really difficult."

"Environmental hurdles?"

"Yes. Among other things. But whether Xandex is in it or not, it's important to our country to make development of our own oil and gas reserves easier, not harder, don't you think?"

Cortez watched Andrew lock his blue eyes onto the congresswoman's and put his hand on top of hers. *Damn his good looks,* Cortez thought. *He doesn't even have to work at it and they fall all over him.*

"I think it's important to protect the environment as well," the congresswoman said.

"Couldn't agree more, but we know how to do that. The important thing now is to create jobs and protect our national security. We shouldn't be beholden to the Middle East to keep our economy humming."

"I'd like to talk to you more about that." She turned to Cortez. "Why don't you call my office next week and set up a time?"

Cortez smiled and poured more wine into her glass. *This is how it's done,* he thought. *One small, masterminded step at a time.*

Peg woke up and reached across the bed for Lee before remembering that he hadn't made it back the night before. She checked the cell phone that she'd kept beside the bed, in case he managed to get coverage and call. But there was nothing. She dressed for the cold ride out to the canyon to help with the calving and met Manny in the barn.

"No word?" he asked.

"No, but I didn't really expect any. You know there isn't cell coverage out there."

"Should we take the snowmobiles, or do you want to ride?"

"I'd rather take the snowmobiles to get there faster, but if we have to go into the canyon, we might not get through with the rocks and early melt. I think we'd better ride, don't you?"

"Yup. I've already got us both saddled up and ready to go."

They rode silently, and Peg was thankful for the monotonous rocking of the horse. The sun was bright but gave no warmth. When they got to the cabin, it was clear that Lee hadn't been there. They got back on the horses and rode into the mouth of the canyon.

A few hundred yards in, they heard the distinct bellowing of a cow in distress. "I think we've found our problem," Manny said. "That sounds like a cow that's been working hard all night. Must be a breach birth."

As they approached the laboring cow, there was no sign of Lee. Manny got down from his horse and peered at the ground. "I'll be damned," he said, "but I don't think he's been here at all. There must be another one further up."

They left the cow to nature and rode farther into a side slot of the canyon so deep and narrow that sunlight barely hit in the middle of summer and never graced the ground during this time of year.

"Good thing we brought the horses," Manny said.

They rode for another ten minutes before Manny saw tracks in the snow. "He's gone in here," he said, "but he hasn't come out. Can't be far now." He whistled.

There was no response.

He called out Lee's name.

Still, no response.

"There's his horse," Peg said, pointing at a shadow in the distance, relieved that they'd finally found him. They went quickly toward the horse. Something didn't feel right. They could still hear the bellowing of the cow they'd left behind echoing in the confines of the canyon, but otherwise it was quiet. The cold air had a chill unlike anything she had felt before. She shivered involuntarily and pulled the zipper of her jacket completely closed.

Lee's horse trotted toward them, still saddled and bridled, the reins hanging loosely by its neck. Why hadn't Lee taken the bridle off for the night or tied the horse to a tree? It was so unlike him, she thought.

Manny was off to her left picking his way through sagebrush and boulders when she saw him pull his horse to a stop and jump off.

Peg wheeled her horse around, spurred it over to Manny, and saw him huddled over Lee's inert body. She was off her horse in an instant.

Manny looked up at her in horror. "My god, Peg," he said. "He's dead."

CHAPTER 30

Leslie slipped quietly into one of the few seats remaining in the back row of the church. The room buzzed with hushed whispers and stifled sobs. Women sat with their hands protectively on their husbands' arms, as if the touch could prevent them from enduring a similar fate. Men sat stoic in their mourning, staring straight ahead as they fought, sometimes unsuccessfully, to keep tears from escaping.

Peg sat stiffly in the front row, flanked on both sides by her sons and their families, including Will, without Kelly, who was in the middle of midterms. The church was full yet people kept coming. Soon, it was standing room only. The ranch hands, tugging at the necks of shirts and ties they were unused to wearing, congregated at the back, shuffling from one boot to the other. The whispering quieted as the pastor approached the pulpit to begin the service.

Leslie looked at the people in the church. She could see that the women were beautiful despite the deep, furrowed lines on their faces. She could see the strong backs of the men who worked the land and lived by the seasons. She could feel the shock and grief evident on every one of their faces, tempered only by the sense of community that she was just beginning to understand. She saw the book club members scattered throughout the church, and Sam Curtis, in the second pew, right behind the family.

She hadn't done a very good job of accepting these people or their way of life. She realized that she had brought with her a whole range of preconceived notions and biases that she had not even been aware of. She vowed to change and let go of her assumption that they had nothing in common with her or weren't as educated. It was stupid and hurtful to have said what she did to Peg. From now on, she would work on seeing people for who they were and what they did, before making any judgments. Including Will. And Kelly. Death had a way of putting things into perspective.

During the service, all three of the boys spoke. Will went last. His remarks were beautiful and consoling, and even at such a time, he made the congregation laugh with stories of growing up with Lee. He was more uplifting than the preacher, Leslie thought. He was handsome and articulate and Leslie could see why Kelly had fallen in love with him.

When the pallbearers picked up the casket to carry it out of the church, the family followed first, then each of the rows in turn. Leslie could tell that Peg was still in shock, the spark of life missing from her eyes. Sam came down the center aisle behind the family, shaking hands with most and hugging some. He looked comfortable in his dark suit and tie, a stark contrast to the cowboys' unease. *He has such a commanding presence*, she thought.

She could hear people greeting him and heard him respond, calling each of them by name. *Yes, that's what community is all about*, she thought. *When the US senator knows everyone by name.*

Outside the church, Sam came over to Leslie. "I was hoping I'd see you here."

"I'm so sorry, Sam. I know you were good friends with Lee."

"Thanks. It's tragic. Not a finer man in the county. It's a huge impact on the whole community."

"I think everyone who ever set foot in Legacy Springs is here."

"Not to be disrespectful talking about this during the funeral, but I've made some progress on getting information about the company involved in the drilling project. Any chance you're free for dinner tomorrow so we can talk about it?"

"Of course."

"Good. It's a date. Why don't you come by my house around six and I'll cook something for us. I'll e-mail you directions. See you tomorrow." He smiled at her and turned to greet the person who had stepped behind him.

"I'd really like a little bit of time alone," Peg said to the boys the day after the funeral when she realized one son wouldn't leave her side until another one was there to take his place. "Why don't you go into town to Two Whoops and have a few beers and reminisce about your father. The girls and the kids can do some shopping or something. It's too morbid to have everybody moping around here."

"Are you sure, Mom?" Roy said, holding little Jake.

"I'm sure."

She went into the bedroom and tried to nap, but her mind wouldn't let her. She got up and went to Lee's desk and sat down.

She had spent her life in this house, much of it by herself, but it had never felt so empty as today. And this was how it would feel from now on. The numbness was starting to wear off, and she knew that once the kids left, she would have to figure out how to carry on.

I guess I could sell the place and move to Hawaii like we joked about. What would I do in Hawaii though? I would be miserable. No chores to do, no horses to feed, no beautiful mountains to look at. What do people do who move to a place like that and don't work? Not for me, that's for sure.

She moved some papers around on the desk. The foreclosure notice was still on top of one of the piles. How could she possibly save the ranch? No, she realized, the question was different now. The question was how could she possibly live here without Lee?

She loved Legacy Springs. It was home. She loved the feel of the wind in her hair when she rode along the ridgeline and watched the eagles swoop in a mating dance. She loved the solitude of the mountains and the closeness of the community. She loved the smell of ozone after a thunderstorm and the special quiet during a snowstorm. *This land and this place are what keep me alive,* she thought. *It wouldn't be the same if it was overrun by people. I can't sell out and develop it like Lee suggested.* She stared at the papers on the desk. She'd think of something. It was going to be hard enough to live without Lee, but she knew she couldn't live at all if she lost both him and the ranch.

Leslie drove to Sam's house in the fading light and felt a glimmer of hope that maybe spring wasn't far away. It was almost the end of March. The piles of snow on the side of the road were slowly diminishing, and brown earth patches showed through. Even though new snow still fell, the rate of melt kept slightly ahead. The pine trees had a mystical feeling to them, branches starting to spread again, without the weight of the winter's ice and snow. The sky was clear and the early stars were starting to come out. Two deer stood on the side of the road but then hopped easily into the shadows of the forest as she drove toward them. When she pulled into the driveway, Sam was waiting at the door for her.

"Did you have any trouble finding it?"

"No, your directions were impeccable," she answered as he took her coat and hung it in the closet.

"You look great, Leslie. It's a joy to see a woman in something other than jeans and a barn coat."

"Thank you, Senator." She smiled. "It's nothing much." In fact, she had spent an hour deciding on exactly the right thing: a long, tweed, wool skirt with high-heeled boots and a deep V-neck cashmere sweater with a lacy camisole peeking out above the V. She knew she shouldn't think of the dinner as a date, but she couldn't help it.

"It's Sam, remember? We're not on the Hill anymore."

They had cocktails and appetizers in the living room. His house was exactly as she had pictured it. She admired his collection of Western paintings and bronze sculptures, and listened to his stories of each piece. Sometimes he knew the artist personally, sometimes it was a family heirloom, and sometimes it was just something he liked.

"I've got a few things to do to finish dinner," he said when their drinks were empty. "You can stay here and I'll bring you a glass of wine, or you can keep me company in the kitchen."

"Much as I love this room, I'm happy to help get dinner ready."

"You don't need to work. Just keep me company." They picked up the empty plates and glasses and she followed him into a large, modern kitchen.

"This is a cook's dream." Leslie ran her hand over the large island's granite countertop and noticed the copper pots hanging from a wrought-iron rack. "It's gorgeous."

"Karen and I both liked to cook, so we had it completely redone. I'm afraid I don't cook quite so often anymore, but tonight I'm making my specialty, so hopefully it will turn out okay."

"It smells wonderful. What is it?"

"Coq au vin." He motioned to the barstools at the island. "Please, have a seat." He grabbed a black-and-white striped apron and tied it around his waist as he went around to the other side. A large pot simmered on the six-burner gas stove. He lifted the lid and stirred the contents.

"It's such a shame about Lee, isn't it? I don't know what Peg is going to do without him. I don't know a lot about ranching, but it seems like it would be pretty hard for her to run the place by herself, wouldn't it?"

"Peg's quite the woman. If anybody can do it, she can. But it will still be damn hard. Maybe now one of the boys will have a change of heart and she'll get some help. But that's not the worst of her worries right now." He took a large bowl of salad out of the refrigerator and began to toss it.

"I know. I can't even imagine how hard it must be to deal with the emotions."

"It's been almost five years since Karen died, and that part's still hard. But what I meant was the financial situation. They're on their last legs, you know. Selling to you was supposed to be their salvation, but it wasn't enough." Sam stuck salad tongs into the bowl and turned off the burner under the chicken.

"What do you mean, 'it wasn't enough'?"

"Lee told me last week that unless Peg agreed to sell some more parcels, the bank was threatening to foreclose on the ranch. They'd lose the whole thing. He wasn't sure Peg understood the seriousness of it, but she insisted she wasn't selling any more. You know, she was never happy about letting that parcel go to you."

Leslie shifted uncomfortably on the stool. "I always sensed that. But I had no idea about a possible foreclosure. Peg had made some vague references to financial difficulties, but I assumed it was like everyone else—there's never enough money for all the things we want to do. What will happen now, with Lee's death?"

"It's not going to be any easier, that's for sure. Unless Lee had some life insurance that could pay the bills. But I suspect it won't be enough. Around here, people think of life insurance as something you get so there's money to bury you, not to keep your business alive. I just hope this doesn't cause her to make some bad decisions. It's hard to be rational when something like this happens." Sam got a serving platter from the cabinet. "I know when Karen died, I wasn't really at a hundred percent for quite a long time. And I didn't have financial issues to worry about."

"What's so difficult about making money on a ranch of that size? And why do they even have a mortgage? Didn't they homestead the land?"

"If only it were so simple. Ranchers in the valley have had their property mortgaged to the hilt since the beef market tanked five years ago. They needed the money to cover leasing fees, feed for the animals, paying the ranch hands, keeping the equipment running, things like that." He took pieces of chicken from the pot and placed them on the platter. "The general pattern is cyclical. In bad times, the land becomes the collateral to tide things over until the good times come back, and then it's paid off and the cycle starts all over again. Unfortunately, this bad cycle came soon after the last three downturns, so people didn't get back to square one quickly enough and the debt kept mounting." He got a ladle and began spooning liquid over the chicken.

"So why are the Hamiltons any worse off than the other ranchers?"

"Mostly because they've been stubborn. They refuse to routinely use growth steroids, or to fatten the cows with corn, so they often get less at market. It's the old-fashioned way to raise beef, but they insist on keeping the tradition going. They think it's healthier and that it makes their meat taste better."

"But people will pay more for grass-fed beef, not less. It does taste better you know."

Sam looked at her with surprise. "I don't think anyone even knows it's grass fed, so it certainly hasn't been a marketing point. And how do you know it tastes better?"

"I've eaten both and much prefer the grass fed. I get mine from Argentina. I didn't know anyone in the US was raising grass-fed cattle, let alone my neighbors. Once you've had it, everything else tastes off—artificial."

"I'll have to try it sometime. But for now, let's get this chicken on the table."

Sam took off his apron and they carried the food to the dining room together. Sam had already set the table and dimmed the lights. "Would you mind lighting the candles while I get the wine? The matches are right there." Two candlesticks with white candles were in the middle of the table.

Sitting in the glow of the candlelight, Leslie felt like she was on a date. Sam brought the wine in from the kitchen and poured them each a glass.

"To old friends," he toasted when he sat down.

She liked the way their conversation weaved among memories from DC, current events, and Sam's interest in how she had decided to come to Montana and how she was faring. They talked about everything except the natural gas development. He hadn't brought it up and Leslie didn't want to spoil the easy mood by asking about something she thought of as business.

They were almost done eating when he finally raised the topic. "I think I've found out who's behind the project," Sam said.

"So was our theory of a shell correct? Is it a big company that Harbinger's working for?"

"Yes, and a Montana company at that. Xandex Exploration."

Leslie froze. *Oh, shit.* "Did you say Xandex?"

"Yes, do you know it?"

"I know the president, Andrew Macfarlane," Leslie said. This couldn't be true, she thought. Harbinger couldn't work for Andrew. He said he didn't even know him. "But that's a mining company, not an oil and gas firm."

Sam looked at her questioningly. "That's right, but they've been venturing into natural gas exploration. How do you know Macfarlane?"

"I'm . . . Well, I'm . . ." She hesitated, not sure what to say or even what to call what she was doing with Andrew.

Sam waited.

"I'm dating him."

Sam sat back in his chair, eyebrows raised. "Dating? You've got to be kidding. Did you know him from DC?"

"No, I met him when I first moved here." Her mind was racing. *How could Andrew be involved in such a thing? Maybe he didn't know it was happening,* she thought. *But, no. No way.* She didn't know what to do with the sinking feeling that she had somehow been taken in by Andrew. And now Sam was going to think she was a jerk. "I met him at the airport. Actually, I ran into his car in the parking lot."

"Well, if you're dating him, does he know about your opposition group?"

"No. At least I haven't mentioned it. We really don't talk about his work much." She felt funny talking to Sam about Andrew. She wanted the information to be wrong. She searched for the right thing to say. If Sam had been interested in her, he wouldn't be now.

"Have you been seeing him for a long time?"

"Not long. A few months. We don't see each other very often." She tried to make the relationship seem less than what it was.

"Leslie, I need to be straight with you about something." Sam leaned forward across the table.

"Yes?"

"I'd like to know how serious you are about him." He stopped and waited a moment before going on. "I feel a bit awkward asking you, but—"

Leslie interrupted, relieved that he was interested after all. "It's no problem, Sam. I don't mind telling you." She put her hand over his as it lay on the table. He pulled it back and ignored the gesture. She sat back, unsure again, and continued. "We've been seeing each other for a few months, but it's very sporadic, and it's not serious."

"I guess what I really need to say . . ." Sam hesitated again. Leslie waited; maybe she had been too forward, touching him. "I guess I really mean to ask . . . Well, this is very difficult for me."

Leslie waited. Dating again in your late fifties was not so different from in your youth, she thought. The same insecurities and jealousies, the same shivers and thrills, and the same delicate dance.

"What I need to know is whether you've told him about my affair with Abby," Sam blurted.

"Your affair? Why would I have told him about that? Of course not." The memory of her last evening with Andrew, the gift of the diamond bracelet, the probing questions about Sam, came flooding back. "Why do you ask?"

"I'm going to be perfectly honest with you. And only because I trust you. I believe that Xandex Exploration is looking for information so they can blackmail me into supporting legislation they want. They know they can't get it passed without me, and they've made some threats." He took a deep breath. "The affair was a big mistake and I regret it. If it came out . . ." He stopped, leaving the thought hanging.

Leslie's heart sank. He wasn't interested in her. *All he wants to know is whether I've told anybody anything.* "I've never mentioned that to anyone. And I don't see any reason why I ever would." She felt sorry for him, living in fear of a scandal breaking over something that had happened so many years ago. And Andrew. *How could he!*

"I appreciate that, Leslie. I hope you'll continue to stay quiet about it."

"I will. I respect you too much to say anything to anybody." She was feeling more than respect for Sam. But it was clear that he saw their relationship as strictly business. So it wasn't a date after all, she decided. She'd made a fool of herself putting her hand on his.

"Thank you." He poured more wine into their glasses. "Shall we talk about something else?"

She gratefully changed the subject, resolving not to think about Andrew until tomorrow, and they were soon back to an easy camaraderie. She liked the way he laughed when she told him the story of her first meeting with Peg and how she'd fallen down on the sidewalk.

"I think Peg is an interesting woman," Leslie said. "She's very creative and a great cook, but she also seems really smart. She could have been something in the world. Why did she waste her life on the ranch?"

Sam laughed. "Wasted her life? Could have been something? That's an interesting perspective."

Leslie looked at him with surprise. "How so?"

"Peg's done quite a bit with her life. She served in the state legislature for a few years before she had kids, she's the biggest fundraiser for all of the local charities, and she's served on several statewide commissions appointed by the governor. She had a weekly column about politics in the local newspaper for years. Haven't you two ever talked about any of that?"

"No. Never. I had no idea. Did she go to college?" Leslie felt stupid again.

"Of course. Stanford." Sam laughed again. "Majored in literature, I believe."

"No way! So that's why she's the unofficial leader of the book club." *Another surprise.*

"I don't know about that, but you shouldn't underestimate her. She's quite a celebrity in her own right." He paused, refilling their wine glasses. The candles on the table were burning down.

"Celebrity? Because of the ranch?"

"No, because of her writing, of course," he answered as a buzzer sounded in the kitchen. "That's the timer for the dessert tart. Let's clear these plates and head back into the kitchen so I can get it out of the oven."

Sam stacked the plates while Leslie took the glasses. "Just put them on the counter for now. Have a seat while I put these away." He motioned to the barstools. "What is it between you two? Why don't you like each other? You should have so much in common."

"Until tonight, I didn't think we had anything in common."

"Don't be silly. You are two highly intelligent, energetic, talented women. You have more in common with her than with Edith and Emma, and that hasn't kept you from becoming friends with them." He handed her a plate with a piece of warm pear tart on it, a scoop of vanilla ice cream melting on top.

"I guess I really have misjudged her. We had an argument recently and I said some things that not only weren't very nice but, given what you've said, weren't very true either. I feel like such a fool."

"She's going to need all the help and friendship she can get over these next few months. If you really want to help, you should use your business acumen and help her prevent foreclosure. She's going to be devastated if she loses the ranch."

"But I don't know anything about how to make money on a ranch. And if she and Lee, with all of their family experience, couldn't figure it out, how could I?"

"I didn't mean in that way. I meant by helping her overcome her aversion to selling off parcels to pay the bills. You might help her see that it's better than losing the whole ranch."

They finished dessert and Leslie rinsed the dishes before handing them to Sam to put in the dishwasher. She dried her hands.

"It's getting late, Sam. I've got to get going. Thanks so much for a lovely evening."

"My pleasure, Leslie."

"We never did talk much about the opposition group," Leslie said as she put her coat on. "I'm sorry I had such a bad reaction to hearing it was Xandex behind the project. I'm going to have to come to grips with that."

"Me too." He paused before continuing. "I had a really nice time. It was great to catch up. Will you have dinner with me again?"

"Of course, Sam," she said, wrapping her scarf around her neck. "Next time, it will be my turn to cook." It would be nice to be friends with him, if nothing else, she thought.

"If what you said about Andrew Macfarlane is true and you're not serious about him, then would it be moving too fast to have dinner again one day next week?" Sam moved slightly closer to her.

"That would be great," she said, surprised. "How about next Tuesday? My house at seven?"

"It's a date," he said, repeating the phrase he had used before. Then, as if to confirm its meaning for her, he leaned over and kissed her lightly on the lips.

When she got home, she went straight to the dressing table and picked up the Tiffany box with the bracelet Andrew had given her. It *was* a bribe. *I could never wear this. I'm giving it back the next time I see him. And I'll be telling him a thing or two when I do.* She carried it out and put it on the kitchen counter so she wouldn't forget.

CHAPTER 31

It was Saturday night and Leslie curled up in front of the fire with several cookbooks, the TV on mindlessly in the background. It had been a few days since her dinner with Sam and she found that the angrier she got with Andrew, the more she thought about Sam. *I'll find something interesting to make for dinner next week,* she thought. *Something I can do mostly in advance.* She smiled, remembering the kiss he had given her.

She promised herself she wouldn't make a big deal out of seeing him again or blow it out of proportion, but she couldn't stop thinking about him. She had to admit that, no matter how comfortable she had become being alone in her house, it was always nice to have somebody else there with her. She imagined Sam sitting next to her on the couch, rubbing her feet and telling her about his day.

But then, she thought about Peg, alone in her house with a huge gaping hole of loneliness. She wondered what she would have felt if Hugh had died while they were still married, and if it would have been worse than the ache she had when he left. *I've got to try again to be friends with Peg. I've got to make amends.*

She heard the sound of a revving motor coming up the steep road to the driveway. *Damn*, she thought, realizing that she didn't want just anybody there with her; she wanted Sam. She got up and looked out the window. It was Andrew's car. *What the hell is he doing here?* Not only had he not called, but he never came on a weekend, only during the week when he was here on business. She wasn't ready to talk to him yet, or to say anything beyond the angry voice mail she had left him the day after she learned that Xandex was behind the natural gas project.

Andrew walked in like he owned the place, the chill of the winter night reddening his cheeks, despite the short distance from the car to her door. He had a cloth tote bag with him; his company's logo was emblazoned on the side. "Think Green" it said above the logo, and "It's Your Planet" below.

"You look delicious." He eyed her cleavage, and she pulled up the neck of her sweater. "You're not still mad at me are you?" He didn't wait for an answer and tried to kiss her, but she resisted.

"Yes. I am."

"Here, I've brought a really good wine for us to try." He handed her the tote bag and began to take off his coat.

"I wasn't expecting you tonight," she said coldly, holding the bag without looking into it. "And you didn't respond to my voice mail."

"That voice mail is exactly why I'm here. You sounded so angry I thought it would be better to talk in person." He took the bag from her and walked toward the kitchen.

"It is better to talk in person. But I'm still mad at you. I want some explanations."

"Let's have a drink first and then we can talk and I'll tell you anything you want to know. It was a long drive and I don't want to start the evening with an argument." He went proprietarily to the liquor cabinet, took out the single malt scotch, and poured himself a drink. "What would you like? Want me to make you a martini, or should I open this nice old wine I brought for you?"

"Wine is fine."

She wasn't ready to kick him out, but she wasn't going to make it easy either. She stood with her arms crossed and watched him get a wineglass from the cupboard, open the wine, and swirl and taste it before pouring her a full glass. The thought of what could have happened to Edith and Emma made her want to slap him. Instead, she watched him maneuver his way around her kitchen, kicking off his shoes in the meantime. She used to like the fact that he felt comfortable in her house, knowing where things were, not waiting for an invitation from her for something he may have wanted. But tonight it felt possessive. Tonight it felt invasive.

She sat in a chair, instead of on the couch with him, while he told her about the condition of the road on the way over and how he had canceled all of his weekend plans just to come see her. "Paid a pretty price for it too," he said, but she didn't ask him to elaborate. "Because you were so angry when you called, I got something for you. I hope you like it." He pulled a small velvet pouch from his pocket.

"I don't need any more presents. I need answers. Is your company involved in this natural gas project? Yes or no."

"The Tiffany bracelet looked so good on you, I couldn't help but get something to go with it," he said, ignoring her question.

He opened the bag and pulled out a string of hand-stamped silver beads. "This will look gorgeous on you. Try it on."

"No. I'm not going to try it on. In fact," she got up and brought the bracelet over from the kitchen counter, "I'm giving this back too."

"How come?"

She sat at the other end of the couch and put the box on the coffee table. She, in turn, ignored his question. "Cortez Harbinger has been all over the valley, getting people to sign contracts that are bordering on unconscionable. You told me you never heard of him, but I understand he works for you. Is it true? Is this the project that has been bringing you to town so often?"

She wasn't sure if she expected a denial or a confession. And she certainly wasn't sure which she preferred.

Andrew looked at her quizzically. "Does it matter?"

"Yes, it matters. I want to know."

"And if the answer is yes, then what?"

She took a deep breath. "Then I'd like to know how you justify taking advantage of these poor people."

"Advantage?" he said with clear disdain. "Advantage? The law is clear; the subsurface ownership is up for grabs. If they weren't smart enough to secure their own rights, then it certainly isn't taking advantage of them if I come in and see the value in something they didn't recognize. It's called capitalism and good business."

"So I guess the answer is yes."

"Look, forget about that stuff, Leslie. Righteous indignation doesn't suit you. Here, try on the necklace."

"I don't need any more presents," she said again quietly. "I need you to be honest with me."

"If that's what you want, then so be it." He let the beads fall back into the pouch. "Yes, my company is behind the project, and it'll be a good thing for everyone involved. It'll bring jobs and prosperity back to Legacy Springs. It isn't as bad as you make it sound."

"Why are you using a sham company name?"

"Simple: negotiating strategy. If people heard the name Xandex, they would expect to be paid more."

"Does Harbinger work for you?"

"Yes."

"Is there really a natural gas field here in the valley? Or is it speculation?"

"It's real. But I need access to enough properties to make it worth developing. Once I've got that, there's only a small legal issue that will make the difference between being profitable and extremely profitable." He paused, as if considering whether to keep going. "And Sam Curtis is key to getting the law changed. That's why I'd like to know how best to influence him."

Leslie was silent. Everything he told her made sense. It was a business strategy not unlike what she probably would have advised him to do if he were her client a few years ago.

He reached over and took her hand in his. "That's why I want to know what you know about him."

She stiffened and pulled her hand back. "You have no scruples, do you? There is nothing to know. Sam Curtis is an honorable man. Unlike some other people in the room." She stood up and walked into the kitchen.

"Okay, forget that," Andrew said, following her with the necklace in hand. She poured herself another glass of wine. She hadn't even tasted any of the first one. "Since I'm being honest, what else do you want to know?"

"How can you live with yourself?" she asked angrily. "Bilking old ladies and hard-working ranchers out of their rights."

"I live with myself just fine," he said matter-of-factly. "Regardless of what you believe, this project could help a lot of people. Like your neighbor Peg Hamilton, for instance, who so desperately needs the money. Seems like selling this land to you wasn't enough to keep her and her husband from running the ranch into the ground."

"Has Harbinger been bothering Peg? Her husband just died!"

"No, it's only an example. But you shouldn't be so quick to judge whether this project is a good idea or not. There are a lot of people in Legacy Springs who have already had their hands out waiting for the money to flow in. Look around. There's nothing here anymore. This town is dying, and when the ranching goes under, that's the end. Anybody who isn't in on this project is just too stupid to realize they have nothing else." He held out the necklace. "Come on. Put this on and let's make up and go to bed."

Leslie moved away, repulsed. Who was he to judge the people of Legacy Springs? "I told you I don't want your necklace—or your bracelet. And I don't think I want you here either. Maybe you should get your stuff and leave." She picked up the tote bag and went over to the table to get the bracelet. He followed her. She put the bracelet in the bag and tried to hand it to him, but he didn't take it.

"Come on, Leslie." He sat on the couch and put the necklace back in its pouch. "I drove all the way over here to see you. Sit down and let's talk about this like adults."

She threw the tote bag on the couch next to him. "I've asked you to leave. You weren't invited here tonight anyway." She got his shoes from the kitchen and dropped them in front of him.

"I never needed an invitation when you wanted me in your pants," he said, settling back and putting his feet up on the coffee table.

"It's always been just about the sex for you, hasn't it?"

"I never led you to believe otherwise, have I? I thought it was clear that this was just a way to pass the time when I had to be in this cow town."

"Pass the time? I can't believe I ever got involved with you." Leslie paced back and forth.

"Come on. It feels good to have a younger man, doesn't it? And you're certainly not going to find anyone else around here to be with. Even at your age, you're too much of a thoroughbred for these work horses."

Leslie felt an icy calm. "At least these workhorses have a sense of ethics—and manners. Which is more than I can say for you." She went over to the door and stood with his coat in her hands. "It's over, Andrew. I'll say it one more time: I'd like you to leave."

"You'll be sorry." He leaned over to put on his shoes. "Pretty soon Legacy Springs is going to be the biggest boom town in Montana. There will be trailer courts and man-camps all over this valley, and I'll be looking pretty good to you compared to the roughnecks that'll move in. The good news for me, and Cortez Harbinger for that matter, is that there are always a lot more bars that pop up, too. It sure won't be the quaint little town you thought you were moving to." He stood up, put the necklace in the tote bag, and walked to the door.

"You're obnoxious. Get out."

She thrust his coat at him and he looked at her with the steely blue eyes she had previously found so irresistible. They looked menacing now. She opened the door, and shivered with the blast of cold air.

"Well, I hope the sight of all the drilling platforms in the valley doesn't ruin your precious view. Goodbye, Leslie. It was fun while it lasted. But, oh well, I'm sure my wife will enjoy her new necklace."

She slammed the door and stomped into the kitchen. *A wife? What a complete and total ass he is! And what a fool I've been.* She poured herself another glass of wine and practically chugged it. *Damn him. Damn the day I ever met him. I will not let him ruin Legacy Springs. I will not let him ruin the life I'm building here. I'm going to kill that project, no matter what it takes.*

CHAPTER 32

Peg moved through the days following the funeral in a haze. The boys stayed for a few days but had to get back to work. The ranch hands gave her room to grieve, moving out of the way when she came to the barn, except for Manny, who stayed close and talked to her about Lee and the ranch.

When it had been more than a week, she realized she was restless. She finally felt like doing something. *Maybe this is the beginning of healing*, she thought. She went out to the barn where Manny was cleaning tack. "It's such a nice day today, I think I'm going to ride out to the bottom forty this afternoon."

"Peg, with all due respect," Manny said, "I don't think that's a good idea."

"Why not? A ride will do me good. Help clear my mind."

"Truth be told, me and the other cowboys have been talkin' and we don't think it's a good idea for you to be out ridin' by yourself. I mean," he stammered a bit, "look what happened to Lee and all."

"Lee had a heart attack, Manny. It had nothing to do with him being alone."

"That might be true. But if one of us was with him, then we might have been able to save him. And we don't want anything to happen to you. The ranch needs you now. More than ever."

Peg dipped a bucket into the bin of oats and poured them into the feedbag at the first stall. "You know we can feed the horses," Manny said.

"I want to do it. The chores keep me sane." She filled the second bag. "And so does riding, Manny. You can't expect me to stop going out by myself. I've done it since I was a kid. Nothing's different now."

"Somethin' *is* different," he said. "You just lost your husband. And you're not yourself yet." She looked at him, startled. "You need some down time. It'd be hard for anybody to concentrate. By summer, things'll be different, but for now, me and the boys don't think you should be out by yourself. If you wanna ride, one of us will go with you."

"But you all have too much work to do."

"We'd be so worried, we wouldn't be able to get anything done while you were gone anyway. Promise you won't ride alone, at least for the next month or so?" He looked her in the eye. "Do you give me your word?"

Peg let out a sigh as deep as those that came from the long necks of the horses beside her. She nodded. "Okay. For a month, then we'll see."

She went back to the house. Even in the kitchen, nothing seemed right. It was empty. But, she told herself, there was work to do. She made coffee and spread the ranch account books on the kitchen table. She crunched numbers and ran columns, but they always ended up with a minus sign in front of them. Lee was right, the only way to save the ranch was to sell more parcels and hope things turned around in a few years. The boys had told her the same thing after the funeral. They'd all offered money, but she'd turned it down. They were young, without reserves, and besides, it wasn't enough to make a difference. And none of them was willing to come back to the ranch. That was clear. Not even Will, her last hope. Especially not now that he was living in DC with Kelly and planned to marry her.

She was surprised when she started to cry. After the first day, when the tears came in such volume she thought they'd never stop, they suddenly did. And she hadn't cried since. Even at the funeral, with all of the eulogies, when the boys stood up to speak and there wasn't a dry eye in the house, she didn't cry. But now the tears were back again. She felt despair deep in her soul and had no idea how she would get through it without Lee there to help her. She wiped her eyes with one of the kitchen towels and forced herself to concentrate on the numbers again.

Lee had suggested the idea of a golf course development. It would give her the most cash immediately, if she could find a developer. But then there would be scores of homes on her land. Selling large parcels, like the forty-acre section she'd sold to Leslie, was a better option. Fewer people. But substantially less cash, and maybe not in time. She needed the money soon. Even a dead husband didn't buy her any more time. *I wish there was a way to keep the ranch intact,* she thought over and over again.

She heard a knock at the front door. She couldn't imagine who it could possibly be. Even Leslie now knew to come to the back. Peg made her way through the living room and opened the door to see the face of a man she didn't know.

"Howdy, ma'am. Sorry to drop in without notice, but I wonder if you might spare a few moments. My name is Cortez Harbinger."

"You'll be pleased with the deal once you've had a chance to think about it," Cortez said to Peg as he stood to leave two hours later. "It's the best option for keeping the ranch in one piece with only a modest intrusion of a few wells. And I'm sure I can get authorization to accelerate the payments to you so you can get the bank off your back."

Cortez couldn't believe how easy it was to get Peg to reveal details of her financial needs as he talked to her about the value of her mineral rights. Andrew had authorized him to quadruple the normal payment to bring in this major property that would cement the project. Cortez had told Andrew that the community was growing restless and he worried that others would break their contracts, even though the penalty was high. When Cortez had presented his plan to approach Peg Hamilton just days after the funeral, Andrew agreed. The rumors about the Hamiltons' financial woes were all around the valley. But as long as Lee was alive and so vocal in his opposition to drilling, neither Cortez nor Andrew believed they'd ever get the mineral rights to the Hamilton ranch. Andrew had told Cortez that the bonus would be big if he brought this one in. Cortez could taste the money the whole time he was talking to Peg.

"I know your word, as a true Montanan, is as good as gold," he had said. "So, I wish I didn't have to ask you to sign anything today. But I'm afraid the lawyers won't let me do that. I'll just need your signature on this preliminary agreement to get things moving. And the confidentiality agreement of course. I'll bring the contracts back for final signature a week from now—next Monday."

They shook hands as he stood at the door to leave. "I am truly sorry about your loss, and may he rest in peace knowing that now you will be taken care of. Thanks for your time, ma'am. And again, my condolences to you." He tipped his cowboy hat respectfully.

Peg stared at the account books after Cortez Harbinger left. His offer was too good to refuse, she thought, and good thing, because now she couldn't refuse. Even though she knew from Edith's experience that she'd have three days to renege, she'd given her word and couldn't go back on it. Regardless of what her children might say, regardless of what her friends might say, and even regardless of what her attorney might say. The details might be tweaked, but overall, the core of the deal and the fact that there was a deal would remain unchanged. As he'd said, a Montanan's word is gold.

She envisioned the wells that Harbinger had described, quietly sitting on her property and doing their thing. No matter how ugly or imposing, they would still be preferable to hordes of people building big, fancy houses on a golf course. She worried that Lee had been so opposed to the project, saying it was unfair, but it was only unfair to those people who didn't own the rights in the first place, she rationalized. Those who were only given token payment for access to property. For Peg, who owned the rights, the amount offered to buy them seemed astronomical. It would be enough to pay off the mortgage completely and still provide a guaranteed income for years to come. Any profit she could make from the ranch would be extra. It was just what she had wished for.

She heard a car pull into the driveway. The stream of visitors had slackened since the funeral. *Of all the people*, she thought, annoyed when she saw Leslie's face peer through the back-door window. *Well, at least with this new deal, there won't be any more close neighbors.*

Peg went to the door and opened it almost before Leslie could knock. She didn't ask her to come in.

"Hello, Peg. I dropped by to give you this." She thrust out a beautifully wrapped package, a small square that could only be a book. "It's something I've loved for years that has gotten me through many a rough time. I thought you might enjoy it."

Peg wore her rudeness like a too small sweater. It didn't fit. "Thank you," she relented. "Please, come in and have some coffee."

"I can't stay long," Leslie stepped in as Peg went to the cupboard for a mug.

"You take it black, don't you?" Peg poured from the half-full pot.

"Yes." Leslie sat at the kitchen table. "Peg, I want to apologize again for what I said that day you came over when the kids said they were going to get married. I was completely out of line saying what I did to you. Every time I talk to Kelly she tells me how happy they are. And when I talked to Will at the funeral, he couldn't stop telling me how much he loved my daughter. I had no right or reason to react the way I did and I'm sorry."

Peg listened, feeling sorry for Leslie and for herself and for the situation they were in. It was the first time since Lee had died that she'd felt an emotion that wasn't grief. In fact, since that day when she and Manny found Lee's body, she had felt as if she was watching her life from somewhere else. She went through the motions, she carried on the conversations, she told everyone she was doing fine, but she was hollow. For some reason, this conversation felt real to her. Maybe it was because her money troubles would soon be over. There was a light at the far, far end of this tunnel she was in.

"I know you don't particularly like me," Leslie continued. "And I've said things I shouldn't have. But it turns out I'm not a very good judge of character."

"Let's forget it." Peg sat down at the table, coffee cup in hand. "Tell me about Kelly. If she's going to be my daughter-in-law, I'd better get to know her."

Later that night, Peg saw the small package and carried it with her into the bedroom to open it. What had Leslie said about it? Something she'd loved for years? That had gotten her through rough times? She unwrapped it to see her own favorite volume of poetry. It was the one she had been reading every night since Lee died. She picked up the well-worn copy from the nightstand and compared it to the shiny new one, both with the same title: *When Times Are Tough*, by Maggie Madison.

Cortez Harbinger felt like he was flying. The Montana highway opened up ahead of him for what seemed like forever. He was heading east, back to Xandex, wanting to tell Andrew in person that he had clinched the final deal. The cherry-on-top deal. The one that would get him the biggest bonus he'd ever made.

His oversized SUV responded to his lead foot on the pedal. The speedometer moved from eighty to eighty-five and finally to ninety, where he felt the speed matched his mood. The sagebrush plains stretched in front of him, the mountains a mere suggestion in his rear-view mirror. *At this rate, I should be there in less than three hours,* he thought. *Just hope Andy is still there. I don't want to wait until tomorrow to tell him.*

"Doesn't matter, though," he said aloud. "No need to hurry, since I have her word, which a Hamilton would never break. Silly people." He chuckled and broke into a huge grin. *"Yahoooo!"* he shouted at the top of his lungs.

It was like taking candy from a baby, he thought, still smiling. A grieving widow staring at the bank on her doorstep. What could be easier? He congratulated himself on being the master of good timing—not too soon after the funeral but soon enough to be the savior. He watched the speedometer climb to ninety-five, then touch a hundred. He was a happy man.

CHAPTER 33

Leslie got home after taking the book of poems to Peg, her mind spinning. So much had been happening. Kelly and Will. The fight with Peg. Lee's death. The wonderful dinner with Sam. Then the awful fight with Andrew. Seeing Peg brought home the reality that life was fleeting and things could change in an instant. She was restless and couldn't settle on anything. She remembered Peg's advice about cabin fever and decided that a walk would help clear her mind.

She put on her boots and headed down the road. The sky was muted, a dull pewter color. The needles on the trees beside her were green, but the mountains in the distance, with the same trees, loomed an ominous black, still accented with white. A storm was predicted to hit sometime late tomorrow, according to the TV news, but she was learning the signs herself, paying attention to the precursor clouds and the wind direction and the feel in her bones of the barometer dropping. She thought about how much more aware of her surroundings she had become, and not just the views. Walking and noticing this storm, she felt like it was the first time she truly understood the description of a coming snowstorm in one of the Maggie Madison poems.

Equal parts anticipation and longing,
Waiting for the mistress.
Waiting for the love, the white virginity.
I taste her before I feel her,
I feel her before I touch her.

Maybe Peg was right when she said I didn't understand about the love of the land, she thought as she noticed fresh droppings on the road and instantly stopped to scan the trees in case she could see the deer, but they were either gone or hidden. *I've been here almost a year and feel like I'm just starting to scratch the surface of something I used to think I understood. Peg's lived here her whole life, so her connection with this land must be so intense that I can't even imagine it. What a small and narrow view I had, thinking that words of a poem gave me the same depth of feeling as her first-hand experience.*

Leslie got to the bottom of the switchbacks and waved at Manny when he drove by in his pickup. She walked a while longer before turning around to head back up the hill. She was out of the big trees now and on a flatter stretch with an open field on one side and thin aspens on the other. She noticed a movement in the field and stopped. There, standing atop a small mound of dirt not far from her, was a fox. She wasn't sure whether foxes would chase her, or if only wolves did that, but it was so small and cute that she didn't move, and it didn't either. Within a few seconds though, the fox darted into a hole in the mound and then two heads peeked out to look at her. *It must be a den! The first foxes I've ever seen and their den is on my road. Cool.*

She walked up the hill and was breathing heavily by the time she got to the final switchback. Still exhilarated by her sighting, she made a mental note to tell Peg about the den. *We'll all need to drive slowly when we go by there to make sure we don't hit one of them.* Of course, maybe the den was there every year and Peg was well aware of it. Didn't matter. She wasn't going to make assumptions anymore—either way—and would tell Peg about it.

If this is what I see on a short walk, what must Peg have seen in all the years she'd spent on this ranch. What else haven't I been noticing? Or feeling? As if to punctuate her thought, a flock of bluebirds swooped around her before flitting into the trees. *Gorgeous! I don't remember seeing any all winter. These must be the first of the season. Maybe I'm getting the hang of this.*

Cortez Harbinger swaggered through the halls of the corporate headquarters of Xandex Exploration, Inc. He practically knocked down two people who came around the corner and into his path. His excitement was fed by the high-speed drive from Legacy Springs. He strutted into the suite outside the president's office.

"Hello, sexy," he said to the pretty, blonde secretary. "Tell Andy I'm here."

"He's in a meeting, Mr. Harbinger," she said coolly.

"Who's he with?" He pulled a cigar from his inside jacket pocket. "We've got something to celebrate."

"You can't light that in here," she said, wrinkling her nose and motioning her head toward the stogie.

"I know. I know. You antismokers don't know what you're missing. I'll wait until I get in there," he said, gesturing at Andrew's closed door. "So who's he with? He won't mind if I interrupt him."

"I'm certain that he would *not* like to be interrupted. It's almost five, and I suspect that he'll be quite a bit longer. I can schedule you for some time tomorrow morning."

"Damn," he muttered, his exuberance waning. "Nah. I'll just wait." He plopped into a large leather chair and pulled a book of matches from his pocket. The secretary's look was enough to make him put it back.

"You're sure in a foul mood today," he said to her. "What's up? You on the rag or something?"

She ignored him and continued working on her computer.

He picked up a magazine and pretended to read, his eyes peering over the top of his glasses at the secretary's breasts.

Shortly after five, she got up and took her purse out of her desk drawer.

"Nice butt," he said as she reached for her coat on the rack behind the desk. "You sure you don't want to ditch that boyfriend of yours and have dinner with me tonight?"

"Make sure you don't light that thing in here," she said as she left.

It was over an hour before Andrew's door opened and three impeccably dressed men came out with him.

"Always best to do business with a principal," one of the men said in a British accent. "I knew that the way to get this resolved was to come over here across the pond myself and take your measure."

"I agree and appreciate the gesture," Andrew said. "It's the fact that you came personally that persuaded me to settle. Have a good trip back tomorrow."

Andrew did not acknowledge Cortez until the men had all left.

"What are you doing here? Weren't you supposed to be meeting with Peg Hamilton today?"

"Yes, I was, and I did. I drove back because I wanted to give you a report in person."

They went into Andrew's office. A small conference table on the far side of the room was covered with papers and used coffee cups from the previous meeting. Andrew motioned him into one of the two large leather chairs that sat in front of a fireplace. Cortez decided to wait until he broke the news before offering one of his Cubans to Andrew.

"I thought I told you to stay out there until you finalized at least one more deal."

"I got the deal," Cortez said simply, without aggrandizement but with a big smile. "With Peg Hamilton." He watched Andrew's face. During his drive, he fantasized about how fast he would be able to go if he had one of those little Mercedes sports coupes. Surely the bonus would be enough to buy one outright. He steepled his hands and waited for a reaction.

"What are the terms?" Andrew asked, clearly pleased.

Cortez explained the details. Andrew nodded approvingly. "Well done. Did she sign the preliminary contract without any changes?"

"Yup. And better yet, she gave me her word. That's as good as money in the bank."

"She still has three days, so it's not sealed yet. We'll see if it sticks once she talks to her lawyer."

"I'm not worried. The word of a Hamilton is golden. She'll never break it. She can talk to god himself and she'd still keep the deal."

"What do you know about some opposition group forming over there?" Andrew switched subjects abruptly. "Have you heard anything about it?"

"Oh, yeah, but no need to worry about that either. Two old biddies are behind it. Everyone goes along with them because they've been around there forever. But when push comes to shove, it won't amount to anything. Everybody in that valley needs money, especially Peg Hamilton. And once word's out that she's signed, everybody else will go along. It'll be fine. Let's have a cigar to celebrate, Andy." He pulled two of them from his pocket.

"No, thank you. And you'll not have one yet either," Andrew said sternly. "Not until you get a signature on the final contracts and three days have passed."

"Okay," Cortez said, deflated. The new car would have to wait, too. "But hey, speaking of push coming to shove," he grinned lasciviously and made a lewd gesture, "how's it going with the Montgomery babe? In addition to getting some, are you getting any of that dirt we need on the senator?"

"Cortez, sometimes you just don't know when to stop, do you?" Andrew stood up. "When are you going back to Legacy Springs?"

"I told her I'd be back next Monday, but if you're nervous about it . . ." he paused as Andrew nodded. "I'll go back as soon as the lawyers get the documents drawn up." He trusted Peg's word and didn't feel he had to hurry. Besides, there was another storm due and he wanted to wait until the road was clear and dry again so he could enjoy the speed. During the winter, it was hard to drive fast.

"Go as soon as you can before she has a chance to change her mind," Andrew growled at Cortez. "Now, get out of here and don't come back until you have everything signed."

CHAPTER 34

The day Sam was coming to dinner, Leslie spent the afternoon in her kitchen, three different cookbooks spread out on the counter, preparing a meal that she hoped would taste as good and look as effortless as his was. She felt a tingle of excitement when she thought of him but remembered her vow to take things slowly. Her emotions were still raw from the debacle with Andrew.

As the light started to fade, she went out on the deck to get logs to replenish the supply she kept next to the massive stone fireplace. It was cold, but she stood for a minute and looked at the dark clouds that already encapsulated the distant mountains. *These shades of gray are like a black-and-white photograph. I love this place, and my view. Now if only I can get the rest of my life in order.* She shivered as a gust of wind hit her and she felt the cold air burn her nostrils.

She carried the wood inside, stacking it neatly. She crumpled some newspaper and laid it beneath the grate, then carefully arranged the kindling into a teepee before lighting a match to start the fire. Within minutes, she had a good base and was able to add some logs. *I'm getting pretty good at this,* she thought, admiring the growing blaze.

Before returning to the kitchen, she stood a while longer looking at the view. A few twinkling lights were starting to come on far off in the valley. The clouds seemed to be getting closer and dropping lower. As she watched, the clouds let loose and big thick beautiful flakes began to fall like dandruff on a dark suit. She went back outside and stuck her arm out, admiring the symmetry of the flakes that landed on her sleeve. It was hard to believe that each one was different and unique. Just like people.

Within an hour, the storm had already dropped an inch of snow on the railing of the deck. The big flakes had turned to icy pellets, the wind driving them against the window, the scraping sound like a dog scratching to come inside. It was dark now and she turned on all of the outside lights. Sam was due at seven and she still had plenty to do. She was startled when the doorbell rang at twenty of.

"Hope I'm not too early," Sam said when she opened the door. "I allowed extra time because of the storm, but the roads weren't bad at all."

"Not a problem." She was glad that she had gotten dressed early and hadn't put it off until the last minute. "But now you'll have to help with the final touches since things aren't quite ready yet."

"My pleasure." He took off his coat and looked around. "This place is fantastic."

"Thank you. Feel free to walk around and take a look while I open some wine."

Leslie poured wine and gave Sam a knife and cutting board to chop vegetables for the salad. She was surprised when Sam started talking about the drilling project almost immediately.

"I've had Brenda doing some research," he said. "There are quite a few folks that have already signed contracts. Combined with the people Edith and Emma have talked to, we're getting close to having a handle on the big picture of what's going on."

"I've been so busy all week I haven't had a chance to talk to Edith or Emma. What's the next step?"

"Putting a map together. Brenda's working on it. So have you gotten over the shock of it being Xandex's project?"

"I don't know if I'm over the shock, but I want you to know that I won't be seeing Andrew Macfarlane anymore. In fact, I've broken off the relationship completely." It felt good to say it out loud.

"Well, that's great news. It will make things a lot easier for you to be involved in the group trying to bring his project to a screeching halt."

"That's for sure. Now let's get this dinner on the table."

She didn't mention the project or Andrew again, and neither did he. They lingered over the meal, and when Sam offered to help clean up, she accepted. Andrew had acted like he owned the place when he was there, but he never helped with the cooking or the cleanup. She opened another bottle of wine and they sat in front of the fireplace talking easily. Leslie didn't want the evening to end.

"A brandy for a nightcap?" she asked when the wine was gone. "Or a cup of coffee? We can put another log on the fire and sit for a while longer."

"No, I need to get going. It's got to be close to eleven." Sam got up from the couch.

"Try twelve fifteen," Leslie said, looking at her watch. "But I'm not tired. It's no problem to stoke the fire."

"Twelve fifteen? How did it get to be so late? No, I've already overstayed my welcome." He took his coat from the peg and put it on. "I really enjoyed the dinner, Leslie. I feel like I've known you forever, but without the gap."

"Me too. Maybe it's our common background in DC that makes it so easy. In any case, I'm looking forward to having you as a friend here in Montana."

He looked at her with raised eyebrows. "Leslie, if you really have broken it off with Andrew, I'd like to see if we could be more than friends. I'd like to date you. Which sounds so awkward." He laughed. "How are we supposed to have these conversations at our age, anyway?"

"I have no idea." She laughed. "Dates, boyfriends, girlfriends. It all sounds so juvenile."

"Well, whatever we call it, would you like to get together again?"

"Absolutely," she said, completely forgetting her resolve to just be friends when he put his arms around her and kissed her. It wasn't like the friendly kiss he had given her last week but was long and languorous and exploratory. He held her close and she returned both his embrace and his kiss. Then he left.

There was no way she could go to bed. She was energized and her mind was spinning. She put another log on the fire and sat down to think. How different Sam was from Andrew. Andrew hadn't waited for niceties and dates; he had made love to her on the kitchen floor after their second dinner. In spite of his faults, Leslie had enjoyed his sexual assertiveness. Most of the time. She wondered what Sam would be like in bed. She had to admit she would have liked to have found out tonight. She laughed at herself. *I get rid of one man on Saturday and by Tuesday I'm ready to jump into bed with another. After thirty years with the same man. What a difference a year makes,* she thought. *No,* she told herself firmly, *you will take this one slowly. You will not screw up a potentially wonderful friendship by letting things move too fast.*

She jumped when she heard the doorbell.

Oh, no, she thought. *Not Andrew showing up again. Or maybe Peg. No, it was too late for that.* She went to the door and opened it, startled to see Sam.

"I'm glad you're still up," he said as he came in. He shook snow from his shoulders and stamped his feet to knock snow from his boots. "The drifts on the switchbacks were bad enough, but the road is completely impassable down below. Not to mention your steps up to the door. Can I sleep on the couch?"

"No way." She laughed when she saw the look on his face. "I mean I have a perfectly functional guest room. No need to sleep on the couch. Take off your coat and boots and I'll just go check to make sure there are towels in the bathroom."

She had finished putting things out for him and was fluffing the pillows when he joined her in the guest bedroom. "There's a razor, shaving cream, and a comb in the basket in the bathroom, but let me know if there's anything else you need."

"There's only one other thing."

"Oh, of course, a toothbrush. There should be one and some toothpaste in the top drawer. Let me check." She went into the bathroom and pulled open the drawer. "You're in luck. Here's one still in the plastic."

She walked back into the bedroom. Sam was leaning against the doorframe, one foot crossed over the other, hands stuck in his pockets, his lanky figure accentuated by the silhouette of the framing. "Thanks. But that wasn't what I was thinking about."

"Something else then?"

He slowly walked over to her and put his hands on her shoulders. "I need another good night kiss. It got awfully cold out there since our last one. Okay?"

He waited for her to answer.

"Okay. I mean, yes. Sure."

Sam started at her earlobe before tenderly working his lips across her face until he reached her mouth. He kissed her for a very long time, his hands exploring the curves of her body. Eventually, when she could hardly breathe, he stopped, but only long enough to slide her sweater over her head. He kissed her again and opened her bra from the back. Somehow, his shirt was off and she was surprised when she felt her breasts touch bare skin. They stood pressing against each other, Sam's actions slow and deliberate.

He licked the side of her neck, softly nibbling her skin, working his way down until he reached her nipples. She ran her fingers through his hair, moaning softly. His hands moved down her belly and he undid the zipper of her jeans. He pushed her pants down, and then lifted her easily, putting her on the bed and pulling the pants over her ankles.

He quickly unbuckled his own trousers and slid them off while she lay naked on the top of the coverlet, not daring to move and break the spell. Within seconds, he was naked beside her, continuing to smother her with kisses, his fingertips tracing swirls along her body. She wasn't sure how it happened, but they were under the covers exploring each other with the wonder of a new book, all the while being certain of what the ending would be.

It was still dark when Leslie awoke the next morning. Sam was entwined around her, fast asleep. She lightly stroked his hair as she studied his face. Sam was so much more delicate with her than Andrew, so much more caring about her and her pleasure. She felt as if she had been made love to.

"Let's go over to my bedroom," she suggested when Sam woke up. "It's a bigger bed and better view when it gets light."

"That's a great idea. I haven't seen that part of the house yet." They scurried to the other room and quickly slid under the down comforter. Leslie was eager to feel the warmth of Sam's embrace again. She could see out the window that it was still snowing, and for once, she was happy that it didn't show any signs of stopping.

CHAPTER 35

"There isn't anything you can do," Manny said to Peg. "That heifer's gonna take care of her own calf, and if he doesn't make it, then he doesn't make it. We can't get out there for at least another day because we've gotta get the fence repaired down where most of the stock is. Otherwise, we'll lose a lot more cows than just one sickly calf."

"All it needs is a shot," Peg said. "I can do that in ten minutes."

Manny looked at her skeptically. "I know, but remember your promise? Not to ride alone? It's barely two weeks since Lee passed and besides, there's another storm comin' in."

"Hello," a voice called, and Peg saw Leslie peeking into the barn.

"Hello," Peg said. "Be with you in a minute."

"No problem. Take your time." Leslie went to the horse in the first stall and stroked his neck while she waited.

"It's not that far," Peg said to Manny. "The calf is up by the old shepherd's cabin, so I can get there in an hour, give the shot, and be back before dark. Or before a storm could cause any trouble. If it's snowing a bit on the way back, that's no big deal. Nothing will happen in such a short time."

"Lee was only supposed to be gone a short time too," Manny said bluntly. "Besides, you promised. If I let you go alone and somethin' happened, there's not a man on this ranch that would forgive me and I wouldn't be able to live with myself either. But none of us can go with you right now."

Peg knew Manny had won the argument. She had given her word and she had to live by it. But she'd done this kind of thing a hundred times and she wanted to save the calf if possible. She looked around, saw Leslie, and had an idea.

"Leslie can go with me," she said to Manny, as if settling the matter once and for all.

Leslie looked over at the mention of her name. "Go with you where?" She hadn't been paying attention to their conversation.

"Up to the old cabin," Peg said. "I need to give one of the new calves a shot of antibiotics. It's an easy ride of about an hour each way and the shot won't take long once we find the calf. Let's see, it's just after two now, so if you go home and get into some warm riding clothes and get back here in fifteen minutes, we'll have the horses all saddled and ready to go. We can be back by five o'clock. Will you come with me?"

"I was going to make a pumpkin pie. That's why I came over—to ask you for your recipe. Sam Curtis is coming for dinner tonight."

Peg wondered what that was all about, but was more concerned with getting her way. "I'll put out a pie from the freezer and it will be thawed by the time we get back."

"You know, I've only had a few riding lessons. Do you think I can handle the terrain?"

"It's an easy ride and we'll be walking and trotting most of the way. You can trot, can't you?"

"Oh, yes."

"Good." Peg was satisfied that she was going to get her way. She looked pointedly at Manny. Of course, she didn't want to take Leslie along, but it was better than not going at all. "Go change your clothes and be sure to dress warm enough. Manny is right that there might be a few flakes falling by the time we get back. Skedaddle now," she said in the same tone she used to use with her children as she shooed Leslie from the barn. "We've no time to lose or we'll run into dusk. See you back here in fifteen minutes."

Leslie was happy she'd put on an extra layer of clothes for the ride with Peg. The heat from the horse kept her legs warm, but the wind was biting cold. She wasn't thrilled with the idea of spending the afternoon looking for a sick calf and would rather have stayed home getting ready for dinner with Sam. But she felt like she couldn't refuse the one request Peg had ever made of her. And now that she was here, she hoped it might be a chance to make up for her past mistakes and start the friendship anew.

"I talked to Kelly this morning," Leslie said to Peg's back as they rode single file. "She said Will had been down to Georgia and Texas to compete in some rodeos and that he'd done really well."

"Yes, he told me. Took first in one and second in the other," Peg said over her shoulder.

"I was surprised when she told me he had been there. I had no idea there were rodeos any time other than in the summer."

"There are events all year round and all around the country. The professional circuit can be pretty grueling. I hope Kelly understands how much travel is involved."

"I'm sorry. I could barely hear you. What did you say?"

Peg slowed her horse and allowed Leslie to come up beside her. She repeated what she had said.

Leslie was grateful for the easier way to have conversation. "She seems to be good with it. In fact, she seems really happy overall. I've never seen her so head over heels before. How's Will coping with living in the city?"

"I have to admit, he seems really happy, too. I can't quite believe it, but I guess being in love changes everything. Will told me that they want to have children soon after the wedding. I told him he needs to take one step at a time."

"That's Kelly's doing. She's always said she wants to have kids while she's young. I try to tell her the same thing you told Will, but she's stubborn about it."

"Will's always said he wants to have a lot of kids. He's great with his nieces and nephew. So I'm sure it's not just Kelly."

Leslie felt like she and Peg were finally connecting. Nevertheless, she wanted to be careful about what she said so she didn't inadvertently offend Peg again. "I might be old-fashioned about it, but I think they should wait until they have some income and savings before having kids."

"You know Will makes a good living already, don't you?"

"Actually, I've never asked and Kelly's never said anything about it. I guess I didn't know that. I really don't have a clue how somebody makes money in rodeo. Who pays their salaries?"

Peg laughed and Leslie was relieved that she hadn't put her foot in her mouth. "It's not like other professional sports where the players get a salary. Instead, they win prize money. The cowboys actually pay to enter each rodeo and so every time they compete, it's a gamble whether they make money or lose their entry fee and travel expenses. It's not the kind of thing you dabble in. The stakes are high."

"I had no idea. So, Will does well at it?"

"He made over a quarter of a million last year." Leslie gasped, but Peg went on. "After expenses, it wasn't so much, of course. But he's a good saver and has quite a bit in the bank. And he's got a few sponsors, so the better he does, the more he can make from that."

"Well, there goes my argument why they should wait." Leslie laughed. There was so much she didn't know. "You must be proud of him to be so successful."

"I am. But I have to admit that I'm secretly hoping Kelly rubs off on him and that he decides to go back to school. It's just that I place such a high value on education."

"College isn't the only place to get an education." Leslie surprised herself when she said it. "From everything I can tell, Will is one smart man. After all, he fell in love with my daughter."

This time Peg laughed. "And vice versa. Let's get a move on and find that calf." She kicked her horse into a trot and Leslie followed.

They reached the mouth of the canyon and easily found the ailing calf with its mother. They stopped and dismounted, and Leslie rubbed her sore backside. She hadn't been on a horse for over a month, and she was feeling it.

Leslie watched as Peg got supplies from the saddlebags and prepared to give the calf the shot. She looked up at the high walls of the canyon and thought the weather seemed more threatening. "It's funny, but I feel a little bit claustrophobic up here."

"It's always darker in the canyon. Makes it feel smaller than it really is. But it also looks like this storm is coming in faster than I thought it would. We might want to pick up the pace on our way back."

Leslie took a couple of deep breaths and felt calmer. She watched Peg cradle the gangly calf and stick the needle in its hindquarters. The wind whipped small snow pellets into their faces.

"This place reminds me of a passage from a poem," Leslie said. "By the author of that book I gave you. It goes something like this:

> When the canyon walls crowd in around me,
> A contrarian's sense of space evolves
> The blotting of the sun . . .

"I can't remember the last line, but it's something like *makes me feel cozy.*" Leslie looked up and realized she couldn't see the tops of the canyon walls anymore. The dark cloud layer had dropped.

"Creates a cocoon of calm," said Peg, gathering the supplies that were strewn around her on the ground.

"Yes, that's it. Creates a cocoon of calm. I can't believe I couldn't remember that. I must have recited that verse to myself hundreds of times over the past years."

"You did? Why?"

"There was a lot of stress in my job. Sometimes I felt the pressure was like the walls of a canyon closing in on me. I used to recite that passage to calm myself."

Peg was putting things into the saddlebag, but Leslie noticed her glance up with an odd look. Peg took out four apples and handed two to Leslie. "One for you and one for your horse."

"Thank you." Leslie put one in her pocket and held the other out in her palm for the horse to eat. "That poem goes on with a beautiful description of the landscape. Nobody does that as well as Maggie Madison. In fact, it's fair to say that the reason I'm in Legacy Springs is because her poetry made me fall in love with the West. But more than that, she was almost like a spiritual lifeline while I was juggling a career, a kid, a husband, and everything else in the pressure cooker of DC."

She felt Peg was looking at her as if she was crazy. Maybe Peg thought she was being—what word had Peg used?—*uppity* to be talking about poetry. She decided to stop talking.

"It's starting to snow. We've got to get a move on." Peg was busy putting the rest of the things into the saddlebags. The calf was calmly suckling its mother.

Leslie tried to jump up onto her horse, but quickly realized that she couldn't get on alone. She was used to having the step stool provided at the riding class. Or at least the rungs of the buck and rail fence. When she mounted the horse at the barn,

Manny had provided two gentlemanly cupped hands for her to step into. She had never done it from the ground, but she didn't want to ask for help. She wanted Peg to see her as a self-sufficient Western woman. *Maybe if I stand on that rock over there,* she thought, looking for a solution.

She led the horse to the boulder and perched precariously atop it. One foot in the stirrup, she was almost there, the other leg stretched across the broad back of the beast. She grabbed the mane and tried to haul herself up. She managed to get atop the horse and was practically lying on its back, neither foot in a stirrup. She and the horse saw it at the same time, a small gray bobcat, perched on a ledge just ahead of them, ready to pounce on the weak calf for a warm meal on this cold day as soon as the horses and riders left.

Her horse reared and snorted with fear, then bolted. Leslie had not held on to the reins when she mounted, so she grabbed in vain at the mane. She hit the ground and everything went black.

CHAPTER 36

The first thing Leslie felt was the warmth on her feet. She wriggled under the covers without opening her eyes, but her foot hit something hard and she felt a sudden jolt of pain in her ankle. She reached down to find a warm brick wrapped in a towel. She didn't know where she was, but could see that she was in a small bedroom with wooden slat walls and a low ceiling. She could hear the wind howling outside.

She lay for a moment and tried to remember what had happened. She knew she had been riding with Peg, and then, then, what? The last thing she remembered was seeing the bobcat. She moved her arms and felt a twinge in her ribs. "Peg?" She called out tentatively.

Peg appeared in the doorway. "You're awake. That's good," she said. "I've got some tea ready for you. I'll go get it."

"There's a brick in the bed." Leslie felt silly saying it, but Peg only laughed.

"It's an old trick to keep the bed warm. I heated it in the fireplace first. It was so cold when we got here that I thought you'd need some extra warmth. I'll move it if it bothers you."

"No, it's fine as long as I don't kick it. I was just surprised by it. I've never heard of such a thing, but it makes sense."

Peg left and returned a minute later carrying a tray with a cup of tea, a glass of water, and three ibuprofen tablets. "First, take these anti-inflammatories. Do you think you can hold the glass by yourself?"

"Yes, I think so." Leslie slowly maneuvered herself to sit up in the bed. She hurt all over. "What happened? How did I get here?"

"A bobcat spooked your horse and you got bucked off. You hit the ground pretty hard, but I helped you get on the horse so we could come here. You've been sleeping for a few hours. Don't you remember?"

"I remember the bobcat." Her mind was hazy, but it started to come back to her. "And I remember how much my ribs hurt riding here. Now my ankle feels pretty stiff," she said, trying to turn it from left to right, grimacing. She gave the glass of water back to Peg and took the cup of tea.

"I checked you for concussion, but you knew who you were, so I don't think you have one. That's why I let you sleep. But we should probably check again. Do you have a headache?"

"No."

Peg peered into Leslie's eyes. "Do you know your name?"

"Of course, I know my name."

"Then tell me."

"Leslie Montgomery."

"Very good. What's your address?"

Leslie told her.

"Final question: what day is it?"

"It's Friday," Leslie said, then with a bit of panic she added, "Oh, shit."

"What?"

"Sam is coming for dinner. At seven. What time is it now? Can we call him?"

"It's almost eight and there's no cell coverage here. But don't worry. When we weren't home by five, Manny came up to check on us. I told him we were okay for tonight and made him go back right away so he wouldn't get caught in the storm. I asked him to call Sam and tell him what happened. I didn't think you were hurt badly enough to have Dr. Bob come out now, but Manny's going to ask him to come tomorrow once the storm dies down. I want to make sure it's okay to move you."

"Thanks. I think I'll be okay, but I'm not sure about these ribs and riding on a horse *or* a snowmobile. It'll be good to have him take a look." Leslie sipped at the tea and felt the warmth flow into her body. She couldn't remember a cup of tea ever tasting so good. She looked around the cozy little room. "What is this place?"

"We're at the old shepherd's cabin," Peg said. "Luckily, it's only about a half mile from where you fell. There was no way I was going to try to get you all the way home. Especially not with the storm."

Leslie groaned as she reached over to put the empty cup back onto the tray.

"If you're feeling up to it," Peg said, "I've got dinner cooking in the next room. You could either try to sit at the table or I'll bring it here to you."

"Let's give it a try out there. That way I can also test out which of my parts are working." She moved slowly to get out of the bed.

"Let me help you. By the looks of your ankle, my guess is that you won't be able to stand on it."

Peg was right. With her help, Leslie hobbled into the other room and sat on a couch beside a small potbelly stove. Peg put an afghan over her and then went into the kitchen. Across from the couch was a well-worn leather chair, the edges frayed and a bit tattered. On the other side of the room, the wall had bookshelves from floor to ceiling, crammed full of books. Leslie was too far away to read any of the titles, but it was clear that whoever spent time here would have plenty to read.

The kitchen area was open to the living room, and Leslie could see Peg at a small stove. "We'll start with some soup," Peg said, stirring something in a saucepan. "Then I've got red sauce heating up that we can put over pasta. It's not much, but it will have to do."

Leslie couldn't believe how much fit into the small kitchen space. There were shelves filled with cans and jars lining either side of the window above a large sink. A small refrigerator sat next to the stove, and in the middle of the room was a butcher-block table on wheels. Beneath the butcher block, steel storage shelves held several lidded plastic tubs through which Leslie could see dishes, glassware and silverware. Above it, cast-iron pots and pans of all shapes and sizes hung from a round rack.

Peg went over to the door carrying a large container and stepped outside. A few seconds later, she was back, the container filled with snow. While the door was open, Leslie could see the snowstorm raging outside. The rush of cold air made Leslie pull the afghan closer around her. The simple movement caused her ribs to ache again. A small drift of snow came in with Peg and settled around her feet as she pushed the heavy wooden door closed with a resounding clunk.

"We've got to get some ice on that ankle of yours." Peg packed the snow into a plastic bag.

"Thanks. I feel so silly having gotten into this predicament."

"Accidents happen. I guess the guys were right that it's a risky thing to be out here alone." She turned away and Leslie thought she might be wiping tears from her eyes. "If Lee wasn't alone . . ." She let the sentence drift off unfinished.

"Peg, I'm so sorry. You must miss him terribly."

"Yes, I do." Peg straightened up. "But there's no point in crying. I've got to check the soup." She went back to the kitchen.

Leslie looked around the room. "This place is amazing. Why is it here?"

"It was built for anybody who works the far reaches of the ranch. A cowboy can spend the night or a few days here rather than ride the extra hour back home only to come out again the next day. We call it the shepherd's cabin."

"Why is all this food here?"

"For circumstances like this. It can be a refuge from a winter storm or a place to crash after eighteen hours on the range in the summer. You can see that everything is in tins or bins, since the mice would chew through anything to get at food."

"It seems so remote, but there's electricity."

"That's been in for years. It's finicky though and might go out during this storm, but that's why I've got the lanterns at the ready." Peg pointed at several kerosene lamps lined up beside the door. "The electricity isn't the best part though, it's the indoor plumbing. When I was a kid, we only had an outhouse. Even though I loved being here, I hated that part. It was either freezing cold or dark and scary, or both. The summer the septic tank went in, I rejoiced as if it were my firstborn child."

"Do you spend much time here now?"

"Not enough. Sometimes I ride up for the day, to read or write. And a couple times a year, I'll come for a few nights by myself. Kind of like a retreat. I'm the one who insisted on adding the bookshelves and hauling all these books up here." Peg got up and went to the stove. "I think this is ready. Do you want to move to the table or stay on the couch?"

"I think I'd rather be on the couch, if that's okay."

"Sure." Peg ladled the soup into bowls and brought one to Leslie. "I'll get you a spoon."

Leslie cradled the bowl, enjoying the warmth on her hands. Peg handed her a spoon and sat in the leather chair across from her, holding her own bowl of soup.

"My grandmother used to cook in this cabin for as many as thirty men working the ranch during roundup. I used to wonder how so much food could come out of such a small place."

"The first Thanksgiving I was married was like that," Leslie shared. "My husband and I lived in a tiny apartment, but we decided to cook for our extended families and then invited friends to boot. I think there were over twenty people in a space as small as this kitchen."

They finished the soup and Peg traded the bowls for plates of pasta.

"This is delicious," Leslie said after the first bite, realizing she was still hungry even after eating the soup. She also realized how much she was enjoying talking to Peg. "Tell me more about your history. Sam said you were in the state legislature at one point. What was that like?"

"I spent six years there. I had just finished college and was trying to figure out what to do with my life. I got appointed by the governor to fill my uncle's spot when he unexpectedly died. I won the next election and became the youngest elected legislator ever. Then Lee and I got married, and by the time the next election rolled around, I was pregnant and didn't want to be away from home so much, so I gave it up."

Leslie felt like an idiot thinking of her misconceptions about Peg. She vowed again to rethink every impression she had of every person she'd met so far in Montana. If she could be so wrong about Peg and Andrew, she could be wrong about anyone.

After dinner, Peg stoked the fire and refilled the ice bag for Leslie's ankle. She went into one of the bedrooms and came back with a bottle in her hand. "I found some of Lee's whiskey. Since you don't have a concussion, I think you can have a drink. We deserve one, don't you think?"

"I sure could use one," Leslie said as Peg poured the translucent brown liquid into two glasses. "Do you mind if I ask you how you met Lee? If you don't want to talk about him, that's okay. I don't mean to be insensitive."

Peg set the bottle on the butcher block and handed Leslie a glass. She sat in the chair with a heavy sigh. "On the contrary. I feel like I want to talk about him all the time, but everybody's afraid to even mention his name. It's more painful to ignore it and pretend it hasn't happened than it is to talk about it. Talking about him keeps him real for me."

Peg told Leslie how she met Lee and about the early years, her face animated as she recalled the good times.

"You are so lucky to have had him. I wish my relationship with Hugh had been half as good."

"I was surprised when you got here last year and said you were divorced. What happened?" Peg got up and poured them a second glass of whiskey.

"I guess I didn't pay enough attention and got caught up in my career. One day when I was talking about moving to Montana, he announced that he didn't want anything to do with Montana—or our marriage. It was quite a shock. But I was lucky enough to be able to do this alone. So I guess there was some payoff for all those years of work."

"At least you got a payoff. Lee and I worked our fingers to the bone for this ranch, and all we got is trouble from the bank."

"Oh, Peg. I'm so sorry. Listen, this might sound strange, but Sam told me that you don't use steroids and that your cows only eat grass, instead of being corn-fattened. If you don't mind my asking, why aren't you marketing your beef as grass fed? You could get more money for it, and it would fit right in with the sustainability movement and people's desire to eat healthy."

"What's the sustainability movement?"

"It's the new thing in the urban areas now. In a nutshell, sustainability is running your business in a way that it will last for generations. It's sometimes called the triple bottom line: in addition to the normal financial one, you add two more. One for the environment—so you make sure you protect the natural resources your business depends on—and one for the community and your workforce. If you pay attention to any one without the other two, it doesn't work in the long run. A lot of companies are now touting their environmental and social responsibility as a marketing tool." Leslie stopped and looked apologetically at Peg. "Is this too boring? I can get on a soapbox sometimes."

"No, I think it's interesting. After all, it's the way we've run the ranch for a hundred years, although we never called it sustainability. But I don't see what difference it makes. The buyers of our beef don't care how we run our business. They care whether they can sell the product. And right now, the market for beef is just bad."

"It's only bad because of the fear of disease and effects of steroids. Since Sam mentioned it to me, I've been doing some research. The grass-fed Argentinean beef sells for four times more than traditional US beef. You've been focused on the Japanese market, but I think there's a play here in the US for sustainably-raised beef." She watched Peg's eyebrows shoot up. "You could establish your own brand around this as different from what everyone else is doing. And the point is that you would drive the market, instead of letting it drive you."

"I'm not sure I understand what you're thinking. Can we talk through some numbers?"

"Sure. Get some paper."

Peg opened one of the plastic bins and got a couple of tablets and pens. She picked up the whiskey bottle and joined Leslie on the couch. They scribbled numbers and went back and forth, creating a new business plan for the ranch.

"Do you really think this could work?" Peg asked incredulously.

"I do. As you know, grass-fed beef tastes so much better, but the real marketing hook is not just that. It's the story of the ranch, your stewardship, and your refusal to use steroids. People want to know where their food is coming from and what's gone into it. It's been a foodie gourmet thing for a while, but now even the better chain groceries are starting to feel the demand."

"Are you sure this isn't the whiskey talking?" Peg added another splash to each of their glasses.

"I'm sure. The most important thing we'll have to do is establish the brand quickly," Leslie said, unconsciously using the word *we*. "That's what'll allow us to drive the market. I haven't found anyone else in the US who is marketing beef this way, so if we get on it, we'll be first and that will be huge for market share. We'll call it sustainably raised beef, and we'll define for the industry what that means. Then everyone else will be chasing us as we keep upping the bar with the profits we'll make."

"What about my sheep?" Peg asked, almost as an afterthought. Lee had told her that they were losing money on them and they would have to go. "I do love having the sheep around."

"I don't know. Tell me about them."

"Well, that afghan you're wrapped in is made from their wool. Isn't it soft?"

"It's fantastic. Did you make it?"

Peg nodded. "Yes. I use natural vegetable dyes to get the rich colors."

"Perfect. What if we use the wool to make high-end garments? We'll just need to find a factory."

"We don't need a factory. Every ranch woman for miles around Legacy Springs is a skilled knitter. What if we hire them? Most of them could use the money and besides, we all run out of things we need to make. Wouldn't hand-made items be better or do we need mass production to make money?"

"We'll have to run some numbers, but I love the idea. We can sell at a higher price point if each piece is hand crafted. We could do custom orders as well as a standard inventory. Women in the cities will pay a lot for a one-of-a-kind garment. Besides, the concept fits perfectly with the sustainability brand. It supports women in the community and lets them to stay on the ranch, despite the economic downturn."

"And you really believe it will work?" Peg asked again.

"I believe it so much that I'd like to become a partner with you. My initial investment could be enough to get the bank off your back."

"I really appreciate that. I think this is a great plan to keep the ranch profitable for the future and I'd like to have you as a business partner. But I already found a way to take care of the bank. I guess we should talk about whether it contradicts the sustainability brand, but I've agreed to sell the mineral rights under the ranch."

"*You what?*" Leslie said involuntarily. "Sorry, I didn't mean to say it that way."

"No problem. I feel the same way myself now that I know there's a different solution."

"I thought they were only looking for properties where the mineral rights were unclaimed. I thought you already owned yours."

"That's just it. Because I do own the rights, I can get a lot of money for them. Enough to pay off the mortgage. And keep the ranch from being sold out from under me. I didn't tell you, but we got a foreclosure notice the day before Lee died." She looked down. "I've been wondering if it was worry about it that caused his heart attack."

Leslie felt sick to her stomach. She didn't know where to start. She wanted to lean over and give Peg a hug, but it didn't feel right. Instead, her lawyer instincts kicked in. "Have you signed anything yet?"

"Only a preliminary agreement, but I've given my word, and I can't break it."

"Oh, yes you can, and until you sign the final papers, that preliminary agreement is no problem."

"But Leslie, when a Hamilton gives their word, it's as good as a signature. I promised, and so I've got to go through with it. I was so grateful when I was offered the deal. It was the only way out that I could see. God, I wish he had never shown up."

"Who?"

"Cortez Harbinger." Leslie cringed as Peg went on. "That's who I've given my word to. And now he can hold me to it. And he knows it. The only way I would break it is if he personally let me off the hook. And somehow, I don't think that's going to happen. He'll be here tomorrow with the final papers."

"You might not be there tomorrow. I need to think about the best way to handle this," Leslie said, using her tried-and-true "buy time when you don't like the answer" approach. *Damn Harbinger and Andrew Macfarlane. The snakes.* She didn't want Peg to see how angry she was at this news. "For now, I need to use that indoor plumbing."

Leslie held onto Peg as she hobbled to the bathroom. With Peg's arm across her back and under her armpit, she didn't need to put any weight on her ankle. "Yell when you're done," Peg said, "and I'll come and help you back. I'm going to check the windows to make sure there's no snow getting in. This storm looks as bad as the one we had a few days ago. I think there's already a foot of new snow out there, and it's still coming down hard."

The remnants of the storm that came after Cortez had driven back to the Xandex headquarters did not take long to clear, and the lawyers had rushed to get the documents done. It was Friday and another storm was predicted for later that night, so he knew he had to get on the road to Legacy Springs. He'd meet with Peg Hamilton for the final signing tomorrow. She had told him she would be home when he called her yesterday. And yes, she was still prepared to sign the contract.

It was a beautiful, sunny day and the road was completely dry. Cortez put on his sunglasses and opened the sunroof. No, snow on the road was not a problem today. The yellow and white lines were a welcome sight after their months of absence. The temperature by midafternoon was warm enough that the snow was melting fast, forming small rivulets across the road and pooling in the low spots. No, snow on the road was not a problem.

He patted the bright red folder on the seat beside him. The legal department used that color to signify something that was ready for signature. Cortez liked to think it signified the blood that was about to be signed away. He only had a few hours before dark, but with the road clear and the pedal to the metal, he would easily make it, maybe in record time.

When I get that bonus check, he thought, *I'll be flying down this road in half the time.* He pictured himself behind the wheel of the sports car he would buy, women lined up in every town wanting to be with him, men staring at him just wanting to be him. The speedometer leveled out at his favorite number: one hundred. He was cruising.

As he neared the mountains, the straight road turned into curves and he reluctantly slowed to seventy. The shrubs and sagebrush that had been on the side of the road gave way to towering pines, casting long shadows across the rivulets and pools of water from the day's earlier snowmelt. He sped up on the short stretches between the curves, braking only at the last minute to slow his speed going into the next one. *I can't wait until I get my sports car and can do this by downshifting instead of braking.* He came into a curve shaded by trees, where the temperature had already dropped and the melting water on the road had formed a sheet of black ice.

Cortez never felt the impact of the tree that he hit after the car flipped several times. He never felt the branch that impaled him through the airbag. He died with a smile on his face, flying to his end in his imaginary sports car as the hero and lover that everyone adored.

The contents of the red folder were shredded and strewn across the landscape.

CHAPTER 37

Leslie stood on one leg, leaning on the bathroom sink to wash her hands. *I don't need to bother Peg,* she thought. *I can make it to the couch by myself.* But after a few hops, she knew she'd made a mistake. Her ankle throbbed and her legs felt weak. She leaned against the wall of bookshelves to wait for Peg, and scanned the spines of the books.

The first few rows were novels by a broad assortment of authors. *I could spend months working my way through these,* she thought, seeing many she'd read and many more she hadn't. She hopped a few steps to the next section, using the shelves for balance. There, in chronological order, were two copies of every Maggie Madison book. *Peg must love her too,* she thought, wondering why there were two copies of each. Her gift now felt silly and redundant.

She remembered their conversation before she was thrown from the horse, when Peg finished the passage from the poem. She hadn't commented on it then, perhaps hadn't even noticed it, but the scene came back to her now. Had she found someone who loved this poet as much as she did? If only she had known this when she first met Peg, things might have been different between them.

"What are you doing trying to move around by yourself?" Peg scolded when she came out of the bedroom.

"I thought I could make it alone, but I was wrong." Leslie laughed.

Peg helped her to the couch. "It's almost eleven o'clock," Peg said. "Do you want to get some sleep?"

"To tell the truth, I'm wide awake." Leslie's stomach was full and she had a pleasant buzz from the alcohol. "I'd just as soon stay up and talk if you're up for it. I'd forgotten how nice it is to spend hours solving the problems of the world with another woman."

"I'm wide awake too. And hell," Peg pointed at the bottle, "we haven't even made a dent in that yet."

"That's an impressive array of books," Leslie said as Peg sat on the couch next to her, wrapping a fresh ice bag around her ankle. "I can't believe you have a complete collection of Maggie Madison. I have every volume but not a duplicate set like you. There must be a story there——"

"There is," Peg started, but Leslie cut her off.

"No, you can tell me in a minute. First, will you let me tell you why her poems are so important to me?"

"Okay." Peg picked up her glass, settled back into the couch and curled her feet under her.

"I first started reading her when I was in my early thirties. I'd been practicing law for quite a few years and Kelly was maybe a year old. I was so busy and felt like I'd lost all sense of myself—I was a lawyer, a mother, and a wife, but *Leslie* was buried under all that. For my birthday that year, my friend Cynthia gave me *Venus is Singing* and when I read it, I remembered who I was. It saved me—Maggie Madison's words anchored me."

Leslie took a sip of whiskey, putting her hand up when Peg tried to speak. "Over the years, I bought every book as soon as it came out, and it seemed like Maggie was a mirror spirit, going through the same phases of life I was. Her beautiful descriptions of the land and the way of life were an added bonus."

"Leslie," Peg tried again.

"Just one more thing, I promise. When I bought your property, I thought I was buying that way of life: quiet and creative, full of love and beauty, with scenery, not stress. I realize now that it doesn't just happen, I've got to work at it. Being in this community and watching the people here, I'm learning I can't selfishly sit back and look at the view; I've got an obligation to understand this place, this life, and participate in it and protect it. Maggie's poems have said that all along, I just didn't get it. And maybe that's why I still read at least one poem every day, because she's always teaching me something new and reminding me of who I am, or maybe who I *could* be."

Leslie took a deep breath. "Look, if we're going to work together on this business plan and if our kids are going to get married, we need to clear the air. I know I've been a jerk and you don't like me much, but maybe we can get past that." Leslie picked up her whiskey and held it out in a toast. "Deal?"

"Deal." Peg leaned over and clinked her glass against Leslie's. They drank together.

"We do need to clear the air, and I owe you an apology," Peg said as she refilled their glasses. "At first, I didn't like you because you bought my property but, since I didn't want to sell it, I wouldn't have liked anybody who bought it. Then I tagged you as an outsider, and, without even knowing you, as an obnoxious Easterner. I thought you were a prima donna trying to live a fake version of life in Montana. In fact, I thought a lot of other worse things about you too." She smiled ruefully. "But I was wrong. You're a nice person, a savvy businesswoman, and you love all that's precious about living here more than I've ever given you credit for. I'm so sorry and I hope we can be friends."

Leslie smiled. It felt good to finally understand why Peg had been so standoffish. "I'm sorry too. Seems we've both been working on bad assumptions."

"Yes, that's putting it mildly." Peg laughed and took a big swallow of whiskey. "There's something else I need to tell you. Something important. You know Peg is a nickname for Margaret, right? Well, my given name is Margaret. Margaret Ellen. My maiden name is Madison."

Leslie looked at her with slow comprehension.

"Yes, Leslie. I should have told you long before. I am Maggie Madison."

CHAPTER 38

Leslie tightened the scarf around her neck and pulled up the collar of her coat as she walked down the main street of Legacy Springs. The wind was fierce and biting. The color of the sky mirrored her gray eyes. *There'll be snow by tonight,* she thought. As she approached the corner, she noticed a woman standing still, staring at the mountains in the distance. The woman wore an expensive camelhair coat, which, Leslie thought, might be enough for a few minutes outside in today's wind. She had on red calfskin gloves, the kind Leslie knew did not keep your hands warm on a day like this, and hard leather cowboy boots, the kind that Leslie knew caused you to slip and slide on the snow and ice. The woman's hair was whipping about her face; she didn't have on a hat.

"Pretty blustery, isn't it," Leslie said as she stopped at the corner with the only stoplight in town. Several cars and a few pickups passed through the intersection as they waited to cross.

"I love it," the woman said with enthusiasm. "It makes me feel so alive. And the view! Everywhere you look, mountains in every direction. It's so fantastic."

"Yes, it is."

"Are you from here?"

Leslie thought for a minute. "Yes. I guess I qualify as a local. Been here for almost six years." She realized she was proud of it.

"So tell me, do you ever get tired of the view? I can't imagine getting anything done with this to look at every day."

"I haven't gotten tired of it yet and it changes all the time with the light and the seasons. And, yes, I do sometimes find myself just sitting and staring." She laughed. It actually happened to her a lot. "Where are you from?"

"LA. I've got a small solar-panel research company and I'm going to move my operation here in a few months. I'm here to find a place to live."

"That's fantastic. How did you find Legacy Springs?"

"I wanted somewhere with a great quality of life. It'll make it easier for me to attract the kind of top talent I need. And the economic incentives offered by the town were too good to pass up. I can't wait to be here."

The woman's enthusiasm reminded Leslie of herself when she first came to Legacy Springs. She remembered her misconceptions about the people who lived here and what her life would be like.

Could it really be five years since she and Peg had spent the night in the shepherd's cabin? It had gone by so quickly. The timing had been perfect for the business plan they hatched that night. People everywhere were starting to demand what Peg and Lee had always had—food from the land, free from chemicals, and raised with integrity. And, as the new Lee's Legacy brand took hold, ranchers came from around the country to learn how to emulate their practices.

But that was only the beginning. Success begat success. The whole town got in on it and became a green business incubator as well as a year-round recreation hub known for amazing restaurants and a thriving arts community. When tourists came, they ate local foods, like the best grass-fed beef in the nation, and drank craft beer made with local hops. They bought beautiful, hand-knit sweaters made by one of the hundred women across Montana and Idaho who Peg and Leslie employed, and some of the visitors stayed to become part of the still tight-knit community.

"You don't think you'll be bored in a small town?" Leslie asked, remembering her first winter and how she fell into bed with Andrew, searching for companionship and affection. But now she didn't have time to be bored, or lonely. She traveled across the country to market the beef and the sweaters, and when she was home, she and Peg worked tirelessly to keep growing the business.

"No, I'll still be running my company. I know the pace will be slower than in the city, but I'm looking forward to that. And, I can always visit LA if I need a fix of activity or warm weather. This may sound silly, but I love the poetry of Maggie Madison, and her descriptions of the landscapes and the seasons are what made me explore Montana in the first place. I know she lives somewhere around here. Do you know her?"

Leslie laughed. "Yes, I do."

"How exciting! What is she like, if you don't mind my asking?"

"She's everything you'd expect. She's talented and tough and strong and sensitive. I love her poetry, too, and I think it just keeps getting better."

"Apparently the world agrees. Seems like everybody I know is reading her books after her newest one, *Lee's Legacy,* made it to the best-seller list. I hadn't heard of her before that, but now I've read everything she's written."

"Yes, it's funny how that happens. You know she started publishing books almost thirty years ago, but people think of her as an overnight sensation." Leslie had gotten one of her old clients, a publicist, to get Peg the visibility that made the difference.

"Does she ever do local readings? I'd love to meet her." The woman shivered, but made no sign of moving, even though the light had changed again.

"Yes, of course. But even if she didn't, you'd meet her eventually. It may seem like there's a lot happening here, but it's still a small town."

"How do you know her? Is she a friend of yours?"

Leslie smiled. Not only was Peg her friend and business partner, but their children were married to each other. This woman's simple questions brought back a flood of memories. Leslie had given her house and property to Will and Kelly as a wedding gift, so the Hamilton ranch was once again intact. Will had 'retired' from bull riding and now ran the daily workings of the ranch. Kelly joined Dick Henderson's law practice, working three days a week so she could stay home with the baby the rest of the time. "I've known her since I moved here. She's a dear friend," Leslie answered, knowing that to say anything more would be complicated.

"I know I'm taking up all of your time, but do you mind if I ask you one more question?"

315

"Of course not." A gust of wind made them both tuck their heads into their shoulders. Leslie was perfectly warm, but could practically hear the other woman's teeth chattering.

"I just got divorced, so I'll be moving here by myself. Do you think that's crazy?"

Leslie laughed again. "No. Not at all. I was newly divorced when I moved here. Then I met the love of my life, and he's now my husband. He'll be your senator once you get here. Sam Curtis."

Leslie smiled warmly at the woman standing next to her, full of hopes and expectations. She took off one glove and rummaged in her purse, pulling out a business card. "Here," she said, handing the card to the stranger, then quickly putting her glove back on. "I'm Leslie. Call me and we can get together for coffee or dinner. It can be kind of hard to make friends in a new place. I'd be happy to get you started."

"I'm Caroline." The woman took the card and put it into her purse. "Thanks. I'd like that. It will be nice to know at least one person in town." She smiled, pushing her windblown hair out of her face and trying in vain to keep it behind her very red ears. "Even though I'm freezing right now, I think I'm going to love living here. I can hardly wait. A town like this is exactly what I've been looking for."

The light changed yet another time. "Let's cross while there aren't any cars," Leslie said. She grabbed Caroline's arm when her new friend started to slip on the icy road.

"Guess I'll have to get some different boots," Caroline said when they got safely to the other side of the street. "And serious gloves. And definitely a hat! Thanks again, Leslie. I'll call you."

"Welcome to Legacy Springs, Caroline. I think you'll like it here. It's a great place to live." Leslie pulled her hat farther down over her ears. Her hands were warm in her fleece gloves. She thought about all the things she loved about this valley, this town. Everything from the silence of the snowflakes to the smells of the summer; but most of all, the serenity of the scenery. In spite of the storm moving in, she could see for miles down to the end of the valley, the glorious, snow-covered mountains rising on either side. And not a drilling platform or natural gas well in sight. She turned her face up into the wind and smiled. *Yes, my life here in Legacy Springs is everything I could ever wish for.* Taking a deep breath of the sharp, cold air, she walked confidently toward her car, her bulky boots crunching on the snow.

CPSIA information can be obtained at www.ICGtesting.com
Printed in the USA
BVOW021044050713

325047BV00001B/1/P